I0557594

MYKING

KANE

Kane's Publishing Company

ISBN-13: 9781732602700

Cover design by: Passion P.G.M. All rights reserved
WWW.PASSIONPGM.COM
Library of Congress Control Number: 2018960230
Printed in the United States of America

This book is dedicated to black girls all over the world. You are Art! You are Magic. You are immortal. The beauty and talent you have is unmatched. With God, you will not fail. Thank you, Jasmine Derrick, for simply believing in Kane.

CONTENTS

PROLOGUE

MyKing

I was born April 29th, 1989 to Arlene Saunters and I never knew my father. He was killed by his ex before I was even born. All I know is my momma and she doesn't fuck with any of her family as far as I know, and I am ok with that. I never bothered to ask why because I never really cared. And I can't say it's because she is a bad mother but she just wasn't the mother I thought she should have been. Growing up, I saw her run through men like no tomorrow. As a kid, I had a different "uncle" every week. By the time I got into my teens, she just stopped giving me kinfolk and bullshit introductions altogether. I always thought the loss of my father set her on the path of being a ruthless hoe. Either that, or she was a hoe all along. Whatever the case, moms is loose, and a part of me always hated her for it. I never complained because she kept food on the table, and as a kid that's all I could ask for. But It started to become more complicated when I started growing up and was no longer a kid. The fact that I had no pops, a hoeing ass mama, and lived in the Slater Mills housing projects was motivation enough for me to become the hustler I was born to be. Hell, I really ain't want for shit but to be better than my situation. So, I did what I had to do. My name is MyKing by the way. Yeah, I know it's unique but as you enter my life you will realize it fits me.

I was sitting in my U.S history class checking Toni out. She was this fine lil bitch that sat in front of me. She had these sexy light brown eyes and pretty full lips, and whenever I see her I get an instant vision of her sucking my dick. She noticed me looking at her and smiled at me. I smiled back because I knew she wanted me. The class was almost over and I was glad this was my last period before I got to go home. I had business I needed to handle and I was tired of being in this hot ass class. Tevin had just hit my line letting me know we had to handle some business later and I couldn't wait to get it over with.

The bell rang and I was glad. I was so ready to go I barely paid attention. The summer was approaching swiftly enough and it was getting hot in my city. I hit my locker putting my books back. When Toni walked up behind me grinning I smiled back.

"So, what you doing today King?" Toni asked.

"You if you'll let me," I replied.

"Mmm maybe..." she smiled.

I closed my locker and proceeded towards the door. I stopped once I realized she wasn't with me. I turned back around to find her still standing there looking lost.

"Come on baby." I smiled.

She started walking towards me and out the door, we went. I unlocked my truck and let her in.

"Ooooh I like your truck King, it's nice." She said.

"Thanks."

Every bitch here in Marshall High School wanted to be in her spot. Sitting comfortably on the peanut butter leather seats of my fully loaded 2006 Cadillac, Escalade. I found it comical when she rolled down the window so she would be seen riding shotgun next to me. She thought she was special because she was sitting here and she wanted everyone to know it. The funny thing was I'd never give her that impression. I just want some head and some pussy. Nothing more, nothing less. I ain't never fell hard for no bitch and didn't plan to. I like making my money and that was good enough for me. I fuck these bitches and dispose of them. Ain't none of these hoes worthy of my time, but every once in a while, I take them to the crib and use them up until I can't cum no more.

I turned up the radio and jammed as Gucci blasted until we pulled up to the buildings. There was no conversation while in route. The weather was nice, which meant my moms wouldn't be home anytime soon. She never was home but I didn't miss her. I opened the door to my apartment, took off my shoes, and headed straight to the bathroom for a shower. That low budget ass school don't even got a dependable air conditioner, so I been sweating all day. I won't stunt. Sometimes I ask myself why I even bother with school. Tevin got kicked out our freshman year and didn't bother returning. Kevin dropped out as soon as we started getting money last year and I'm sure he ain't even thought about school since. I kept going to school, but in my head, it was because I figured slinging was temporary. I promised Rita aka "Ma", Tevin and Kevin's mom, way back I'd graduate from high school. Even though I don't give a fuck about what my momma feels, I made that promise to Rita and I planned to keep it. After all, I wasn't a bad student. I never did bad in school. I did get in trouble often enough but my grades were good. I didn't think it was because I was smart but rather the workload was just simple. It wasn't hard enough for me to fail and too easy for my grades to be below 3.0. My GPA was a 3.8. and I scored a 29 on my ACT and even though every now and then I get into trouble, I was not a dumb nigga. That's probably why I stayed on top of the streets. Well at least with the money.

I had one more year of high school before I graduated. I already had a few colleges in mind. But right now, all I want is to make this money. I washed down and hopped out the shower, dried, and walked out the bathroom into my room. Toni was sitting on my bed. She smiled when she saw me wrapped in my towel.

"What? You like something you see?" I asked, smirking at her.

"Yeah, I do." She admitted

"Well then, show me." I tested.

I let the towel fall exposing my long dick. She looked shocked to see I hung low. Guess in her head the shit was impossible.

"Suck it," I instructed.

She didn't say a word. She just got on her knees in front of me and proceeded to do what I'd asked. She slowly took me into her wet mouth. Shit, the feeling was good. I grabbed the back of her head directing her to the base of my dick. And she starts choking immediately and that excited me. I ain't let go of her head either.

"Open up your mouth and relax," I instructed.

Most bitches have a hard time taking all of me in, but I'd planned to coach this one. She followed my instructions and before long she had a nigga ready.

"Fuck girl, suck this shit." I groaned. She was handling the dick.

"Damn." I started to fuck her mouth and she let me.

"Fuck." I groaned because I was about to bust. So, I kept pumping thrusting my dick straight into the back of her throat.

"Shit." I came in her mouth some before I pulled out and shot on her face. She swallowed and got up towards the bathroom to wash up. I smiled, heading to my top drawer to grab a condom. I opened the wrapper and slid that joint on. She came out of the bathroom and made her way to my king-sized bed.

"You ready?" I asked her. She ain't say shit, so I grabbed her. She had this uneasy look on her face.

"What's wrong?" I asked, only half giving a fuck.

"Nothing," she said uncomfortably.

"Cool," I said and proceeded to take off her clothes; her pants, and her panties. I kissed her neck and she moaned. I laid her on my bed ready to penetrate and she stopped me.

"What's wrong?" I asked again. She was starting to piss me off.

"You're big, King." She said referring to my penis size. I smiled because it wasn't the first time I'd heard it. It was something I'm sure she had already heard about too. She knew what she was getting into before she sat her ass in my truck. I was blessed with a big dick and I'm proud of it. I found it funny that she was afraid suddenly when she was literally just throwing her pussy at me an hour ago.

"Lay back sweetie, I got you," I told her just so she would calm her ass down.

She laid back and I was on her. I slid in and started to stroke her and she whimpered. She was tight. Nice, I thought. I stroked her until she got wetter and I sped up. She started moaning and I was glad she could take dick. I started fucking her harder and she moaned louder. Her pussy was decent, I thought.

"King... ooooo...King" she moaned.

I love when bitches say my name. So, I flipped her on her knees in the doggy style position and proceeded to knock her walls a loose. I slammed her hips into my body and thrust inside of her. I wanted all of me inside her.

"Ahhhh... King, I'm coming baby." she moaned.

I ain't give a fuck as long as I got my nut. I fucked her like that for about five more minutes and pulled out before I started to cum. After I busted that nut, I was straight.

I got up and headed for the shower right away. I walked out of the bathroom back to my room to find this bitch dressed sitting on my bed.

"You still here?" I screwed.

"Um, can you take me home?" she asked.

"Do your legs work?" I asked her.

She sucked her teeth." Are you really finna make me walk home?" She asked.

"Um, why can't you?" I asked her.

"King, I live in the village, that's almost ten blocks away from here." She exclaimed. I chuckled.

"Well bitch you better get to stepping. Hop on the bus!" I told her.

"With what money?" she sighed. I started laughing.

"Oh, so I'm supposed to give you some?" I asked amused.

"Nigga really? We just had sex! You cannot be seriously about to make me walk home!"

"Bitch, I don't pay for pussy. Get the fuck out my shit, shorty." I frowned. She smacked her lips and walked towards my bedroom door.

She was leaving out when I called her. "TONI!! "

"Yeah?" She came back a little more hopeful than she looked before.

"Make sure you lock my door, ok." She frowned and walked out the second time. I heard the door slam and I drifted to sleep.

I woke up to the sound of my phone and I picked up.

"Speak!" I growled.

"We ready to move," Kevin spoke.

"Cool, meet me at the spot in a ten" I told him.

"Ten-four," he replied, and I hung up the phone.

I got up right away and went to the bathroom, washed the sleep out my face, and brushed my teeth. I threw on my jeans, pulled out a fresh white T from the pack, ironed it, and threw it on. I pulled my dreads into a band making a mental note of a well-needed lining. I jumped in my Mikes, grabbed my phone, and headed out the door. As I approached my truck in the project lot, I realized the clucks were out running rapid tonight, tryna get that shit. I nodded at a couple of homies serving on the edge. And I still hadn't seen my mama since I been home from school and that was hours ago. "Something is seriously wrong with that broad." I thought. I got to my truck and jumped in traffic.

I finally checked my phone. Had a couple missed calls from a couple of broads. Got a message from Toni telling me how bogus I was. Oh well, I thought. Bitches these days kill me. They fucking and sucking every man on the block like hoes but expect me to treat them like wifey. The fuck outta here with that shit. I ain't wifing no bitch. Ever. All women are the same and I done had the baddest and still ain't wifing no broad. I shook my head as I pulled into the trap just five minutes later. I walked up the stairs of the porch and opened the front door. I walked in to see the guys drinking and smoking weed. That's all they ever did. Rayvon, Travis, and Shaun were the homies.

"What up!" I spoke to everybody. They all seemed to be in a good mood. It was all good. I headed to the backrooms where I came to handle my business. When I walked into the last room where my right-hand Tevin was, he and KC were bagging up. I looked over the product and my insides jumped. I got excited when I saw drugs. The profit always would trump my nerves about the risk that came along with doing this shit. The money was what I pushed to the top of my mind. The drugs weren't even a problem once I thought about the cash. Hell, I love the shit almost as much as the clucks do, if not more. Shit, at least what I get out of it benefits me for the better.

"Tevin, my nigga!" I said as I gave him a pound and we embraced.

"What up, how you living bro?" He asked as he accepted the brotherly love.

"Nigga you know me, I'm just living," I said with a smile. He asked me the same thing every day.

"Good, good."

"What you on K?" I nodded my cools over at KC.

He nodded back and we started working. They bagged the product and I worked on the numbers. It was my job to make whatever we had work. Math was my thing so the measurements and weight along with the money was my expertise. I was trusted with the most important job here and I was proud of that.

These were my niggas. Tevin, Kevin, and I had seen it all together. If I didn't have anybody else, I had them. I fucked with them hard. They momma always looked out for me when we were younger, may God rest her soul. She is just about the only woman I respected completely. She treated me like her son. If I was with Tevin and Kevin, then I got just as much as they did. She made sure I felt some love. When she died of cancer about two years ago, it hurt. Right before she died, I promised her that I'd have a family one day, and Kevin and Tevin would always be my brothers. That promise still stands as far as the brothers go. But the family thing was the furthest thing from my mind. Shit, I ain't wifing no bitch. Ever. I couldn't imagine making babies with nobody so it was dead before I let that come out my mouth. Point was, the only woman I had love for was dying. I woulda said anything to make her more comfortable. If letting her believe I was gone start a family did that then so be it. She dead now anyway so she will never know I lied.

After my count was right, Tevin put all the product in the duffel bags. KC and I snatched them up to put them in the truck. They had to drop on all our lil niggas to be distributed. Tevin grabbed the weight from the plug. We brought it back to the trap, broke it down, and handed it out for sale. While Kevin supervised the way the drugs were sold through the projects, I stuck with what I knew and I ain't have no intentions of standing on nobody corner or over another nigga. I didn't know anything about the drugs or selling them but I could tell you exactly how much was gonna be made before it even left my view. I held my own when it came to the measurements and money. My business ended there. But the streets ain't know that and I was immediately labeled. I'd never admitted it, but I wasn't really cut out for the work. It was just my only real means of income and the only reason I could stomach the shit in the first place is because I trusted my best friends and they needed me. We all needed the money because we lost our support when Ma died. Wasn't nobody trying to help us. I ain't feel like selling a little bit of drugs was so bad at first. Nobody using handled me directly and I enjoyed being the money man. You would never find me on the corner. Nor will you ever see me conversing with a cluck. I attempted to handle the drugs as less as possible because I didn't plan to sell them long. It was just the quickest source of income I had and I needed it. We all did. In truth, Tevin did most of the work, and Kevin and I simply had his back along with our crew. This wasn't my hustle and I knew it right off. But the money was worth all of the risk.

CHAPTER ONE: KING OF THE HOOD

MyKing

The drop went smoothly as always. KC dropped the weight to Kev. Tevin picked up the money after everybody got they weight and we dropped the cash to our connect. He sends us our weight the way he always did once he counts his bread. It had become really simple. Shit was so easy that it made me feel uncomfortable. I and Tevin got into his whip and pulled off to go back home. I was quiet because I was in my own thoughts.

"What's on your mind, Bro?" Tevin asked.

"Nothing," I told him.

"You stunting. Boy, I've been knowing you since you use to pee in the bed. Wassup?" He looked at me seriously.

"Bro, I don't think we should keep doing this shit. We ain't hurting. We did what we had to do. I just don't think it's necessary now." I told him honestly. I had been feeling that way for a minute but the re-up always changed my mind.

"King, you eating because you work. You stop working and yo

ass gone starve. What, you don't remember what that feels like? Huh? Oh, you got your truck paid off so now you wanna quit? King, be for real, this is how we are able to fucking live. What the fuck will we do without this bread? Go back to juggin? Huh? Cause I know you ain't finna work nobody's nine to five. So I'm listening…"

"I'm just saying…shit too sweet…"

"Exactly. Shit is good and you tryna stop now. Nigga we're making money! More money than I expected going into this thing. I ain't tryna quit now. Shit, I'm tryna be the plug! You playing."

"Look Tev, all I'm saying is this shit ain't supposed to be sweet. If we keep this up something is bound to happen; I can feel it. I like the money too, but I just don't think our lives are worth it. That's all I'm saying."

"Nigga look around. We live in Chicago. It's only one way to live and that's to survive out here. To be aware is to be alive! I used to go to bed with my stomach growling. Hungry. Felt as close to death as I can comprehend. I ain't going back to that. If you want to quit, then I can't stop you, but King, I won't ever go to bed hungry again. Not when this money this simple."

I didn't respond. Didn't seem like I could convince him. He was the hard-headed one out the group. He didn't learn until it was too late. I knew that about him, but he was my best friend, and I wasn't going to leave him hanging. He knew that.

"So, what's it gonna be? You out?" he asked.

"Nah, you know better," I said.

"Right, now let's get this fucking money!" he said before he pulled in front of the lot where I parked my truck.

"Aight bro, hit you tomorrow," I told Tevin as I got out.

"Ten-four." He replied before he pulled off and I hopped in my truck. I couldn't stop thinking about how this shit all started.

Tevin Rashaan Woods was my best friend. We'd met in the first-grade class of Randolph Elementary on the south side. He and I hit it off instantly, but his identical twin brother was not a friend as easily. Kevin Rashaad Woods was the opposite of Tevin. He was quiet and reserved and mugged me whenever I looked up at him. Tevin and I would play together but Kevin was completely against us being friends. However, the longer I stayed around Tevin, the closer me and Kevin got. Eventually, we all became the best of friends and I could honestly say I had never been closer to anybody else in my life. The craziest thing is the older and closer we got, the more the twins started to change. Although Tevin remained outgoing and vocal, he started to become ruthless and mean. He was the one who would start the shit we always seemed to get into. Kevin, on the other hand, was the peacemaker. When it came down to throwing hands and fighting with the local niggas who tried to step to us, he would, but only after he couldn't do anything but fight. And I was simply me. I wasn't as vocal as Tevin nor was I as reserved as Kevin but those were my brothers, and we just rode for each other. As years passed, our bond only got stronger. Like I said, we weren't the same at all but we had one thing in common. We all wanted a way out.

It was Tevin's plan to rob Meechi. He was a local drug dealer who had just come up in the hood. Nobody cared for him because he was one of them grimy type of niggas that you couldn't trust, and everybody knew it. Nobody wanted to fuck with him because he had a bad reputation. He'd sell drugs to his own mama for a dollar and not give a fuck if she OD'd on it. He was all about the almighty dollar and didn't give a fuck about shit else. He talked shit and toted a pistol around like he was gone use it. But he was a bitch ass nigga, and we all knew it. That is exactly what made him a target in the first place. Tevin ain't fuck with him because he liked to talk shit. He ran his mouth too much and because of that fact neither did me and Kev. The plan was simple. Catch the nigga slipping and stick his ass. He was the type of nigga that was always slipping. He was stupid, and he moved recklessly anyway. We knew he wasn't smart enough to not shit where he slept. He was gone get stuck by somebody anyway it went. Fortunately, we thought of it first. Tevin had made it his mission to watch his every move until finally, he saw what he was looking for. Meechi had made moves twice with Tevin on his tail. Every time he got a payoff, he brought the cash back to his crib. We'd watched his dumb ass do just that for the third time and we chose to make our move at that moment. So, we trailed him. He lived in the grounds behind Slater Mills. It wasn't actually a part of the projects me and the guys stayed in, but it was so close it might as well have been. Meechi got out his car without even noticing we were behind him. He popped the trunk and grabbed the black duffle bag. As soon as he shut the trunk, Tevin had his pistol at the side of his head.

"Drop it bitch!" he said easily as he shoved the pistol further into Meechi's nappy uncut head.

"Man, what the fuck? Yo, do y'all know who you fucking with?" he asked angrily as he looked at the three of us dressed in all black with peek a boo ski masks covering our faces.

"Yeah, a stupid muthafucka." Kevin joked and we all start laughing. Before he could say another word, Tevin hit him in his shit and I grabbed him up as I matched my pistol to the back of his neck.

"Walk nigga," I told him as we walked him through the back door of his crib.

"So yall really finna rob me at my own shit?" he asked stupidly.

"Nigga, shut the fuck up before we do more than rob yo dumb ass," I told him as I pushed him down the stairs of his entrance. As much as we had stressed how little we thought of him, his dumb ass still had the audacity to talk shit. So, after the threat of his retaliation, we all agreed he needed his ass whupped. We walked him down to his basement apartment and beat the fuck outta him.

Tevin smacked him across the face with the hi-point 9mm pistol. Before he could recover, me and Kevin started hitting him too. I found it funny because I knew that after all that shit he talked, his bitch ass still wasn't finna do shit. He didn't even attempt to fight back and was so fucked up by the time we got done we didn't even have to tie him up like we planned to. We walked outta that muthafucka so easily it was crazy, and that was all the come up we needed. We counted out a nice amount in cash. Along with a bag full of cocaine and right before we split that money three ways, Tevin had a better idea.

"Yo, I was thinking. Why don't we flip this shit?" he started.

"Here he goes! Nigga, you got a bag of coke. You don't even know how much is in that bag and now you ready to sell it?" I asked as Kevin burst into laughter.

"Naw for real, why don't we just take this and cop some more product and sell it. We can at least get bout ten thousand and we can keep flipping until we straight.

"Aye nigga, I ain't tryna sell no drugs. I said I'd rob that pussy ass nigga but I ain't on that." Kevin started.

"Come on, is y'all for real? We got the opportunity to get this bread and now y'all wanna act scary?" Tevin asked looking at me and Kev like we'd lost our damn minds.

"Naw nigga I ain't scared at all, but I don't know shit about none of that. I ain't' tryna go to jail or lose my life in the process of me tryna come up. I ain't for none of that. You don't know shit about selling no drugs, Tevin. That shit just ain't realistic. Besides, Quan got that shit on lock. He owns this side of the E-way. And we just robbed the nigga running for him. We start moving anything and its gone be obvious we took his shit! You don't want problems with that man." I stated.

"What? Fuck Quan! I need this bread. That man doesn't move me. He ain't putting food in my mouth. I been looking to do this shit for a while. I was just waiting until I got the ends to make my move. I know a nigga who can get us a connect. The thing is he's over in Mexico, and that shit ain't gone be no quality shit. We can use it as the foot in the door though. Take this lil money, flip it and make it a couple more G's, and take that and buy some real quality from a different connect. By the time we work it down, I'll have had time to find him." He explained.

"Nigga you been sniffing in that fucking bag? How the fuck we gone move this shit? I ain't' finna stand my muthafucking ass on the corner so 12 can lock me up. Tevin, you fucking tweaking." Kevin commented.

"We can easily recruit some lil niggas to do that shit for us. You know it won't be shit. I'll put up the money we have left and we can use it to pay they lil ass to stand outside. Muthafuckas hungry around this bitch; everybody wanna eat. Quan don't give a fuck about Slater. He ain't from this block because he woulda known buddy he trusted with his cash was a goofy. We can lock the house down or blow this lil bag. I'm tryna get this money." He said seriously.

I sat quietly and thought about it. I was tryna find a reason why this wasn't a good idea, but he had me considering it. Then I realized that Tev might've been on to something. I was nervous as hell about the whole thing, but I ain't feel I had much to lose. So, I went ahead and agreed to it. It didn't take much more convincing of Kevin before he was in too, and we met up with the connect Tevin had in mind shortly after. That went smoothly and we copped a lil weight from him. The nigga Meechi got killed shortly after we robbed him so he never had the chance to retaliate. After the cop, we linked up with our homie KC who was known to hit a bitch in the mouth and dare anybody to question him about it. He and his brother Keith were cool, so we brought him in and he was part of our crew. Keith was the one who had been taught how to cook crack cocaine. He learned from an uncle who'd learned the trade serving overseas. Keith was the one who cooked the rocks down, and that was his importance in our organization. His brother KC was the one who weighed and bagged the product along with the help of Tevin who eventually learned how to break it down. I came behind them with the final weigh before sending it to the block. In the beginning, we never really had any problems. Quan never came at us for taking his shit and by the time we copped everything had been lowkey. We used the drugs we'd copped from our Mexican connect and it sold.

I learned quickly there is always money to be made. After I started, I was willing to sell it. Shit, it had become real easy, and eventually, I and the twins had put in so much work, we were the niggas to come at for the good. At least we were on the blocks surrounding the projects. Now, that nigga Quan ain't like that at all but by the time he realized we were making moves we'd already found a better connect. All the niggas in Slater were tryna fuck with us and it eventually got to the point if Quan decided to move on us he would have to be prepared for a war because we rode deep as hell. It wasn't an easy job but it was lucrative. We weren't pushing any major weight so it was alright. I had been hesitant about selling the shit at first, but I got over it when I realized how much money I could get from it. I was known around the hood as King. A shortened version of my name and I believed me and my guys were the realest niggas to ever set foot in Chicago's south side projects.

Now, the Slater Mills housing projects were the grimmest, meanest, nastiest place you could ever live. It was set directly across from a slab of two flats that were abandoned. Behind sixteen high rise buildings sat a dozen low rise set of buildings that everybody called the grounds. Slater was so wild; everybody called it the Jungle. I grew up here, so me and the twins were pretty much accustomed to the ways of the land. The pissy stairways, dark alleys, and broken elevators didn't even faze me. It didn't seem all that bad once we start making money. I had grown accustomed to it quickly. In fact, the sounds of gunshots were more of an expectation than a scare. I won't lie and say I didn't want better, but I had fully accepted the way shit was a long time ago. And in all honesty, this place didn't bother me. As long as I had my brothers and a little money in my pocket, I couldn't care less about the dozens of people dying. The lifestyle was what we considered a game. Only the strongest would survive. I deemed this my own personal palace, and this was how I was able to eat. It was how we all ate. It's been that way since we started.

I got in the house around four am. I went straight to my room but not before hearing my hoe ass mama moaning some niggas name. Nasty bitch! I often wished my dad was alive. Shit, I wish I knew that muthafucka. I'd ask him what exactly did he see in my mama? She was nothing but a nasty hoe with a big ass. Any decent man could see that. I went in my room and just got in bed. What the fuck else could I do? I'm past fucking tired and I just wanna sleep.

"Ahhhh shittt Nathan fuck this pussy, baby". She moaned. I frowned and got back up. "Fuck this shit." I spat as I grabbed my shit and left. I went to Tevin's crib and slept on the couch.

I woke up around nine the next morning; I normally don't sleep late. Tev was still sleeping so I just left and went back to my crib to get dressed. I was planning to get my hair tightened then probably hit the mall. I got in and headed straight for the shower. Once I got out, I picked out my fit and turned on my iPod like I did every morning. Gucci started playing and I rapped along to the lyrics as I ironed my clothes. I dressed and headed to the shop where my nigga Rex hooked me up as usual. I hated having to sit there damn near two hours, but I loved my hair. I start growing it out two years prior and since I've kept my locks clean and done. After he finished my hair, I paid him and hit the mall. It was early so it wasn't as crowded. I walked through hitting a couple of stores and bought some shoes and a watch. Wasn't shit spectacular though. I was just about to leave when I saw this sexy ass broad.

Now, this bitch was bad as hell, but not in a tryna be sexy type of way. She was built up like Keisha from the movie Belly. Dark skin with some long ass hair and clear skin. I don't usually like dark skin broads but this bitch did something to me. Then, she had on this short ass dress that had those long pretty ass chocolate legs out. The bitch was a dime. I had already got in my mind I'd be hitting that before the night was out so I watched her as she walked into Zale's and followed right behind her. Keeping my eyes glued to her fat ass. Damn, I thought. The man behind the counter saw her and asked could he help her. She smiled and told him yes. I'm eyeing her the whole time. Then another man walked up to me asking me did I need something.

"Umm yeah, get me some screws." I spat trying to get him the fuck away from me so I can get at shorty.

"Sir, which ones wou...." he started. I cut him off.

"Look I don't give a fuck which ones you get just fucking get some screws and ring'em up, ok." I snapped. He nodded his head looking all scary-eyed and shit. I was too busy staring at this girl. I mean she was as sexy as I thought she was. But was more beautiful than anything. She wasn't like the broads I see around and I could tell just by the way she talked. She was smiling and laughing with the salesman like they were old friends. His old ass looked amused like he wanted to just hop over the counter and hump her. Shit, I wanted her too so I knew how he felt. The man that had been my salesperson walked up to me.

"Sir I have your earrings ready." I nodded at him and proceeded to the register. He rung me up. Then the other salesman that was with the girl I had been eyeing walked up to the next register holding a box. At first, he looked as though he was ringing it up, then he'd tried to put it away back into the glass case. I turned back around to see the girl leaving out the store. She was so angelic looking but seemed disappointed. She never even looked my way. My salesman spoke. "Your total will be five forty-five, sir," he said.

"Did she want that?" I asked the other salesman.

"Oh yes, but she said she couldn't get it," he said. I thought for a second.

"Alright, I'll take that too," I told him. He smiled and nodded then rung that up with my screws.

"That'll be six eighty-five sir." The salesman said and I hurried up and paid him and left. I was looking for the girl. But by the time I'd made it out the jewelry store she'd disappeared.

"Damn," I thought. Then thought about it. The fuck did I just buy? I couldn't believe I had just bought a broad some shit, and on top of that, she ain't even look my way. I didn't even know what she wanted. I reached into the bag and pulled out the box. I opened it and it brought a smile to my face." It was a gold necklace that said mom in a gold heart. It also had an aquamarine birthstone in the middle. I knew because Tevin and Kevin's mom's birthday was in March and I bought her an aquamarine and diamond ring. I smiled just thinking of the look on her face when I gave it to her. She had it on when she died and I thought it was only right she was buried with it on. I closed the box and shook my head and proceeded to the food court to get me a drink and maybe a bite to eat. While standing in line at Steak Escape, I looked around the food court at all the other restaurants. That's when my eyes landed on her. I got out the line instantly and headed her way. Some nigga was all in her face cheesing hard as shit. She politely shook him off, thanked him for his compliments, and that was that. Buddy couldn't take the fucking hint though and it pissed me off. I walked up to him and asked him to move around. He was about to say something until he realized I had pulled up my shirt to expose the 45 calibers I had tucked between my jeans and boxers. He noticed and got out that jam quick. I pulled down my shirt before I turned towards her to speak. When she looked up at me and smiled, I lost all train of thought and just stood there.

CHAPTER TWO:
DIAMONDS TO DIRT

Jasmine

Every light further into the city made my stomach turn a little more. I was scared out of my mind. There were bums begging on the street and people populated around the front of businesses like a bunch of insects. The sidewalks were littered and junky and traffic was horrible. I didn't speak about it because my mother was already discouraged as it was. "Jasmine, this place will not be what you are used to, but it's temporary until we can afford something better." She said as we passed a woman yelling and cursing herself out. I shook my head because I was mortified. I knew I was not going to like it here. We made a few quick turns before we finally stopped in front of a row of concrete buildings that were gray and disturbing. The sign out front read Slater Mills and you could tell where some of the letters had been removed. Sixteen high rise buildings were stacked high and in order. I could tell by the lack of grass and littered grounds that I would hate it here. My mother took a deep breath before getting out of the rental car. I sent a small prayer up to God just in case he decided to listen to me today. I stood at the front entrance of building six of the Slater Mills housing projects. As I walked towards the door a tear rolled down my face. My entire world had changed and there was nothing I could do. Nothing I could have done would've prepared me for what my world had become. I was sad and broken.

My name is Jasmine Monique Davis. I was born March 29th, 1990. My sixteenth birthday had just passed and it was perfect. My whole world was perfect a month ago. I woke up happy to have made it another year. I didn't want anything because in truth I had it all. My father was one of the lead financial advisers for many of the Illinois elite. He owned several businesses and invested hundreds of thousands into different stocks and bonds. He always use to say "investments keep your money working." I never had to worry a day in my life. I was raised wealthy. I went to one of the finest private schools and lived in one of the best neighborhoods the state of Illinois had to offer. My daddy had always taken care of my mother and I.

I made my way down the stairs of my vast four-bedroom house skipping around like I always did. My mother was sitting at the kitchen table in Chanel slips, her long silk maroon robe, and diamond earrings, sipping a machine-made Frappuccino. She smiled the moment she saw me.

"Happy birthday Jazzy!" my mom squealed as she got up to hug me. I hugged her tight because I appreciated the affection my mother showed me.

"Thanks, mommy!" I replied

"Sooo, how does it feel? Sweet sixteen! Oh, my God, I remember being your age! I am so proud!" she laughed. I laughed too.

"Wait, let me go get your gift! Byron! She is awake!" My mom yelled down the hall to my father who was more than likely in his den. She ran towards the stairs and I stood there excitedly.

"Baby girl! Come on, I got something for you!" My dad motioned towards the front door.

"Oh my God. Daddy! You didn't!" I squealed as I ran towards the front door. I opened it and a little pink toy jeep was sitting out front with a big red bow wrapped around it.

"Nope!" my dad said before he burst out laughing. I pouted because I thought I'd gotten a real car, but the fact he had gotten me so excited was funny so I laughed just as hard as he was laughing.

My mother came back down and joined us at the door carrying a small perfectly wrapped box.

"Byron, I know you did not!" she chuckled as she looked out the door at my tiny Barbie Jeep. "Here baby, you know your mother loves you!" She said as she handed me the box.

"Thanks, mommy!" I said as I pulled the paper away from the box. I opened it and a beautiful diamond charm bracelet wrapped in velvet laid Heavenly in the box.

"Whoa!! Mom...I think I'm going to cry!" I said as I pulled it from the box and inspected the two charms on it. One was a diamond encrusted number sixteen and the other was a heart. I turned to hug her, and she helped me put it on.

"You are the best!" I stated, admiring the way it looked hanging from my dark chocolate wrist.

"Oh so you didn't like my present huh!" my dad teased.

"No dad, I liked your present too! Thank you. I always wanted a toy jeep." I smiled and gave him a hug too.

"No, you are just like your mother. All you care about is diamonds!" He joked.

"Awe, come on dad, diamonds are a girl's best friend, right? I still love the car too!" I laughed.

"Yeah, whatever! Here." He reached into his pocket and handed me a box. I snatched it up knowing already it was the matching necklace to mom's gift. They were so predictable at times. I giggled as I opened the box. It wasn't a necklace. It was one single key.

"Daddy! Oh my God, daddy don't play with me!" I screamed.

"Go check the garage girl!" My mother said as they both laughed. I ran towards the garage, almost busting it down, and screamed to the top of my lungs when I saw the silver and black 2007 Jeep Wrangler sitting in there. I opened the door and jumped in. That new car smell along with the leather seats made me feel like I was in heaven. If I would've died right then, I would have died a happy girl. Everything was perfect. I drove my truck every day for about two weeks. I'd been in class one day completely focused on the lesson when my friend Casey tapped me on the shoulder.

"Jasmine, isn't that your car? She asked.

I turned to look out the window as my baby was being hauled onto a tow truck. I excused myself and ran outside with tears in my eyes.

"Wait! Sir! What are you doing? Put my vehicle down now! What is wrong with you?!" I yelled at the tow truck driver.

"Ma'am, I'm just doing my job! I was instructed to pull it. You might want to call your parents sweetie," He said.

"No! This has to be a mistake! I just got this truck! It's paid for! Put it down, please!" I cried.

"I can't do that. I'm sorry. Contact your folks, ok?" He said and then loaded my new truck and pulled away. I called my father first, but I didn't get an answer. I called my mother, and I knew the moment I heard her voice something was wrong.

"Mom, some man just took my truck!" I cried.

"Baby, I'm coming to get you right now." She said sorrowfully.

"What's wrong? What happened?" I asked her.

"I will explain it to you when I get there," she said before she hung up.

My stomach was in knots, and I knew nothing good was going to come from this situation. I've never not had it good, but I knew things were about to be really bad. She pulled up to my school and I got into her Benz. She had her silk scarf wrapped around her head where her rollers were barely holding onto her hair. She didn't have on makeup or jewelry, and her tear filled eyes made me worry.

"Mommy, what happened?" I asked her as she pulled away from the school.

"Jasmine…your father…is dead." I started crying right away.

"What! What happened to him?" I cried.

"He jumped from the fourth story of one of his construction sites." She sobbed.

"What happened? Why would he do that? Why?" I exclaimed.

She chuckled. "He was drunk! The IRS has seized all our shit! They were investigating your father of money laundering and running some sort of Ponzi scheme. I had no idea he was even accused of it. I did not prepare. I have thirty-nine dollars and twenty-three cents in my purse and they threw me out of my got damn house with a fucking housecoat and slippers on! All of my accounts are frozen! Everything that we have has been taken away. I don't know where to start to fix this. The only reason they didn't take this car is because it is in my name and the moment they realize he paid for it we won't even have it." She cried.

"Daddy would not do that!" I cried. I was overwhelmed with emotion.

"He did, and he has left me to deal with all this crap alone. Jasmine, I don't know what to do. His mother won't dare lend a dime to help me. I don't know what we are going to do." She cried.

"I have some money just take me to the bank. I have a safe deposit box!" I stated.

"I doubt you can get to it. If your father signed anything for you it has been seized." She shook her head.

"No, I mean he gave me the money, but I'm pretty sure it's in my name. It's not much, but I remember getting the box. He made me as a lesson when he picked me up from school."

"A lesson? Hmph! Your fucking father always had a lesson, didn't he? Well, I hope his ass has taught you well enough to get us out of this shit!" She hissed as she pulled away from the private school I'd attended since I started high school.

I was able to attain the money I deposited in the bank. It was in my name and it was mine to withdraw. However, up against what we were facing, the $10,000 was chump change. Thinking of our overall wellbeing, my mother decided we should go to a hotel to crash until she could figure out what we were going to do. Because of the amount of money we had, we couldn't afford anything we were used to. I'd say that night was the first I'd slept on cheap linen in my life. It didn't get any better despite the effort my mother put into trying to stay ahead of things. The IRS seized everything. They even took the cash from my father's life insurance policy. That ten grand was gone before we could even think to do anything. Daddy's people didn't like my mother one bit, and the moment they realized they would have to pay for my father's burial, they didn't bother hiding their disdain. My parents had been married eighteen years but not a single picture of their union made the obituary. Shit, my mother was barely mentioned and her being allowed was only because of me. Regardless of what my grandmother felt for my mom, she loved me. She even offered for me to come live with her. After all, I had a substantial amount of inheritance that would come on my 18th birthday regardless. I had to decline when she made it perfectly clear that my mother wasn't invited. In desperation, my mother went looking for a job. Once she had gotten a series of rejections in the small suburban city in which we lived, and after basically being blackballed from the area, she finally was able to attain a position in the city of Chicago. She took a job at a southside hospital called The University of Chicago, and we went searching for residence there.

Things got even worse from there despite the fact my mother, a registered nurse, was educated and highly capable of providing. She had made one mistake. She didn't have shit in her name. Nothing but that damn car to which she had to sell to get us the money to move. With no credit, no one would allow us to lease the type of properties we were considering, and with the high demand of apartments around the hospital area, we couldn't afford shit in our price range. We had no car, little money, and a messed-up situation. Eventually, after just about all the money was depleted from staying in the local Holiday Inn, my mother finally found us a place to stay that offered the convenience of location and stayed within our budget. The complex was only a ten-minute bus ride to the hospital. I was relieved until I was standing in front of what was proclaimed the Slater Mills housing projects. My stomach tied itself in knots as we rode the raggedy, pee infested elevator to the 11th floor. We walked from the elevator down a concrete hall that reminded me of a prison until we stood in front of apartment 1107. My mother opened the door and handed me a key off her key ring. A tear rolled down her face when I stepped across the welcome mat.

"This is temporary until I can find something better." my mother said shamefully.

I stepped in and looked around the apartment. My mother had gotten it furnished with the little money she had left from selling her vehicle. It wasn't the type of shit we were used to, but it felt like it was ours. Like home. I looked around the tiny apartment again and realized this was just fine. It wasn't that bad. It was small. There were only two bedrooms, a small kitchen, and a living room, but it was ours. It wasn't raggedy and didn't look half bad. After staying in hotel rooms for damn near a month, I was grateful. The outside of this complex looked like shit. It was littered with trash and rodents, and the smell of poverty lingered like the plague. But the inside looked decent. After placing my small bookbag of clothing into my neatly decorated room, I went back to my mother and hugged her for a job well done.

"Thanks, mommy, this is perfect. I like it!" I said as I buried my face in my mother's chest.

"Thank you Jazzy for having my back!" she replied.

"I love you!" I told her.

"I love you too, we're going to be ok!" she smiled once she broke our embrace. Although we didn't have any money, I slept well that night.

The next morning, I woke up to extremely loud music. It literally made the headboard pushed up against my wall shake. The damn walls were so thin I could hear the lyrics to the song.

"I'm a dog, I'm a dog, I'm a dog, I'm a dog, I'm a dog, I'm a dog, I'm a dog, I'm a dog

I'm a treat ha like a dog

Feed ha like a dog (Gucci)

Beat ha like a dog

Then pass ha to my dog....."

I popped up from my slumber with a frown on my face.

"Lord, why?" This was just what I expected it to be like here. At ten in the morning, some retard is bumping some gangster rap music like other people don't live here.

"Grrrr!" I growled into my pillow. Why God did you send me here? I got up from the bed and headed straight to the bathroom. I got in the shower and did something I hadn't done in a long time. Cried. I cried for old and new. I cried for the time

I scraped my knee on the playground. The time I sprained my ankle trying to wear my mama heels down the stairs. The time I broke my arm going skating. I cried about my dumb ass daddy and that stupid ex-boyfriend of mine who wanted my ex-best friend. I cried because we lived in the worse fucking apartment buildings in Chicago. I felt like I had nothing. Hell, realistically I didn't have much of anything. I had about four pairs of cheap jeans, two pairs of leggings and maybe a weeks' worth of shirts that I could match with the bottoms. I own one dress and two pairs of sandals. Not anything close to what I'm used to. When I think about it, I suppose, I could be worse off than that. After I had my little fit in the shower, I eventually washed up. I got out just after the hot water ran cold. I was fuming. I hate it here already.

I dried off, lotioned up, and threw on the flowery mini sleeveless dress that was on the clearance rack at Wet Seal. I went back to the bathroom where I'd plugged in my flat irons. I looked in the mirror at myself and sighed. I'm as dark as your darkest chocolate. I have full lips and high cheekbones. My lashes are long and I have a natural arch in my eyebrows. I stand 5"8, 165 pounds, proportioned like a Ghanaian princess. Where I have been raised has taught me to completely hate everything about my features, or at least they tried. My mother, only a few shades lighter, also has my features and she has taught me to love who I am. And I do. I'm beautiful and I know it. I love almost everything about me, but my hair. My hair was the one thing I've always disliked about myself. It is thick as wool and extremely unmanageable. I have a whole lot of length but it shrinks to my head and looks to me like a big matted mess. When I got old enough to go to the salon with my mother, I started to get it straightened. That is how I've been wearing it for the last few years. Unfortunately, after the whole ordeal with my father and us losing it all, I haven't seen the inside of an actual salon beyond watching the movie The Salon on the hotel's TV. My hair looked a mess, and I knew it was going to take me all day to straighten my hair the way I liked it, especially since my flat irons were cheap. It took me forever to flat iron all of my hair but two hours later I stepped out of the bathroom with my dark hair flowing behind me. It wasn't as straight as I liked it but it would have to do. When I walked into the kitchen to eat a bowl of cereal, I found a note my mom left.

Dear Jazzy,

I had to be at work at 8 and I won't be home until midnight, but I left you some money, and I hope you have a wonderful Saturday! -Love Mommy

I smiled and proceeded to eat. Yup, a wonderful Saturday indeed.

CHAPTER THREE:
PRINCE CHARMING

Jasmine

After I ate, I headed out the door and to the bus stop. My mother told me the mall was located all the way across town. I had to catch several buses to get there. I wanted to get something for my mom and something cute to wear to school on my first day. I had about seventy dollars. I was planning to buy her something to cheer her up. I knew she felt bad about our situation and she deserved to feel her sacrifice wasn't in vain. I arrived at the Ford city mall and headed straight for the stores. I walked into Zale's feeling confident in myself. I couldn't imagine jewelry in a city mall would be expensive and my mother loved jewelry. The salesman walked up to help me. I told him exactly what I wanted and he nicely showed me a few options while trying to bust a joke. I thought it was funny so I laughed. He showed me this one necklace that I absolutely loved. It had my birthstone in it and I wanted that one. My mom would love it! But when he told me the price, I was hurt. I knew I didn't have the money for it. I thanked him for his patience and for showing me the jewelry, but I couldn't get it. He nodded sympathetically at me, and I left the store feeling like shit. I knew my mom would have loved that necklace and I felt bad, but I knew I couldn't cry over it. I headed to the food court for a slice of pizza before I headed home. I stood in the line of the little pizza shack in the mall. This light skin boy with pretty-hazel eyes was there trying to talk to me. He was cute but it was obvious what he wanted. He barely even looked in my face. So, I politely dismissed him hoping he'd just walk away but he didn't. Damn my luck. He was still asking me my name. Talking about how he'd love to get to know me. "What the fuck ever," I thought. I was about to tell him off, but when I turned around he wasn't there anymore. I was surprised to see a tall handsome gentleman with shopping bags in his hand. I smiled. Damn, this boy was fine. He had smooth caramel skin and a sexy head of the neatest dreads I'd ever seen. He was handsome. He had the prettiest deep brown eyes, thick shapely eyebrows, and full pink lips. He wore a fitted shirt that showed a toned chest and his tattooed arms were nice too. He wore two gold chains that hung off his neck complimenting the gold diamond earrings he wore. I mean, I've never really thought guys in earrings were a thing, but it seemed to be popular here. I looked him up and down and I couldn't find anything unattractive about him. I thought he'd speak so I waited for him to say something for a while, but he didn't. After standing there longer than it took for a conversation, I got the feeling something was wrong. He was just standing there staring.

"Umm excuse me, are you ok?" I asked. He still just stared like a zombie.

"Excuse me....hellooo!" I said waving my hand in front of his face.

He snapped back out of his trance and took a step backward before smiling at me. When he did, my heart skipped a beat. He had the most beautiful smile I have ever seen. His teeth were straight and white and he had the deepest dimples I had ever seen on a person. He was gorgeous...until he opened his mouth.

"Shit, my bad ma. What's up?" he said. My interest dropped.

Damn, he had to ruin it with the way he just approached me.

Damn it! I thought with the look of disapproval all over my face. But I still thought he was fine so I cleaned it up as I smiled politely.

"Oh, there isn't anything up. I don't think." I said looking up at the ceiling. He started laughing. Why was I so amused by his laugh? He made me laugh as well. After a moment of both of us laughing, we both just smiled at each other. It was this bare silence and we both just stared at each other. His eyes were so... There isn't a word I can think of to describe them. I broke the silence.

"Um...I was just checking on you. You know to see if you were all right..." I stated.

He smiled. "Thanks, I'm fine," he said.

I nodded. "Good," I said.

He chuckled a bit. "Yeah, well, I'll see you," he said before he walked off and I got my pizza. I sat down to eat it when that same guy walked back up to me at the table. I looked up at him and smiled again. He shook his head.

"What's wrong?" I asked more concerned than I should've been for someone I didn't know.

"I forgot something," he said and he sat this little cute polka dot gift bag on the table.

"What's this?" I asked reaching for it.

"That's for you, sweetie. Have a good day!" he said with a smile and just walked away.

I was stunned. I didn't know what to do. I thanked him before I could even consider the gift. What could he have possibly gotten that fast and why for me? I reached for the bag and picked up the box inside. I opened it in shock. I got up almost right away and ran towards where I'd seen him walk but I promise he'd vanished. Damn. I thought. It was the necklace I wanted from Zale's and it was over a hundred dollars. I don't even know him and he doesn't know me. Why would he buy this for me? I don't even know his name. I was so grateful but disappointed in the fact that he had gone and there was no way for me to properly thank him. I left the mall shortly after he disappeared, but I hoped I would see him again one day. He was so sweet. "What a nice person," I thought. As I headed to the bus stop, I couldn't help but smile. Thought my luck was turning around. Didn't come out of the clouds until two women started arguing on the public bus. I sighed as I exited at my stop. "I'll never get used to this." I thought as I walked toward my apartment building up the concrete pathway between a large slab of dirt that surrounded the buildings. People just walked around like nothing was wrong, and here I was stuck in the most unlikely place I thought I'd ever be. I shook my head and hummed Bon Jovi's Livin' on a Prayer because I truly was.

◆ ◆ ◆

MyKing

I cannot believe myself. But that chick was fine. Beyond fine, she was fucking beautiful. I wonder what her life is like? Does she have a man? I laughed. Why the fuck do I even care and why am I spending bread on a bitch I ain't even smashed? I'm tweaking. I thought. That ain't even me and I don't want no bitch that will change me. Shit, I don't want a bitch at all. I shook my head as I started my truck. Heading out the parking lot I spotted the chick getting on the bus. I smiled. That girl is beautiful, I swear. Even though I don't give a fuck about no bitch. I must say she seems like someone special and that's why I can't fuck with her. I realized that right away the necklace was a sign from ma telling me to leave her alone and that's why I had to walk away.

I bullshitted with Kevin and Tevin most of the day. When the time was right, I went through the money and made my count before heading home. I was thinking about what I'd get into or who I'd get into later that night. I decided to call Mya, my go to. No matter what, I can go to Mya. She was bad as hell. Bright, light skin, red bone with thick lips and hips. Ass high enough to play pool on and her pussy was good enough to marry, but we just fucking. I like Mya. She doesn't sweat a nigga. She knows her place. She knows just what to do to get what she wants from me and she freaky as hell.

"Hello?" She answered.

"Wassup ma, what you doing?" I asked.

"Ain't shit baby, I miss you, King." She said.

"Yeah, I know, I'm missing you too, come see me," I told her.

"Ok I'm getting ready now, I won't be long ok." She said and I smiled.

"Aight, I'm waiting," I told her before I hung up.

Mya, Mya, Mya. I thought. If I was gone wife a bitch, she'd be the one. She easy to be with, do whatever to please me, and does it with so much passion you'd think she was put on earth to be my servant. Maybe she's the one, but I just can't commit to no female. I just ain't interested in being in a relationship. I had been fucking with her since my sophomore year. She graduated the end of that school year. She was two years older than me but that ain't seem to matter when it came down to it.

When I finally got in the house I went straight for the shower. I got out and my phone starts ringing.

"Hello?" I answered.

"Yeah, come open the door babe." She said.

I hung up and went to answer my door. She was standing there looking good enough to eat. She favored the singer Ashanti, just thicker and a lil lighter. She smiled and gave me a tight hug and kissed my lips as she entered. I got hard instantly, she always smells so good.

"Baby, I missed you." She said.

"Yeah, I know. I missed you too." I told her. As I pulled her into my bedroom.

"King, I hope you changed the sheets after you fucked them hoes," she said smartly.

"What hoes?" I asked knowing exactly the hoes she was talking about.

"Nigga, you think I'm stupid? I'm not, and I heard you had Toni in this muthafucka recently. Don't even try and lie cause the bitch described yo dick all the way down to the size and mole on the side." she said.

I smiled cause I loved Mya's attitude. She was smiling too.

"Who's dick?" I asked her.

She walked up to me and kissed my neck. She slid her tongue across it then grabbed my belt.

"Mine," she said as she undid my belt.

I was happy as shit. I ain't have to tell her what to do because she knows exactly how I like it. She dropped my pants and boxers and they fell to my knees. She got down to suck my shit. She smiled and blew on it.

"King, you just remember one thing when you fucking them hoes." she started.

I smiled at her. "And what's that?" I asked.

"This is my dick." She said stroking my move. "And ain't nobody gonna handle my dick the way I handle my dick," she said.

"Show me?" I tested.

She looked at me like I was a piece of steak sat in front of a lion.

"Oh, shit" I moaned as she sucked the head of my dick straight to the back of her throat. Two minutes later I was nutting. She can suck it like no other and that's why I keep her on call. It's so good it makes me cum quick, and she drinks it down like its warm milk. She smiled at me when she got up and went over to my dresser. She grabbed a rubber and put it on my dick with her mouth.

"King, you always get me so wet." she moaned.

I smiled because I didn't have to do shit to her.

I grabbed her, then pulled her dress over her head. I first took off her bra and panties. I start rubbing on her clit with two fingers. I smiled. She was wet.

"How you want it, Daddy?" She asked me in her sexy voice.

"Ma, come ride this dick," I told her. She nodded and I laid back. She got on top of me and slid down on my pipe. She starts moving her hips grinding on me slowly at first. Once she got comfortable enough to speed up, it was on. She was jumping on it. You could hear her pussy smacking as she bounced up and down. The feeling was amazing. Her pussy is good. Real good. I grabbed her hips so I could have more control over how much dick went inside her. I start thrusting further inside. She starts moaning louder.

"Kinggggg oh ahhhh shit babbyyyy... I'm cumming don't stopppp." she moaned. I just kept at it until we both busted. She fell against me and I pulled out of her and got up to go to the bathroom. She grabbed me.

"Uh, where you going?" She asked with a smirk on her face. I smiled because I knew what she wanted. She got off the bed and kissed me.

"My dick, all mine she sang." I chuckled.

"Say it, King." She ordered. I couldn't help but smile.

"It's all yours Mya," I told her.

"I know," she said as she bent over in front of me. "Now give it to me." She ordered. I slapped her fat ass hard before stepping towards my draw. She barely gave me time to recover before she wanted some more. I grabbed another rubber and I slid back into her and put in the work though. The best thing about Mya is she can take the dick. Even when I'm fucking her hard she still screams harder. I love that. I was beating her shit up, but she loved it.

Jasmine

I got home and I went straight to my bedroom. I laid on my bed just thinking about the necklace I got today. My mom is gonna love it. I really wish I knew the guy's name. He's so dreamy and sweet. He really must be someone special. I hope I get to see him again. I eventually fell asleep and I don't know how long I had slept before my nap was interrupted. I start hearing sexual noises and someone next door to me banging against the wall. Yuck! This shit is fucking terrible. I hate my neighbor! I snatched my covers off before I decided to go take a shower. I got in and soon after the hot water started to massage my body my mind drifted back to the sweet mystery man. I wonder what his life is like? Does he have a girlfriend? Where does he live? How old is he? Does he go to school? Where does he work? Man, I wish I at least knew his name.

I stayed in the bathroom longer to keep from hearing that dreadful sound of whoever it was next door getting busy. It reminded me of my ex-best friend Britney and ex-boyfriend Ryan having sex the day I caught them in the locker room of my old school. I had been trying to call him but he wasn't answering which was weird considering the fact he was my boyfriend at the time. I was just about to leave school because I and Brit were supposed to be meeting up at my house later for movie night. I realized when I got to the front door of the school, I'd left my house keys in my gym locker after volleyball practice. So, I had to go back. I picked up the phone and tried to call Ryan again as I approached the locker rooms.

I heard his phone. So, I started looking around until I heard voices.

"Ohh baby you feel so good," he said.

"I love you, Ryan." she moaned.

"I know Brit, I love you too," he said.
I walked up to them behind the six rows of lockers and they both jumped off each other. I almost threw up when I saw the wet looking condom on Ryan's exposed dick. I was disgusted. He jumped up to try and explain but I ran to my locker grabbed my keys and left. I was sad that my best friend had gone behind my back and had sex with my boyfriend, but now that I think about it, it might've been the best thing that could've happened. I didn't like him that much anyway. "Fuck them." I thought as I got out of the shower because the water turned cold, shocking me out my lil memory. I dried off and rubbed down in some baby oil and went back to my room. It was quiet so I fixed me something to eat, straightened up the house and laid down in my bed. It wasn't long before I drifted off to sleep again.

The next day started like every day here did. Loud ass gangster music that usually didn't even make any sense to me. One song even talked about bricks! Like who thought it was a good idea to rap about blocks used to build things? And even more retarded is the dumb ass who listens to the garbage. I got out of bed angry that I'd been woken up again. I hated it here. I sighed. I started to get ready because I'd convinced myself that I was really going to find me an outfit or two for school the next day. After all, my initial visit didn't go as planned and I was beautifully distracted by the guy who came to me like a knight in shining armor. My prince charming! However, I can't say I didn't hope to see him again in hopes of thanking him for the necklace he purchased for me. I hadn't had the chance to give it to my mother but I would today when she got off work. I got dressed and walked towards the bus stop at the very edge of the building where I was verbally assaulted by just about every male I walked past. It was a series of comments that let me know that here it was ok to talk up under someone's clothing. And if that wasn't bad enough, the women here looked at me like I stunk with their noses all turned up at me like I'd done something wrong. I just shook my head and ignored them. I figured if I didn't say anything to anyone then I would not be a target but I'd given up on actually making friends here. I just figured we wouldn't be here long enough for me to care. After waiting a few minutes for a bus, I got on thankful that it wasn't as congested as it had been the day before. I road to the mall excitedly anticipating running into my dream guy.

There weren't many people in the mall on this beautiful Sunday morning and it seemed to be the best time to shop. I still only had sixty bucks but after utilizing the clearance racks at some of the stores I found attractive, I'd actually purchased some nice items. I had started to become excited about my first day. Unfortunately, after two hours of being in the mall, I didn't see my dream bae. I left disappointed I didn't get the chance to see him again. I went straight home to get ready for school and help my mother with dinner. We laughed and fooled around as we always did when we cooked together. My mother could cook like no other. My maternal grandmother was a certified big mama. She made my mother learn to cook way before she had even met my dad. Even after she married and attained the rich and lavish lifestyle, she always personally prepared our meals. Cooking was a talent my mother had naturally and luckily, she passed it right down to me. Despite the things that had happened I'm glad our bond had not changed. She was still, very much so, my best friend and I was grateful to still have her. After eating dinner, we both cleaned and prepared for the day ahead of us. I went to my room and attained the box with the necklace in it. I went to her room where she lay comfortably on her bed with a book in her hand.

"Mommy, I got something for you," I told her as I handed her the box.

"Jazzy, girl what have you went out and bought?" she asked as she removed the top from the box. I held my breath nervously as she inhaled sharply.

"Oh my, Jazzy, this is beautiful. Thank you...where did you get it?" she asked almost immediately.

"I saw it in one of the stores in the mall and I thought of you," I told her.

"That's sweet. I think this is a beautiful necklace but where did you get the money to afford it. It doesn't look fake...or cheap." She started.

"It was cheap...I was able to afford it." I assured her.

"Well, ...it looks real." She stated.

"It is. It was just real, cheap, and affordable." I assured her with a big smile.

"Well thank you. I'll put it on and never take it off. She smiled as she held out her arms for a hug. I didn't hesitate to fall in her arms and I just stayed there because I could.

"Mom...how is work?" I asked her laying on her like a small child.

"It's alright, it's tough but I think I can manage. I'm working as much as possible so that we can get out of here quickly. I'm probably going to be working long hours now. I just need to go in and do what I have to do. I have to be at work at six in the morning. Do you want me to wake you up when I get up or do you think you will be ok waking up for school on your own?

"I will be fine, mom. Besides, I am not waking up two hours earlier than I must. That is absurd." I told her.

"Yeah well just don't be late on your first day. First impressions are everything. The bus schedules are a little hectic during the week especially early in the mornings because everybody is trying to get somewhere. The traffic is really bad. I found out from some of my coworkers that the buses can be late at times. So, you might want to be out of the house a few minutes earlier so you won't have a problem with being late for school.

"Ok mom, I'll make sure I get there on time. Goodnight!" I told her before I got off of her to kiss her cheek and go lay my clothes out for the following day. I believed I had everything I needed for a successful first day. And I hoped it would go better than I could imagine it would be here. After all, I had never been to a public school a day in my life. I didn't know what to expect really. I bathed and comfortably got into bed and drifted to sleep.

◆ ◆ ◆

MyKing

I woke up Sunday morning in a good mood. After taking a leak, I went toward the kitchen for a cup of orange juice. At the table sat a tall dark man who looked up at me like I didn't belong. In front of him was a full breakfast. He had a cup of orange juice, sausage, eggs, and my fucking French toast. I got pissed instantly.

"Aye, what the fuck are you doing bruh? Why the fuck is you eating my shit?" I asked as I approached him angrily about to mash his face in the plate of food I bought for myself.

"Um your mama…" he started. I cut him off because I'd already gathered my own conclusion and nothing he said was going to keep me from beating his ass and throwing him the fuck out my crib.

"Nigga I don't give a fuck about what my mama did. You in here eating food I fucking bought." I said as I snatched his ass up from the chair by his collar.

"MyKing, let him go. He hasn't done nothing to you. Let him go." She said as she came in to get me off her friend.

"What the fuck you mean? Why you got buddy in here finna get beat the fuck up, eating my shit?" I asked her angrily.

"Excuse me? Fred is my company and this is my house, therefore, I can do whatever the fuck I want in this muthafucka! You can get the fuck out if you don't like it" she snapped.

"Ma, you got me fucked up. I pay the bills in this house and you ain't bought nothing to have the audacity to let a nigga eat shit that I paid for. You can miss me with that." I told her.

"Bitch watch your fucking dirty ass mouth in my house!" She hissed.

"Ma, you really in here defending this nigga over me like he some fucking don. This nigga got a free fuck and some French toast and you standing here arguing with me like some low budget ass hoe. If you gone fuck at least make you some money!" I spat furiously. As soon as I got the words out my mouth she slapped the shit out of me.

"I am still your mother and I don't give a fuck what you pay. You are going to respect me!" she snapped. I ran my hand across my face with gritted teeth and half a mind to slap her ass back.

"I don't see anything to respect," I told her before turning around going back into my room. I immediately turned on my music to get ready to leave. I hated being in the same city as my mother let alone the same house. But I wasn't gone leave because, at the end of the day, she was my mother. She was the only family I had. As fucked up as a person I thought she was, I knew I was all she had too.

By the time I'd gotten dressed, my mother was gone. So, I took the time to straighten up the house before I left. I had no real plans. Sundays were always chill days for me. I slid down to Keys Detail shop to have my truck washed and detailed and I enjoyed conversing with some of the old heads that were there shooting the shit as usual. I kicked it with Tev and Kevin a little while before just going back into the house to sleep. I had school the following day anyway.

CHAPTER FOUR:
LITTLE RED RIDING
IN THE HOOD

MyKing

T he next morning, I woke up early and turned on my music. It always got me motivated to start the day. I ironed my clothes and hopped in the shower. After getting dressed I grabbed my shit to vacate the house. I hopped in my truck and stopped at McDonald's like I did every morning before finally heading to school. I had become irritated soon after first period.

"Hey King, wassup? You act like you can't speak." Melissa started.

"Wassup?" I asked uninterestedly. Her pussy wasn't good enough for me to care and she talked too much for my liking.

"So, you can't text back?" she asked me.

"For what?" I asked visibly agitated.

"Damn, ok nigga you ain't all that." She said with her nose all scrunched up at me.

"So why the fuck you in my face then bitch?" I asked her before

I walked off leaving her standing in the hallway with the shit face. I walked into second period just to have Toni mugging me the entire time. I really can't stand when I give these bitches the opportunity to fuck and they take it and use it to make it something else. Give a bitch some inches and she takes a mile. But pussy ain't never moved me. Hell, my mama gives up pussy all day long and I still ain't never had a father. It's not really that I hate women, I mean I ain't no faggot or nothing. Just couldn't see past what they can do for me physically. Truth is, I've never felt anything emotionally for a woman beyond Rita. She was just the only woman I ever been around who really seemed to give a fuck about me rather than what I could do for her. I know because I ain't have shit and she loved me just the same.

When the bell rung, I got up to leave and Tony decided she would run into me scuffing the new shoes I'd just bought. Before I could react and snatch the bitch by her raggedy looking weave, Mr. T, stopped me.

"Son, what's going on in your mind today?" he asked as the class exited the room. I gritted my teeth to keep from saying the wrong thing. Reason being because Mr. T was cool. His name was Mr. Thompson and he put you in the mind of Rick Foxx. I called him Mr. T. because I fucked with him. He always made it his business to check up on a nigga. I had a lot of respect for him. So, I always checked myself before speaking with him.

"I'm alright," I told him.

"You weren't even paying attention today. That is so unlike you. Especially in my class." He started.

"Just got some stuff on my mind. But you know I'm going to always get the lesson. I always do." I told him.

"That's true. You thought about filling out those college applications I gave you?" he asked as he started to erase the board.

"Yeah, I thought about it," I replied.

"And? You pick a school? You can definitely get a scholarship."

He said.

"Nah, I haven't but I did think about it," I admitted.

"Ok, well let me know if I can do anything to help." He said.

"Cool. Will do." I assured him before I anxiously left the class. I had lunch third period and I was about to ring Tony's fucking neck. Well, I didn't really plan to put my hands on her but she was definitely about to wipe my fucking shoes off in front of everybody like the dog ass bitch she was. I walked towards the lunchroom on a mission. As soon as I turned the corner, I ran smack into another broad. The bitch hit the floor before I could tell her to watch my fucking shoes. I looked down at her about to go the fuck off but when she looked up at me she broke out into a full miserable heart-wrenching cry. I got stuck in my tracks.

Jasmine

I woke up completely pissed that, once again, I was hearing this dreadful music. My next-door neighbor will not be getting a Christmas card from me. Fucking idiot. I got up already mad. Despite my positive attitude on yesterday, I knew today would be a crappy ass day. I got up and hopped in the shower. It wasn't until I was already washing that I realized I didn't put on a shower cap. My hair is completely natural and had gotten wet and started to curl up. I was freaking livid because I hated my natural hair. When I finally got out to examine the damage I could have cried. Despite the fact that my hair fell down my back straightened, I had a big bushy ass fro sitting on top of my head and it was hideous. Realistically, I didn't have the time to straighten it and be on time. I decided to get some moisturizer and gel and make it look halfway decent for the day. I brushed it up into one big puff on top of my head. I looked like Thelma off of Good Times, looking for my African prince. And it was fitting because I lived in a Chicago project just like she did. "It is going to be a miserable ass day," I thought. I brushed the soft hairs that wouldn't lay down with gel and hoped my classmates were nice about it. I proceeded to my room and realized after glancing at the clock I was ten minutes late for the bus. "Shit!" I hissed as I hurriedly pulled on my clothes. When I put on the shirt I realized it was a size too small and it was tight around my bust area which made me look way bigger than I was. Wouldn't have been a bad thing if it didn't look to me like I was wearing a shirt that belonged to my little sister. But because my wardrobe was limited, I had to ignore that too. I didn't have time to change anyway. I was already late. After getting completely dressed I looked in the mirror to get one final look at myself before I left. All the confidence I thought I'd had was gone. I looked like a black ass poodle. I held my head low as I exited the building. I didn't even get the chance to eat because of all the time it took me to get my puff right. I'd gotten off the elevator and swiftly walked toward the bus stop. When I saw the bus there, I took off running in hopes of catching it. Unfortunately, the bus driver pulled off as soon as I had gotten to the bus stop. I wanted so badly to kick the side of that big ugly ass CTA sign. "Ugh!" I screeched as it rolled away without even acknowledging my effort. And a few men that were standing nearby started to laugh at my misery. I wanted to give them the finger out of pure embarrassment, but I was too fearful of what they might do to me if I did. I held my head down and the only thing I could think to do was pray. I prayed that another bus would come shortly and that my day would get a little better. But the good lord was in one of his moods where he wasn't listening to me. I finally gave up hope after fifteen minutes. When another bus finally did show up I was already nearly an hour late. I was completely over it as I sat in the only vacant seat on the bus. Unfortunately, it was right behind an overweight woman who smelled like a public washroom. I was disgusted and it probably showed all over my face. I turned around in the seat to block the body odor coming from the lady and looked right up at an old man sitting across from me with no teeth smiling and blowing wet kisses. I was mortified. Figured my day couldn't get any worse. I was grateful to get to my stop and got up to exit the bus. When I got off in front of John Marshall High my stomach dropped to my shoes. This school looked like a prison. There was nothing remotely attractive about the bricked building. It was literally one building. I instantly thought about the school Matilda attended in the movie with the evil principal. I was afraid to walk in because I didn't know what to expect on the other side of the door. I walked into the building and was immediately greeted by metal detectors similar to the ones you'd see at the airport. I was trying to quickly figure out why they needed the detectors while walking straight through it. Security approached me as soon as I walked through and the alarm went off.

"Give me your bag." The short stubby security guard growled like he'd smoked way too many cigarettes. I was so afraid I couldn't verbally respond. I handed him the bag and was instructed to walk back through the detector which didn't make a sound. While my book bag was placed on a conveyor belt attached to a monitor that allowed the security guard to see the contents inside, I was mortified. He gave me my book bag and I stood there waiting for him to direct me to the office. He looked at me like I was crazy.

"Um…can you tell me where the office is please?" I asked with the phoniest smile I could muster. He pointed in the direction of the office like he wished I'd get out his face. I frowned and thanked him dryly as I walked toward the office.

Upon entering my palms had started to sweat. I was late for class and I didn't feel all that great about it. I was hoping that after the horrible morning I'd had, getting my class schedule would be the easiest part of this whole ordeal. I didn't realize I'd been wrong until I was rudely greeted by Ms. Boxton. She was a slender bright skin woman with a hanging mole on her chin and a long wavy ponytail. Her glasses hung at the tip of her nose where she peered over the lenses. And wrapped around the arms of her glasses were a beaded chain that also wrapped around her neck. I could tell despite the wrinkles and a permanent frown on her face, she was once a very attractive woman. She had aged well.

"Uh, where are you supposed to be? The bell just rang for third period and I am not writing any tardy passes." She frowned.

"Uh…My name is Jasmine Davis. I just transferred here." I stated.

"Oh yeah, I have your schedule. Why are you late? You've missed your first two classes! Were you not informed that you were supposed to be here by seven forty-five?" she asked rudely. She didn't hide her disgust in my tardiness.

I held my head in shame as I apologized. She didn't care anything about my apology. She handed me the schedule and told me to get to class. Her attitude was abrasive and nasty and I reluctantly took the schedule and left the office. I looked at the piece of paper in my hand trying to figure out where I was supposed to be going and after walking around the first floor looking like a total idiot my eyes had started to water. I realized nobody was going to help me. I turned the corner hoping to find the next class and ran smack into a wall. I got knocked flat on my ass. I could no longer hold my tears. I broke out into the ugliest cry I'd ever had. The tears were rushing down my face so fast I could barely see. I placed my face in my hands and cried like a big ass baby in the middle of that damn floor. I would have stayed down there all day crying had I not heard his voice.

"Damn baby, I'm…sorry. I wasn't even paying attention." He said apologetically. I looked up and my dream guy, the one from the mall, was standing directly in front of me.

"You." I said completely shocked. Where did the wall go?" I blurted lamely. He chuckled.

"You alright? My bad." He said as he reached out to help me up. I took his hand and he assisted me to my feet. I just stared at him. I didn't even know what to say. I can only imagine what I must've looked like with a wet face and red eyes. Hell, I might even have boogers. I thought. I was so ashamed and I knew he could tell.

"Don't be like that...I said I was sorry. You don't forgive me?" he joked as he took my hand again.

"Yeah, of course. I was looking down at this paper. I'm lost and I've had the worse morning of my life. It was completely my fault and I apologize for bumping into you...And I want to thank you for the necklace you bought. I was hoping to see you again to tell you how much I appreciate you. It was extremely kind and my mother loved it." I thanked him.

"It was nothing. And you're welcome. Let me see your schedule." He offered. I handed him the paper and let him take a look. He started laughing.

"What?" I asked confused.

"You have my schedule with the exception of 6th and 8th period." He said.

"Ok, that's good. At least I'll have somebody I know who can guide me in the right direction." I sighed in relief.

"Yeah, I got you. Come on, juniors have lunch this period." He said as he walked away expecting me to follow.

"But it's still morning...why can't we just take our lunch afternoon?" I asked completely confused. He laughed again.

"What's your name and what are you doing here?" he asked. Guess it was obvious I didn't belong.

"Jasmine Davis and I'm a transfer," I told him as we walked towards the lunchroom.

"I'm MyKing, but you can call me King." He said showing those beautiful dimples on his face. I was going to say something because I've heard the name before but got distracted by his smile. I politely extended my hand to him as we stopped in front of the opened door. He looked down at my hand and chuckled before he shook it.

"Where are you from shorty?" he asked.

"Winnetka, Illinois," I stated.

"For real? That's crazy. That fall down must've really hurt." He stated.

"No…I had just been having a bad day. It didn't hurt." I explained.

"Nah, I'm not talking about that…Never mind. I got you. Just stick with me, ok." He said.

"Alright." I agreed as we walked into the lunchroom to have all eyes directed at us. I froze right in that spot and the moment he noticed he grabbed my hand.

"Relax, baby. I got you." He smiled. I had to use context clues to figure out what he meant by that.

◆ ◆ ◆

MyKing

When I realized, this was shorty from the mall, my whole attitude changed. When I helped her off the floor I could see right through her. I could tell wasn't a damn thing malicious about her. She was perfect. I immediately felt bad for her because she didn't realize where she was. It was something about Chicago that could suck the life out of anything. Especially here in the hood. But when I looked at her, all I could see is a light. And she shined. Every time she opened her mouth or looked me in my eyes, I felt something. Like I'd been given a star in a place full of darkness. The only thing that bothered me about her is the fact she was so oblivious. I couldn't figure out why she was here but she stuck out like a sore thumb. She was so beautiful, hopeful, and bright. When she thanked me, I felt like Superman. I guess in her mind she thought a nigga was a hero or something. She never even thought about the fact I was just tryna fuck. And I would never admit that's exactly what I planned to do to her. Now, after all the praise she'd just given me, I felt guilty. Like I owed her something. And my first mind told me to get the fuck away from her then. I have never felt guilty about anything and the feeling was foreign. Everything about her was completely different. She talked with enunciation. She didn't use slang words. She held her head high and looked you in your eyes when she spoke to you. Didn't seem to be afraid to be who she was. Her confidence was undeniable. Even right now at what I presumed to be her most vulnerable state. She comes from Winnetka. The shit is almost comical. Winnetka, Illinois is the richest city in the state. Actually, it's one of the richest cities in the entire country. What that means is the girl standing in front of me comes from an extremely wealthy family. I'm not talking get rich money. I mean that old rich generational money. Her being here meant that something had gone terribly wrong and she was so modest about it. Somebody fucked her money up. And all I could think about is how she should feel. I was born in one of the worst neighborhoods in the city. I ain't never had shit, so if I lose all my money today I would be mad but the struggle would be familiar to me. But I could tell just by her demeanor that this was as close to struggling that she has ever been. It was unfamiliar to her. Even the type of nigga I am is unfamiliar to her. That means she doesn't realize how close to danger she really is. When we walked into the lunch room her presence made it very clear that if I didn't protect her she'd lose all the light she had. I couldn't help but feel like I was leading little red riding hood through the woods. But I was the wolf.

The moment I grabbed her hand I marked my territory. The envy I looked back at made me smile. The niggas were mad and the bitches were jealous and it was something about the way this looked that excited me. I sat across from her at the table and watched her eat. Her skin was dark and smooth and she had brown baby doll eyes. Her hair was long and curly and I knew that was gone piss all these bald-headed bitches off. Her breast set straight up in her shirt and I couldn't keep from staring at her. And when she got up to trash the remnants of her lunch, that fat ass behind her put a smile on my face. Jasmine was sexy as fuck.

◆ ◆ ◆

Jasmine

The rest of the day went by like butter. MyKing stayed by my side the entire rest of the day. And he walked me to and from the two classes we did not have together. And by the time the dismissal bell rung he was waiting at the door for me to step out of the classroom. It was something I really liked about him. Other than the fact he was attractive, he was caring. And I knew that day I had a huge crush on him.

"So, how was your day overall?" he asked as we walked through the halls towards my locker.

"I can't complain. I am so glad you came along to help. I am completely out of my element. But the curriculum is simple and I think I'll be ok with grades." I told him.

"Yeah, it's not hard. Really, all it takes for you to pass is to do the work. That's it. And I got you. If you need help with anything just let me know. He offered.

"Thank you, MyKing. You're the best." I told him.

"You're welcome. Where do you stay? Do you need a ride or something?" He asked.

"Nooo!" I said excitedly. I mean technically I did need a ride but I didn't want him to know where I lived. It was unflattering to live in the projects and I didn't want him to know that I lived there. Slater mills are low income based apartments and I was embarrassed. I guess I just didn't want to lose him before he got the chance to get to know and like me for me. I just didn't want him to think little of me because I didn't have anything.

"Damn…ok, I was just asking," he said sounding almost offended.

"No..no..I'm sorry. I didn't mean it that way. My uh..dad is coming to pick me up. He is really strict and he will literally die if he saw me conversing with a guy he hadn't met yet. So, to avoid any…confrontations. It's best that you go ahead and go home and I will see you first thing tomorrow in first period." I lied.

"Okay cool. I understand. So just give me your number. I'll text you to make sure you got home safe." He said.

"Um..dang…I was grounded and my father took my cell phone. I haven't seen it in weeks." I lied again. The truth was my old cell phone had been cut off for none payment a while ago. I still had it but there was no way I'd be able to text him back. I was ashamed. Honestly, the only thing more embarrassing than having your services cut off is having them completely taken away. I'd experienced both those things in the last few months. And I and my mother were the laughing stock of Winnetka. People I've known all my life has turned their nose up at our misfortune. I just did not want MyKing to look at me like some poor girl from the projects and not be interested in me.

"Okay…well, I guess I'll see you tomorrow." He said. Before he leaned over to give me a hug. I wrapped my arms around him and the smell of his deodorant sent chills down my back. The butterflies in my stomach were flapping around like there wouldn't be a tomorrow. I didn't want to let him go.

"Bye MyKing," I said as he flashed those dimples before walking towards the double doors I'd come through earlier. I made sure he was completely out of sight before I could finally leave. Right, when I got to the exit a girl I'd seen in some of my classes had come and knocked my notebook completely out of my hand unto the floor. I looked up at her expecting an apology because I thought it was a mistake.

"Bitch." She hissed at me before she walked through the door like she hadn't done anything. I bent to pick up the notebook completely confused. I hadn't done or said anything to anyone specifically to avoid conflict. Now I'm getting picked on at random. What did I do to her?" I thought as I walked towards the bus stop alone.

CHAPTER FIVE: BEAUTIFUL LIAR

Jasmine

W hen I got home, I was floating. I couldn't hide the smile on my face. I literally did my homework, cooked, and bathed wearing a smile. My damn face had started to hurt.

"I take it somebody had a good first day." My mother came in from work. She looked tired and I felt bad.

"Yes, it was great…but how was your day? I cooked dinner! Just some green beans, mashed potatoes, and corn. I know it isn't much but there wasn't anything else to cook." I told her.

"Yea well I did attempt to get food stamps but they won't give it to me because of the money I make at the hospital. Apparently, poor people who don't work get more benefits than the people who do. But I get paid Friday so I should be able to stock up on groceries for at least two weeks.

"Well just sit down and eat your dinner. I'll go run your bath water now." I got up towards the bathroom.

"Jazzy you are the best. I sure do appreciate all the support you've given. Even despite the situation." She sighed.

"No problem mom," I said before I kissed her cheek.

"I am so sorry that I didn't protect you like I should've. I truly resent that. I didn't even see this coming." She looked up at me with teary eyes.

"Aw mom...I do feel protected. You know everything happens for a reason and I've had a really good life. I've traveled, shopped, and ate enough for six lifetimes. I don't need any of that materialistic stuff. It's not so bad here. I have one friend. He's really nice. I'm ok. We will be ok. I'll start looking for a job if it will help. Two incomes will be better than one. We won't even need food stamps. "I told her.

"No, I got it. Just worry about school and I can handle the rest." She said before she said her grace. I ran her water and proceeded to my room to start preparing for the next day. I was determined not to have any of the issues I ran into today. I picked out a cute little-fitted top I got the other day and a pair of my jeans. I tried the outfit on just to make sure it would fit right when I put it on tomorrow. Once satisfied with the outfit I had to figure out what to do with my hair. I was planning to straighten it but my mother had gone into the bathroom by the time I got ready to. I fell asleep before I even realized.

The irritating bass of the speaker woke me up. I threw a pillow towards the wall as I made my way to the bathroom. The sun was already shining through my bedroom window. After I hurriedly showered and got dressed, I start working on my hair. I tried my best to comb it down some but no matter what I did I just could not tame my mane. I was so disappointed in the style I was trying to do. Eventually, I just said fuck it and got the brush and gel to make it happen. The only difference between the puff I had yesterday is its position on my head. And although I hated it, it had to do. I got out at the bus stop in time because I didn't eat. There wasn't anything for me to cook anyway. I road to school silently staring out of the window. Thinking about the life I had and my dad. It was still so unreal to me that he was gone. He was still so alive in my head that seeing him in that casket was merely a blur to me. Like a bad dream. In my head, he was going to reappear one day. And my life would go back to normal. I felt something wet fall onto my hand and I looked down to see what it was. I didn't realize I was crying until I felt my face with my hands. It almost felt numb. That was it. I was numb.

I looked up after wiping my face. I saw that the bus was leaving the stop I should've gotten off at. The crazy thing is a ton of people got off at the stop and I just completely missed it. I pulled the string to get off at the next street and after I exited, I just walked the block towards the school. Mentally preparing for the day ahead of me. I did get there slightly tardy but at least I made it in time to go to first period. I walked into class and the teacher introduced herself right away. She was polite and encouraged me to sit wherever I chose. I looked up into the faces of a room full of people. The only smiling face I saw was MyKing. I saw a seat conveniently beside him and made my way towards it. By the time, I'd sat down I was comfortable. Even though I didn't really know him that well I felt protected. He made it his business to make me feel like I belonged. That was what I liked the most about him.

MyKing

I didn't believe anything Jasmine told me. She was so damn cute though. I could tell when she was lying because when she's being honest it doesn't sound the same. I had scoped her out after the first few days. Shorty wasn't even making sense most of the time. Especially when I asked her certain questions. And I would have been told her to move around if I had hit already.

But I can't stunt, I like her. Even though she lies through her teeth every day.

I decided to wait in the parking lot one day after school and watched her tiptoe towards the bus stop. When she got on, I confirmed what I already knew; her daddy wasn't picking her up. Then after two weeks of her being around me all day, every day I realized she ain't have a disobedient bone in her body. There was no way she was being punished for anything. When I questioned why her father hadn't given her phone back, she told me he lost it. I started laughing out loud at how pitiful she is at lying. But I still liked her. And I looked forward to sitting in her face every day. Lies and all. I had gotten used to having her in my space and I didn't want to lose her. The only reason I didn't tell her that I knew she was lying was because I was so amused by her crazy ass stories. Her fine ass couldn't do no wrong in my eyes. I figured she'd tell me the truth one day. Or I'd hit first.

I looked forward to seeing her every morning and missed her when we had to separate. It felt like I was living two different lives now. She makes me feel like I'm somewhere else. I loved it. Especially since when I went home I was in a world of shit. But when I was with Jas ain't none of that shit matter.

One morning I woke up like I did every morning. My music started to play and I start to get ready for school. I had a whole lot of shit on my mind. Tevin had some serious ideas about expansion that would directly affect our territory and protection. And I wasn't interested in being into it with Quan and his people in P-Town. I wasn't scared but I knew it would be problematic if he decided to put some of these plans into motion. And he is just crazy enough to do it. Those ideas had me stressed.

I'd just got out the shower as I heard somebody banging down my door. I was instantly irritated. I already had shit on my mind and I didn't feel like being bothered this morning. I figured it was the police because nobody else was stupid enough to come to my shit like that. I asked who it was before I got too close to the door.

"It's your next-door neighbor and I am sick of your loud music in the morning! Other people live here too and it's just rude and ignorant! I'd like for you to turn it off!" she snapped. I instantly grabbed the doorknob. I snatched the door open so fast it scared her because she gasped.

"Bitch who the...." Before I could get the shit out, I made eye contact with Jasmine. She was standing just as shocked as I was in my face. She was fully clothed with her hair straightened and before I could think to say anything she turned and ran away. She slammed the door to the apartment next door and I watched her disappear. I stepped back into my apartment confused than a muthafucka. I shook my head trying to figure out how she was even here. Or why she had just run away like that as if she didn't even know me. I got dressed with every intention of going next door to talk to her but when I did I didn't get an answer. I figured she either left out for school or she was purposefully ignoring me because I called her a bitch. Either way, I wasn't getting anywhere standing at her door so I left out and followed my routine as I always did. After I bought my breakfast, I realized I was just too anxious to actually eat it. I wasn't even hungry. I pulled up to the school and parked my car in the lot. I knew Jasmine was lying to me the whole time but suddenly the truth bothered me. My first mind told me not to fuck with her no more just because I couldn't trust her. But it was something in me that didn't want to lose her. I walked into the school and straight to first period and when I saw Jasmine I needed her to come clean right then. Wasn't no way around it.

Jasmine

After being woken up by that irritating ass music one too many damn times, I finally got the guts to say something. Might have come a few weeks late but I finally got myself together. This morning I woke up before the music. I showered and straightened my hair as straight as I could possibly get it with my cheap flat irons. I was dressed in the cutest lil outfit I had. After I finished my fringe, I felt like myself again. My confidence had come rushing back at once and when I heard the bass of the music I decided today was the day. I gave myself one last glance over before I strutted towards the door. I walked right up to my neighbor's apartment and banged my fist against the door. I just wanted to be heard over that loud ass music. He obviously heard me because he asked who it was shortly after. I just let him know his music was too loud and I wanted him to turn it off. He snatched the door open and started to insult me right away. Right after he called me a bitch, I looked into the eyes of the guy who'd put butterflies in my gut on every given day. He stood in front of me with a white towel wrapped around his waist. He didn't have on a shirt and his gold cross chain hung from his neck so perfectly. I wanted to just die there. I knew at that moment I'd lost the one and only friend I had here.

"Jasmine." He said as if he couldn't believe his own eyes. I felt as small as a damn roach. I just ran away. I couldn't think of anything to say and I was ashamed. The only thing I could think was what he would think of me now knowing I not only have been lying to him all this time but I also live in the projects. I didn't even realize that means he also lived in the projects until I had gotten on the bus to ride to school. I was not at all looking forward to seeing him. I was still ashamed and I knew that he wasn't going to want to talk to me after finding out I lied. I felt like shit. I planned to just go to class and leave him alone. I sat in the last seat way in the back of the class. The moment he walked into class he scanned the room. My heart was beating so fast I just wanted to disappear. When he found my eyes I lowered my head. He walked right up to me and stood directly in front of my seat.

"Jasmine, come talk to me." He said aggressively. I was afraid to respond just based on his tone. The class got real quiet and it seemed everybody tuned into our conversation. That made me even more nervous because I didn't want him to embarrass me in front of all of these people. I looked up at him and he looked angry. I felt salt rush down the back of my throat as I tried to control the tears that wanted to fall out.

"Come on Jas...It's ok...Just come talk to me." He said before his expression changed. He looked right into my soul with those brown eyes. I swallowed that lump and took his extended hand. He pulled me out of my seat and lead me out of the classroom. We walked down the hallway silently but he didn't let go of my hand. He pulled me through a side door and we walked towards the schools parking lot. I followed until he unlocked the most beautiful white truck I'd ever seen.

"Get in," he said as he opened the door for me. I hopped into the truck and watched him walk around to the driver's side and get in. Once he shut the door he exhaled loudly and looked over at me. I couldn't find the voice to speak. So it was this bare ass silence that took over the space in the truck. That was until the smell of breakfast made my stomach growl loudly. I gasped out of pure embarrassment. He looked at me then shook his head. He reached towards the back seat and handed me a McDonalds bag.

"Here, you can have it." He said easily.

"No, it's ok. I'm good." I told him.

"Jasmine take the food. Don't be like that with me. Eat it." He said before dropping the bag in my lap. I pulled the warm sandwich out of the bag and ate it slowly. He sat back in his seat quietly, seemingly in his own thoughts. Once I finished the sandwich, I closed the bag and handed it back to him.

"Thank you!" I said.

"You're welcome...Now talk to me. Why you run away from me this morning?" He started.

"I want to...I just don't know what to say or where to start. Couldn't think of anything earlier either." I replied honestly.

"Okay...well start from the beginning. Why are you here?" He asked. His eyes locked with mine pleading with me.

"It's a long story and we are missing first period," I said miserably.

"I don't give a fuck about that...I have one of the highest G.P.A's in the school and coincidently the only one higher than mine is yours. We aren't missing anything and you know it! Cut the shit, Jasmine. Tell me what's up with you!" He said seriously.

"I'm afraid to tell you...I've always been afraid to tell you based on what you will think of me later," I admitted honestly. That lump wanting to form in my throat again.

"It couldn't possibly be worse than what I think of you now. Shit, you've sat in my face for weeks lying and I been peeped it. I didn't say shit because I knew eventually the truth would come out. It was bound to and right now I think you are a liar. What I don't understand is why you feel you needed to lie to me. That's not rubbing me right. So let me know something." He said carefully.

"Okay...I was raised in a very wealthy family. My people are filthy rich and my father was an heir. I can't tell you what happened because I still don't have a clue but one day I'm sitting in class, at a private school, where tuition is 69,000 a year. I have on a uniform that cost over five thousand dollars and I'm trying to focus on the lesson when my brand-new jeep that I'd not had longer than three weeks is being hauled onto a tow truck. I never made it home. My father was dead. They said he jumped off a building drunk because the feds had been investigating him for all kinds of fraudulent charges. And the IRS decided that was the perfect time to confiscate all of our shit. They took everything. Freezed all of the accounts. Everything! We didn't have a chance to prepare. And my family has always had money. They still have money and they were able to dodge all of the heat as if my father acted alone. They still have plenty of money but because my father married outside of their wishes my mother was cut out of the fortune altogether. They wanted me to choose between them and my mother. I chose my mother forfeiting my fortune. I had stored some money in a bank off the books in my name. We used that money to survive and we are here now still trying to survive. My mother has a job as a nurse at the university. We at least have a place to lay our heads. It's not home but it's all we have. I'm broke and I have nothing. I'm pissed off. I'm mad at my father for doing whatever he did that got us in this shit. I'm mad at my mother for being so stupid and not saving for a rainy day. I'm mad at my evil ass grandma who couldn't see past the fact my mother wasn't who she wanted my father to marry. Nobody gave a shit about me. Nobody cared about how their actions would affect me. Now I'm stuck trying to live in a place that won't ever accept me. Every day when I wake up it's a reminder that I don't belong here. The only time I feel comfortable is when I am with you. But everything I told you was a lie and I am sorry." I told him as a cried and let it all out. I had tears and snot rolling down my face and for the first time I was honest about the way I felt. I didn't feel so numb anymore.

He didn't speak. He just reached over to me and wiped my tears away with his hands. I couldn't imagine what he was thinking but his touch calmed me internally. It was something about him that spoke without speaking. He wiped my tears away and pulled my face towards his. Before I could think he placed his lips to mine. There was a chill that ran up my spine and made my mouth shutter as if it was below zero inside the truck.

"I got you. I just need you to promise me one thing…" he started.

"Okay."

"Don't lie to me again. You don't have to stunt with me. Keep it one hundred. I'm here for you and I told you that from jump. I got you." He said and I reached out to him for a hug. He pulled me into his arms and not only did I feel I belonged but I felt protected.

"Thank you," I told him.

"No problem. Come on, let's go." He said. I cleaned my face with a napkin before we got out the car to go back to class. We ended up being grilled by Ms. Boxton after entering the building mid second period. But once getting to Mr. T's class the day presumed as it normally did. I still didn't have any friends but MyKing always made up for it. He was kind and dependable and when he offered to take me home that day I didn't hesitate to ride along.

CHAPTER SIX:
OUTSIDE THE BOX

Kevin

I was agitated sitting in the trap waiting on a nigga to bust a move. Wasn't shit special about the spot. We broke our drugs down and did what we had to do in it. It was a fucked up two flat Tevin bought from a cluck. He ended up blowing the whole bill on a crack rock fiesta and gave Tevin his money right back. It has three rooms, a kitchen, and a living and dining room. We had some raggedy ass living room furniture, a foldable table in a few lawn chairs in the dining room. The bedrooms went without furniture with the exception of the tables and scales we use to split the bank. My brother was in the other room with some red thot ass bitch that was going on a mat in the corner. I thought the shit was funny but that's how it be sometimes. I was twiddling my thumbs waiting. Seems like that's what I been doing since we robbed Meechi. I, if nobody else, believed in Karma. I couldn't say I was mad at the fact I had money in my pockets but I'd be a fool to think the sacrifice was risk-free. I mean we ain't really moving no major weight. We push a lil bit, make the money, and be easy but Tevin ass ain't the type to leave well enough alone. The nigga don't think. He got a gambler's heart and he is willing to risk everything for something better. I couldn't figure out what that would cost me. Especially since that nigga wears my exact face. Ma, done tore my ass out the frame plenty of times for shit I wasn't even around to do. You know we look alike when the woman that birthed us got confused. God rest her soul. The point was, Tevin was doing some fuck ass shit. Not only had he allowed the lil guys to go stepping into another niggas territory but he instructed them to do it. And while he might not give a fuck that somebody's son got shot and killed last night. I do. I done told him to stay his ass outta Quan way but he does not ever listen. I ain't no punk ass nigga but wrong is wrong and it was understood when we started it wasn't finna be no bullshit with these niggas over no fucking space. Now, because of a direct violation of that agreement, he starts some shit with them niggas.

"Yo nigga, fuck you on?" King came in just as cool as he always did. The one brother I always had in my corner. If Tevin was the Satan talking shit on my left, King was the angel on the right. The nigga was level-headed and always had a solution.

"Nigga tell me why lil Keith got killed last night." I started.

"You lying! Where? Who did him?" he asked shocked.

"He was outside the box. You already know." I told him.

"Why the fuck would he go outside the box?" He asked angrily.

"Go ask Tev," I told him shaking my head.

"What?" He frowned in disgust. "Bro, your fucking brother gone start a war one day. Where that nigga at?" He asked looking at me crazy. I nodded my head towards the other room without having to mention exactly what he was doing.

"This nigga" King huffed before he made a beeline towards the door. I just sat back and waited for him to get the fool. Tevin walked into the room behind King without a care in the world. And even though he and I are identical twins me and King wore the same scolding look on our faces.

"Nigga why the fuck would you tell them niggas to go outside the box?" King started.

"Aye, them lil niggas hungry." He stated with his hands held out like the Jesus statue in the cemetery. "I told them to go get that fucking bread by any means necessary. If they feel they need to walk outside the fucking territory, who the fuck am I to tell them not to?" He asked.

"The purpose of us telling them to stay outta Quan nem shit is to keep Quan and his niggas out our fucking yard! You fucking up, bringing heat our way!" King spat.

"What heat? The nigga got killed in P-town how the fuck is that my problem?" Tevin argued.

"Think Tevin! For one fucking second, will you think? You know because of the body the guys gone want to retaliate. You got enough guns for a war with a nigga pushing four times what we collectively weigh? Huh? You want war with tall niggas?" King asked angrily.

"Nigga stop being a fucking bitch. I was gone tell you when we re-upped I'm doubling the order. I already let, China, know to press us out a few extra. We're expanding the box. We got the bread and I wanna make more. I don't see why we can't run straight through P- town." He pointed. "Scared money don't make no money," Tevin stated easily.

"Nigga what? King, you hear your brother?" I chuckled. The look on King's face let me know he was two seconds off Tevin's ass. I was waiting on the monster to jump out of him.

"Tevin fucking Woods! How the fuck are you running through P-town with no affiliation? Nigga the reason they got the fucking spot is because they thick as fuck over there. You can't expand our territory without no got damn heat. Bitch, you need more guns to even attempt that and now your stupid ass done doubled our fucking order without even telling me! Nigga, you just cut my fucking pocket and for what? That's a fuck ass move!" King spat pissed. Spit was flying all out his mouth.

"Double the profit. I'm putting more money in your pocket. Tryna help yall scary ass niggas." Tevin said with a mug on his face.

"Tevin it's not about the money. You playing Russian roulette with the lil niggas willing to serve so you can make the money. They got the bag. If you mess with the shorty's not only is it gone change our income but we gotta protect them. If we can't protect them, they won't risk running our shit. How you securing the bag without no heat? Eventually, we gone be in a war we ain't prepared to fight. And you all in my pockets like you sucking my dick. Now you done upped the order and we gotta back you because if you lose, we all do. "I added.

"Okay, then Imma make sure we ain't gone lose. We got guns and shootas! Yall some pussy ass niggas. I'll get more heat but I know I won't hear shit from yall when that cash comes through. Yall always good when the money right." He spat bitterly.

"Tev, that shit ain't fucking free. You gone learn that one day." King stated.

"Aye bitch, shut up. You finished your homework, while you worried about me?" Tevin spat. King ignored his comment.

"I'm up, this nigga blowing me. Imma hit you later." He dapped me without even looking Tevin's way. I gave him some love before he pulled out. King was smart and everybody who knew him, knew that. Had he been somewhere else he'd be a different man but it's no out when you down. He was born down. We all were. But Tevin could never see the bigger picture so when he made a decision that we didn't agree with he always stuck out his chest. We hadn't taken an L yet but I knew it was coming. I was just waiting.

I left the trap with a thousand thoughts on my mind. I honestly just wanted to make enough bread to get the fuck away from here. I didn't plan on doing this shit forever. No, I didn't know what I was gone do after, but I knew it wasn't gonna be here. I pulled into the buildings and parked my car on the street. I pulled out my bag to roll up. I was planning to spark one before I went in to ease my mind but my phone rang.

"Hey wassup," I answered.

"Kevin, what you doing?" she asked.

"Nothing, wassup with you?" I asked her.

"Nothing really...I was hoping I could come chill with you." She said.

"Aight, that's cool. Meet me at the crib." I told her and I got out the car to go upstairs to my apartment.

"Okay, I'm on my way." She said and I made my way towards my door. Once I got in, I sparked my blunt and turned on my music. Boney James played in the background and I could feel a little peace rising in my being. That's what I did when I was stressed. Weed and Jazz music. The weed slowed my thoughts down some and the sultry sound of that sax takes me somewhere else. And all of the problems I had just melted away. When Candice got to my door I let her in and she hesitantly walked into my apartment as she always did. She was real cute. She had golden brown skin and held the complexion of peanut butter. She had big full pretty pink lips and a smile that could bring any nigga to their knees. She was bad as fuck and I knew it but something about her I couldn't get comfortable with. I had been fucking with her for a while but her way with me scared me. Usually, when I'm fucking with bitches I understand why. I break bread. And even though my dick good these bitches really after me because I'm getting money. That's understandable to me. But Candice never asked me for shit. It's like she wants something, but she won't let me know what it is. Like she is waiting for me to let my guard down so she can take it. It's something unsettling about that. So, I didn't trust her. I liked her, but I didn't trust her. And she looks at me like she can see right through me. Her big brown eyes burning a hole in my chest.

"What's wrong? You don't look too happy to see me." She said as she stepped closer to me with a smile.

"I am," I told her as I pulled her into my arms by her hair.

"Kevin...what's wrong with you?" she asked again looking me directly in my eyes. It was something about her ass I couldn't figure out. Something dangerous. It takes one bold bitch to look a man in his eyes. I just needed to know what she wanted from me. But I wasn't gone ask. Figured I'd break her neck before she ever got the chance to try me. And I enjoyed fucking her in the meantime. Being sure to send her ass on her way the moment it was all over. I never let her stay the night. Wasn't that I didn't want her too. Just couldn't trust her enough to close my eyes around her. It's sad to say I even fuck with her when I feel like that, but I did. She sat on my bed before I handed her the blunt. She took a few puffs before handing it back to me.

She'd never really given me a reason not to trust her. Other than the fact I don't know what she wants from me, she treats me good. I just don't trust her. I sat down next to her on my bed after dumping the remnants of the blunt in an astray I had on my nightstand. I was good and high as the music played soothingly in the background. I was thinking about how stupid my brother was as she scooted closer to me. She starts kissing my neck and I got out my thoughts. She pulled at my belt.

"That what you came here for?" I asked as I assisted her by removing her clothes. She moaned before smiling at me.

"I came here to be with you. I figured this was what you wanted." She said. I stopped immediately and took my hands off of her.

"So, you don't want to?" I asked her for clarity.

"Of course, I do, always." She said before she pulled me to her again. We kissed for a minute before she'd gotten me so excited I couldn't wait to penetrate her anymore. I eased my way into her and she moaned against my lips. My heart pounded so hard

I could hear it. I could feel the blood moving in my veins. And her touch sent chills up my back like winter time in Chicago. I moved inside of her like I loved it there. And I did.

"Kevin!" she moaned loudly before halting my stroke with her hands. She pushed me out of her like she was scared for her life.

"What's wrong?" I asked almost homesick. Nobodies pussy was better than Candice and I knew it.

"I don't want you to stop but…you don't have a condom on." She said almost innocently. I thought it was cute coming from her but I knew it wasn't shit innocent about Candice.

I got up and strapped right away. I don't even know how I missed that part, especially since I didn't trust her. But I swallowed my thoughts when she straddled me and got on top to ride. I grabbed a hand full of ass and let shorty do her thing. She bit her lips and grinds on me like she enjoyed it. She was always loud, and she loved calling my name. I kissed her a lot to quiet her, but she loved that too. I couldn't do that long because it usually made her pussy wetter and I'd have to let her go to keep from busting. She rode me until she came all over me. She fell on top of me like a ragdoll and I kissed her forehead before I pushed her into the pillow I was just laying on and got behind her. I pulled her ass in the air and slid in from behind. She moaned and arched her back like she loved it. I grabbed both sides of her plump ass and drove my dick straight into her. Her moans were silenced by the pillow and at that moment, I forgot about all the bullshit. I was high, jazz was playing in the background and I busted peacefully into the rubber. We laid there just talking for a little while before she put on her clothes and left. After the first time of me asking her to leave, she never gave me the chance again.

CHAPTER SEVEN: FIGHTING FOR YOU

Jasmine

MyKing made it his business to be there for me after I came clean about my situation. I road with him to school and back home and he did whatever he thought would help. I introduced him to my mother who adored him because of how kindly he treated me. He started to buy groceries and spend time with me as much as possible and I loved it. I was satisfied and had started to feel comfortable with being here. My life back home seemed to be a boring thing of the past when in comparison with my current lifestyle. I hadn't had any complaints and it seemed ideal after getting to know MyKing. Until one morning when MyKing had an emergency he needed to handle before school. I didn't question him because I didn't feel it was my place. I just got ready and we followed our usual morning routine before he dropped me off at school promising to join me later. I just went to class as I did every day but without him there I felt like a germ. The girls cackled and smirked like they all knew something I didn't. I hated every second of it and I was uncomfortable. But I just ignored them in hopes of MyKing getting there soon. It wasn't until third-period lunch when I was tried. I got ready to sit my lunch on the table when a guy I saw around came into my personal space and grabbed my butt. I turned around shocked before I sat to avoid him touching me again. He sat across from me with a smirk across his face.

"Damn ma…you got a fat ass. I been wanting to touch you for a while. You need to fuck with me." He said arrogantly.

"You are disrespectful. I am not interested in you so you can go right back to whichever hole you crawled from." I spat mortified.

"Bitch, who you talking to? Your man ain't here to protect yo lil stuck up ass today. You ain't all that." He screwed before I saw MyKing out of my peripheral. He didn't say a word. He snatched the guy up by his shirt and started to rain punches all over him. The lunchroom erupted and soon after that security rushed MyKing and pulled him off of the guy. Everything happened so fast it was crazy. I stood frozen in one spot, as the guy yelled out obscenities of how he would hurt MyKing through a bloody mouth. I was terrified. I knew MyKing would be in trouble because of me and I didn't know what I was supposed to do. I lost my appetite the moment the security guards pulled them out of the lunchroom.

The rest of the day was dreadful. By seventh period I was over the day. The girls in my class were so messy, I just needed a moment to think. I excused myself from class and went to the washroom. I had planned to stay in there the rest of the class period before the door opened and in came a bunch of loud mouth girls.

"You know King hit Rico over that black bitch. Both of them fucking her hoe ass and they got into it because King found out."

"That shit crazy…she not even that pretty. I wonder what she'd look like if I snatch all that hair off of her head."

"Right, that hoe needs to take her ass back to wherever she came from. Besides, King is mine anyway."

"Rashiya, King is not yours. That nigga a hoe. He for everybody." The girl stated before they all started to laugh. I stood in the stall listening quietly.

"She probably not fucking with him. He ain't finna fight over just any hoe. You know how he is. She probably his sister or cousin or something."

"Naw, he an only child and all I know is shorty better be the fuck cool and stay out of my way because King and I have some unfinished business. I want that nigga." The girl Rashiya stated.

"Yeah and who doesn't?" another girl said.

"Ugh! Candice just mind your business bitch; nobody was talking to you." Rashiya started.

"Or what? Who finna make me mind my business? You bitch? "She chuckled before she continued. "You just mad that King don't want you or your muppet ass crew. How yall gone talk about somebody you don't know shit about? And just so you know, she is his girl and yall can hate all yall want but it won't change shit. He is taken so back the fuck up off his dick. Hating ass bitches." Candice spat.

"Candice you already know about these hands, bitch. Don't be in here talking all that shit like you tryna thump. I don't know why you even give a fuck about that hoe. You fucking her nigga too?" Rashiya asked smartly.

I stepped out of the stall to see who had defended me. Four girls looked back at me. It got so quiet in the washroom you could hear a pin drop. I cleared my throat before speaking.

"Thanks, Candice...but I can speak for myself." I started as the girl I knew was Candice nodded her head at me and backed away from the other three girls.

"My name is Jasmine. Not bitch. Not hoe. I have not slept with Rico and I am still a virgin if you must know. I didn't provoke the fight so I don't know where you got your information from but it's not true. I don't appreciate you guys spreading lies about me and I'd like it if you would keep my name out of your mouths. Neither of you know me well enough to tell anyone anything about me…And you cannot have MyKing because he does not belong to you." I stated seriously. Technically he didn't belong to me either but they didn't know that much. Candice laughed.

"See told ya!" she mocked.

I went towards the sink to wash my hands when the girl Rashiya spoke.

"Bitch, who the fuck you think you talking to? You must want your ass whupped too?" she asked angrily.

"She was talking to you. Who ass you gone whup?" Candice shot right back before I could even respond. The girls start taking off their earrings and pulling their hair weaves into ponytails and I just stood there silently praying that they wouldn't really try and fight me in school. Candice had made her way directly beside me now. We stood across from them like a team. Rashiya's friends were pumping her up trying to instigate a fight and she walked up close to me and Candice calling me all kinds of bitches and hoes. I was afraid to fight because I didn't want to get in trouble. I had a perfect record and never was a problem in school. Her words didn't bother me and I figured as long as she didn't touch me I had no reason to overact and provoke her. I wasn't convinced she could beat me anyway. I wasn't hood and I never caused any trouble but my dad ain't put me in boxing classes for nothing. I had exactly what she wanted if she decided to advance a fight. I didn't believe it would come to that after her insults had done nothing to anger me. But then she did the most disgusting thing she could possibly do to me. She hacked and spit in my face. When her saliva landed on me, I couldn't think to do anything but fight.

I wasn't just going to fight her but I was going to pummel her ass. I swung twice hitting her in her face before moving out of the way as she swung back. I kept moving back and forth like I was taught and cracked her a few more times before her friends jumped in on me. It happened so fast it caught me off guard. Fighting multiple people at once wasn't a part of the lessons.

One girl grabbed my hair and the other started to windmill me. I momentarily lost my edge on Rashiya and they jumped me until Candice grabbed one of the girls and dragged the girl into a body slam. She started stomping the girl and I did my best to throw my best punches at Rashiya while the other girl pulled my hair. I was able to hit Rashiya hard enough to knock her into the washroom sink and the moment she was away I wacked the girl who was pulling my hair as hard as I could. Her nose made a knuckle cracking noise and started bleeding immediately and security rushed in blowing the whistles. I was grateful too. It felt like we were fighting for ten minutes straight and I was tired as hell. The adrenaline was pumping through me so hard I couldn't stop shaking. I was angrier after the fight than I'd been during the fight. I knew my record was ruined. Candice and I were sat together in the vice principal's office to wait until we were told. The moment I sat down I realized I was in big trouble. I didn't even try to control the tears that came rushing down my cheeks. I hated this.

Candice who had calmed down looked at me like I was crazy.

"Yo...why you crying? You won, Relax girl." She stated oddly.

"My mother is going to be so angry. I've never even been in a fight." I told her sadly.

"Never been in a fight? Girl, I know you lying! Girl you just fucked Rashiya and Sierra up. Bitch, you were handling them hands. Stop playing with me." She laughed. I looked at her this time confused. I didn't even understand what she had just said fully.

"Did you just call me a bitch?" I asked cautiously. She started laughing out loud. When I didn't join in she looked at me with her eyebrows raised.

"Wait...you're serious? Girl...I don't mean bitch like that. It's a word of endearment. Doesn't mean the same thing when you are saying it to somebody you fuck with. Like when a white person says Nigga and when we say it." she explained smiling. I kind of understood and nodded my head. But I didn't think the N-word was okay regardless of who said it, so I didn't comment.

"So, you've really never been in a fight? Because you damn sure know how to handle them thumpers," she said.

"No...I've never been in a fight outside of a ring. I boxed a little in grammar school. But I've never even been in trouble at school. Not even detention. Just a few classes when I was younger. And I quit after getting my eye busted by this mean ass little white girl at my old school." I explained. She laughed harder.

"You let a white girl whup you?" She smirked before she burst into laughter.

"She was bigger than me," I exclaimed before I shook my head.

"Oh girl, It's cool, I'm just fucking with you. At least you know enough to cut loose when you need to. You had to defend yourself and you did what you had to do. They probably won't do shit but give us five days." She said easily.

"Five days what? Detention?" I asked mortified.

"Nah suspension but relax chick its ok." She tried to explain.

"Relax! Girl I can't! Suspension goes on your permanent record. My mother will be pissed!" I sighed miserably before the door opened and the vice principal Mr. Taylor walked in.

He sat down at his desk in front of us and started talking.

"What happened?" he asked looking at both of us. Candice spoke first.

"Rashiya, Sierra, and Page were in the bathroom talking shit about Jasmine trying to bully her. I stepped to them and we start fighting. Jasmine tried to break it up and Rashiya hit her. That's it." She explained and I looked at her crazily trying to figure out if she was in the same washroom I was in.

"Okay well Ms. Davis you can go and Ms. Walker I'm giving you ten days suspension for fighting." He stated plainly as Candice nodded her head at me. It had just dawned on me that she lied to keep me from getting suspended and although I didn't want it on my record I knew it was wrong to let her take all the blame.

"No, that's not what happened Mr. Taylor. Candice is just trying to protect me. The girls were in the washroom talking about me. Candice did come to my defense but Rashiya spit in my face so I threw the first punch. I was getting the better of her so her friends jumped in. Candice helped me. That's the truth." I explained. He looked up at me for a while before writing something on a piece of paper.

"Okay here's what we are going to do. I gave each of the other girls ten days suspension. They will be out for the remainder of the school year. I understand why you were fighting but there is a zero-tolerance policy I have to abide by. Especially when students are injured and as a result of the fight one of the girls, Sierra, has a fractured nose. I'm giving you five days apiece. I won't file it on your record because you have an outstanding resume but you all will have to vacate the premises after the final bell. When you come back off of suspension, do not get yourselves involved in any more trouble, otherwise there will be severe punishment for both of you. Do I make myself clear?" he stated plainly.

"Yes, sir!" I responded.

"Good. You guys can stay here until I've cleared the building after the final bell." He said before getting up to leave. As soon as he closed the door Candice started busting up laughing.

"Bitch! You broke that hoe nose!" she laughed excitedly. And even though we had just got in trouble I couldn't help but laugh at her amusement.

"I'm Candice it's nice to finally meet you." She said with an extended hand.

"Jasmine. Nice to meet you too…wish the circumstances were a little different though." I admitted.

"Well, it be like that sometimes." She said before an awkward silence fell upon the room. I looked up at her, really getting a good look at her. She was pretty. Peanut butter skin complexion with big doll eyes and a big smile. I'd seen her around but nobody has ever said anything to me. Thought to ask why because she didn't seem to mind speaking her mind at all.

"Why is it that nobody says anything to me? I feel like an alien." I stated.

"Oh, girl…it's your man. Do you know who you're with?' she asked.

"What? MyKing is cool. He is a really sweet guy. I don't understand what you mean by that." I laughed.

"Sweet to who? I'm amused by the relationship you guys seem to have with each other. I mean no offense at all but I've known him and his best friends since we were in the third grade. That nigga has never been nice. He fine as hell. Smart than a muthafucka but he doesn't have a sweet bone in his body. Shit, to be real yall relationship looks fake as fuck." She stated. I liked Candice for a few minutes but what she had just said bothered me. It must have been all over my face.

"Nah chick, don't get me wrong. It ain't nothing personal. I don't think you ain't worthy of a good dude that's gone love and protect you and treat you like a queen. I just don't see that in King. Nobody does. You asked me to tell you and I'm just being honest. I don't know how long you've known him or what yall have but most of the people here have known King our whole lives. Nobody believes what you seem to see in him. These niggas just waiting to get their turns with you. These bitches are just mad his attention is somewhere else and you are competition. Them bitches ain't tryna befriend no "opp" so that's why ain't nobody said shit to you." She explained.

"OPP?" I asked confused. She chuckled.

"Opponent." She explained.

"Soooo, what do you think? What's your angle?" I asked her seriously. I remembered Rashiya mentioning that Candice might've been sexually involved with MyKing. She chuckled.

"Honestly, I think you need to be careful with King. You obviously don't know who you fucking with. Or his reputation. And I have no angle. You are not an "opp" to me. To be real, I'm fucking his best friend. I don't want your man chick." She laughed.

I was satisfied with that as we were allowed to leave. I figured I'd be taking the bus home since MyKing had been suspended and left hours ago. So I and Candice walked towards the bus stop.

CHAPTER EIGHT: BEST FRIENDS

MyKing

I had just calmed down enough to chill. My day has been fucked up since I woke up this morning. Stupid ass Tevin got his ass locked up, for some guns, and he called me to bail him out this morning. I dropped Jasmine at school and made my way to the police station to get him. Only, by the time I'd gotten there he'd already gone before the judge who not only denied bail but also accumulated a bunch of bullshit charges. I ain't get many details but I was able to talk to him for a few minutes. It was understood before I left the nigga was gone sit for a minute. Nobody had to tell me for me to come to that conclusion. Considering he had just made a major move with our connect, I was pissed the fuck off that I and Kevin were going to have to handle the shit he started. I was gone do it because I didn't have a choice but I was heated about it. Especially when I wasn't comfortable with doing the shit no more. By the time I got to school, I was already tired. I wouldn't have even come if I hadn't told Jasmine I would. I got there third period and went straight to the lunchroom. I walked towards the table me and Jas always sat and peeped Rico in her face. I was instantly more irritated because I ain't fuck with him and he knew it. The fact he was in her face was a direct violation. But to add to the disrespect I got close enough to hear his bitch ass talk greasy to my piece. I didn't even think to hesitate. I started to beat his shit in because he got slick. I was suspended and asked to vacate immediately. I ain't trip because I figured wouldn't no other nigga think to fuck with Jas after the example I made of Rico. And the school year was pretty much over anyway.

The last day of school was only a week away and I got suspended for the remainder of the school year. I left the school and went to the trap. Kevin was trying to prepare for the next ride. I chopped it up with him for a minute trying to busy myself before that time rolled back around. I headed back to the school to pick up Jas and parked across the street from the lot because I wasn't allowed on the premises. I sat in my truck until I saw my homey, Mark. He walked up towards my truck with his shorty on his arm. I got out and shook up.

"Wassup nigga! I saw you throwing them earlier. Fuck was that about?" he started.

"Man, the nigga was on some ole disrespectful shit. He was talking big shit to my girl." I explained.

"Yo girl?" He looked up at me crazy like he was shocked. I laughed because I ain't plan to explain.

"Wait, is your girl the one with the long hair? The dark skin one?" His girlfriend Denise asked.

"Yeah, Jasmine," I stated matter of factly.

"Oh, she was just fighting too. They got her in the office right now." She said, and I was right back irritated again. I knew Jasmine wasn't the type to be trying to fight nobody which meant somebody had fucked with her. I gritted my teeth at the thought of her being bothered and me not being around to protect her.

"Who?" I asked trying to figure out who else I had to check before the day was out.

"Heard she beat the hell out of Rashiya and Sierra. Broke Sierra's nose." She chuckled.

"Damn, guess your girl got hands too." Mark chuckled. I didn't find shit at all funny.

"They jumped her?" I asked as my blood boiled.

"Yeah, from what I hear they tagged her in the bathroom 7th period," Denise said carefully after she realized I was not amused by her news.

"Aight bet," I said angrily. I dapped Mark before I turned around to get back in my truck. I was pissed the fuck off and even more mad that I couldn't text or call Jasmine because she didn't have a phone. I felt guilty as fuck for not protecting her and I didn't know how she was gone feel about me leaving her to the wolves.

The school grounds were nearly clear as the police officers that patrolled after final bell road off. Jasmine and another girl came out the main door and start walking towards the bus stop. I immediately put my shit in drive and did an illegal U-turn in the middle of the street to ride directly in front of the bus stop. When I got up close to her I peeped the girl she was with was Candice. I rolled down the window.

"Get in," I told Jasmine. She pulled the door open and got in. I rolled up the window and looked at her company standing still at the bus stop. I knew who she was but that was it. I looked at Jasmine and besides a small scratch under her eye and her hair pulled into a ball in the back of her head, I couldn't tell she'd been in a fight.

"What happened?" I asked her.

"I was in the washroom and some girls came in talking shit about me. Rashiya spit in my face and I start fighting her. Her friends jumped in on me." She told me.

"Spit in yo face? That bitch nasty. What friends?" I asked with my face balled up in disgust.

"Yeah. Sierra and Page."

"All three of them jumped you?" I asked her with my teeth clenched trying to control my anger.

"Yeah but Candice jumped in and helped me." She stated as she nodded her head towards the bus stop I purposely left her friend standing at. I looked at Jas good before I rolled down the window again.

"Get in," I told Candice as she nodded her head and jumped in the back seat.

"Thanks." She muttered as I pulled off into the street.

"So, did you get suspended?" I asked her.

"Yeah, I got five days." She admitted.

"I momentarily made eye contact with Candice from my rear-view mirror before I focused my attention back on the street light we sat at. I guess Candice was cool. Especially since she had Jas back.

"Don't trip about it. We gone be on suspension together." I assured her. She looked towards me with those big pretty brown eyes and I calmed down internally.

"Thanks for defending me, he is so rude. He grabbed my ass!" Jasmine said easily.

"Who grabbed your ass?" I asked seriously.

"Rico...the guy you were fighting. I thought you saw that..." She said before looking at me confused.

"Nah," I said feeling like I didn't do enough. My anger had come right back and I was quiet trying to imagine what I was gone do to that bitch ass nigga when I saw him again.

"I'm hungry," Jasmine whined breaking me out my train of thought.

"What you want to eat?" I asked her.

"I want some chicken. But you have to stop at the store so I can pick up some to cook tonight." She said.

"Nah you promised I was getting ribs tonight. That's what I want for dinner. We can stop by Harold's and get you some chicken right now." I told her.

"Harold's? What is that?" She asked. I and Candice start laughing simultaneously.

"Girl, you really don't know what Harold's is?" Candice asked.

"Well no. I've never heard of it. What? Are they any good?" She asked.

"Don't even trip ma. Your man gone get you some chicken, aight?" I told her as I chuckled to myself.

"I pulled up to the restaurant and we all hopped out. I pulled Jasmine close to me and walked her into the restaurant with her in my arms. Lately, she'd been comfortable enough with me to allow me to hold her and it was something about the way it felt that drove me crazy. She always smelled so good to me and she was just sexy. By the time we stood in front of the open window and over-head menu I had to try readjusting my penis in my pants.

"What you want?" I asked her trying to distract her long enough to calm my erection. I needed some pussy because Jasmine tease me every day and it's getting harder for me to ignore it.

"Um…I don't know. Candice, what are you getting?" she turned to her friend who I momentarily forgot all about.

"Well, I usually get a six-piece with lemon pepper and mild sauce." She started.

"Oh okay, well I will try that too. And it's on me because you had my back and I appreciate it." She said to her friend before turning back to the girl at the window taking the order. She went in her purse to pay for it and I immediately felt some type of way. I can't explain if it was anger or embarrassment, but I felt something. I grabbed her hand before she could place her twenty-dollar bill in the cashier's hand and pushed it back towards her purse.

"I got it Jas. You know better." I said as I reached into my pocket to handle the bill. She chuckled before putting her money back as if she didn't even notice how bothered I had just gotten. Candice looked on as if she fully understood and the slight smirk on her face made me wonder what she was thinking. I got lost in my own thoughts before Jasmine was handed her food. We walked back to my truck and I opened the door for Jasmine to get in. Candice starts chuckling and that bothered me too.

"What the fuck is so funny?" I asked with a screw on my face. She looked at me before every ounce of amusement fell from her face. She hopped in the back seat and I didn't hear another peep out of Candice the entire ride back to the P's. I was okay with that considering Jasmine and I talked most of the way home.

When we got to the buildings we all got out and walked towards the elevator. I pressed our floor and Candice pressed hers. She was only a few floors beneath us.

"Dang, I didn't know you lived here." Jasmine tried starting up a conversation with a mute Candice.

"Yeah." She simply mumbled as the elevator stopped on her floor.

"Well, I'll see you later girl. Thanks again for having my back." Jasmine stated awkwardly.

"No problem, anytime. See you." She said before she looked at me and exited without saying a word. The moment the doors closed Jasmine was staring me down.

"What?" I asked with a smirk.

"Was that really necessary? You were really rude to her, MyKing. You hurt her feelings." Jasmine said seriously.

"That girl feelings ain't hurt. I just asked her a simple question."

I chuckled.

"See that's why nobody likes me now." She said before we exited the elevator.

"Nah it ain't me. Them bitches don't like you because you fine as hell and they are all jealous." I told her.

"Yeah well even if that were the case I'm sure having your mean ass around me all the time has something to do with it." She stated before she opened the door to her apartment.

"So, you got a problem with me being around you?" I asked her as I followed right behind her.

"No, that's not what I said." She retorted.

"Well say what you mean then," I said as I sat at the small kitchen table with her.

"Dang...this chicken good." She said as she pulled the chicken apart.

"I see you changed the subject," I stated.

"MyKing stop being so mean. The girl jumped in a fight that had nothing to do with her to protect me. You could be a tad bit friendlier considering I might've gotten my ass whupped had she not snatched one of them off of me." She said between bites.

"The fact that you handled two project bitches in a fight let me know you can handle yourself. I heard you beat they asses. I think I underestimated you. I'm almost certain no other broad will try you after that." I smiled proudly.

"Yeah well. That means I probably won't get another friend either." She laughed.

"You got me. We friends, right?" I asked her before the look on her face humored me.

"Yeah, best friends." She replied oddly.

I had to leave Jas to make some moves with Kevin. By the time

I got back to the crib, I was immediately satisfied. The moment I stepped off the elevator I could smell the ribs I knew Jasmine had cooked for me. I smiled because I fucked with her. I quickly went into my apartment to change and freshen up before I went over to her apartment. Right away I was greeted by Jas mother Jennifer who was just as pretty as her daughter. She was nice and even though I know she works hard she never let it show. I really admired her effort and things seemed ok. I wanted her to think I was good enough for her daughter so I ain't hesitate to help when I could. Jennifer reminded me of Rita and I appreciated the fact she cared. I sat at the table and both Jasmine and Jennifer served me Baked BBQ ribs, baked mac and cheese, green beans, and homemade honey dinner rolls. I felt like the man of the house. I was stuffed by the time the peach cobbler was ready. And her mother let me chill with Jas after dinner. We just laid in her bed caked up watching her favorite movie BAPS.

"What's in the bag?" she asked as she motioned towards the bag I set on her dresser before we sat down.

"I don't know. Go look in it." I told her as I looked back towards the Tv.

"MyKing, stop playing. Tell me what you put in this bag boy!" she giggled before picking it up and walking back towards where we sat on the bed.

"Would you just open it and see. Dang, I'm tryna watch the movie!" I chuckled. She laughed before she pulled the box out of the bag and pulled the new phone I bought her out of the box.

"You bought me a phone? Seriously?" she laughed as she cut it on to inspect it.

"Dang a nigga not even gone get a thank you huh?" I asked with a smirk. She looked around me as if she was looking for something on the bed. I got up to help her look.

"What you looking for?" I asked her.

"The nigga I'm supposed to be thanking. I don't see any niggers in this room so I thought I'd try and find them before saying they weren't here.

"Really?" I asked before I sat back on the bed and pulled her to stand between my legs.

"Yes...you are not a nigga MyKing. You can be called a lot of things but a nigga is degrading and I would rather you simply not use the term." She said carefully. I didn't respond right away because I didn't want to say the wrong thing. I got what she was saying but none of the shit meant anything to me. In many ways, I disagreed but I wasn't gone tell her that.

"Okay," I said before I rested my hands on her ass. She didn't push me away so I leaned in to kiss her. She moved almost immediately.

"Thank you so much for the phone. I mean you really didn't have to buy it. It's not like I have anyone to talk to anyway." She said before laying back in her spot on the bed.

"Don't matter. You can always call me." I told her before I got behind her and comfortable on the bed. Eventually, she fell asleep and I got up to leave. I placed her phone on its charger and before walking out the door, I leaned in to kiss her lips. She didn't move and I walked towards the door to leave.

"Goodnight Best friend!" she said sleepily startling the shit out of me. I chuckled.

"Goodnight Jas," I said before walking out the door.

Candice

I liked Jasmine. She was cool as hell despite what I might have thought of her when I first saw her. She turned out to be completely different than my first impression. And if nothing else, the girl can throw them hands. I didn't expect to have a problem with Rashiya and her crew, but the fight was actually fun. Even though I got suspended, it was worth it. King surprised me when he offered me a ride. I can't lie, being in his truck wasn't so surprising when he wanted to fuck. But in this case, I was amused by his sudden change of heart. I smiled to myself at the power Jasmine seemed to have. Here it was a nigga I've known for over ten years to be the definition of a dog ass nigga, magically turned into a gentleman. I'm talking holding doors open, paying for bitches to eat, the whole damn nine. I couldn't help but laugh. I had planned to give Jasmine her props the moment I could. But King was still King. He made sure to remind me before we got back to the P's. I still wanted to laugh. Could you believe she haven't actually fucked him? I thought.

"I must be doing it wrong," I said out loud as I walked through the door.

"Doing what wrong?" My mama asked as she stood over the sink washing dishes with a cigarette hanging from her lips and Xscape playing in the background.

"Nothing." I laughed before I slid out my shoes to leave them at the door.

"What you got to eat?" she asked adjusting the cig between her fingers.

"Some Harold's...King bought it", I admitted before she could even assume I had some money.

"King? I know you not fucking for no meals? I feed you every day! All that lil nigga do is sling dick and drugs." She started and I laughed. My mama was crazy as hell.

"Ma, no! I don't like him like that. Me and his girlfriend are cool. She was being bullied so I stood up for her and she made him buy us food as a gift." I explained.

"Bullied? Girl if you don't cut the shit. What did you do Michelle?" she asked calling me by my middle name.

"Ma for real, some girls jumped her at school and I helped her," I told her with a smile.

"Ok so you were fighting at school and your ass got suspended?" she asked knowingly.

"Yeah, I got suspended but I helped my friend though." I waved her off.

"Bullshit! That boy ain't got no girlfriend. I can't believe that shit. I don't see how these lil girls letting him run up in them anyway. He so damn disrespectful and his ole hoe ass mama really should be ashamed. That bitch done seen more dick than a little bit." She said seriously.

"Ma you ain't gotta talk about that man mama like that." I laughed.

"I'm just telling the truth, shame the devil!" she said before she starts scrubbing one of her pots. I took my food in my room and ate. I texted Kevin but he didn't respond so I just relaxed thinking maybe me and Jasmine could be friends since we have a mutual interest.

CHAPTER NINE: WHAT DO YOU DO?

MyKing

A few days into my suspension and I was up to my ears in issues. Kevin was doing his best to handle what he could of the extra load we had. It wasn't moving fast enough in the lil area we had but neither of us wanted to expand like Tevin had planned. We had to push everything out as best we could until we could figure out an effective plan that would work for us from now on. I was stressed out and I barely had the time to kick it with Jasmine like I wanted to. She was blowing my phone up every day trying to spend time. I hated I was unavailable and I couldn't be with her long. I knew I had some making up to do when she started ignoring my text messages.

So the day before she had to be back in school I made it my business to spend some time. I woke up early and woke her up so she could fix me something to eat. I loved when she cooked for me and she seemed to like to do it so we had a good thing going. Once we ate I urged her to get dressed. I had an idea and I wanted her to roll with me. I had never been on a date and I couldn't think of a better person to be with than her.

I realized Jasmine was overdressed for what I knew would be a lot of walking at Navy Pier. Her outfit was cool but her sandals had a heel on it and I wasn't trying to hear shit about her feet hurting. That's all she talked about whenever she wore those shoes to school.

"Why didn't you put on your gym shoes?" I asked her.

"Because I don't own any gym shoes. Where are we going anyway?" she asked quizzingly. I wanted it to be a surprise and since I didn't know what the hell I was doing, I thought the less she knew the better.

"We finna just go get you some." I thought aloud as I opened the truck door for her to get in.

"MyKing, would you just tell me where we're going please." She smiled seemingly excited.

"To the mall to get you some shoes." I smiled at her and turned up the music. Once we got into the store I peeped the new mikes on display and picked them up. They were the Omega's and I had to have them. The red, white, and gray shoe caught my eye the moment I saw them.

"I know you don't think I'm wearing those." She laughed.

"Nah. These for me. These the new Mikes that just came out. My favorite shoe." I laughed.

"Mikes?'" she asked confused.

"Yeah. That's what we call Jordan's in Chicago." I explained. I looked back at the other new releases and picked up a pair for her too. "Here, these cute," I said trying to convince her. I held up the silver and white 11s.

"Yeah, they are kind of cute. How much are they though?" She asked. I quickly got confused. It shouldn't have mattered considering she wasn't paying for them. But the moment she found the price on the bottom of the shoe she sat it back down.

"Oh no MyKing that shoe is too much." She said shaking her head.

"Jas chill, I got it," I told her taking the shoes to the associate to bring out our sizes. I turned back to Jas.

"What size you wear? I asked her.

"A ten." She responded and I walked away to obtain our shoes. I paid for the shoes and we walked out of the store with me holding the bags in my hands. Jasmine was quiet for most of the walk. I knew something was wrong by the expression on her face.

"What's wrong with you?" I asked her carefully.

"MyKing...what are you into?" she asked me slowly.

"What are you talking about?"

"Where do you work?" she asked before she looked in my face. I stopped dead in my tracks but I couldn't respond. She waited for an answer while I looked around trying to find one.

"Damn those pretzels smell good. Come on, let's go get some from Aunt Annie's." I stalled.

"Really? You want pretzels conveniently at this moment?" she asked with her mouth held open in disbelief.

"Yeah," I answered shortly and started to walk off towards the restaurant. Each step forward, I was trying my best to come up with something to tell her about how I make my money that wouldn't make her stop talking to me. Everybody around already knew and I never had to explain the shit to nobody. My mama even peeped it and never complained once about me paying the bills. Now I'm stuck trying to explain myself which is something I just don't do. I grabbed the pretzels and we made our way towards my truck. I unlocked the doors and we got in. She was quiet the whole ride. I started to feel uncomfortable and realized what I'd wanted to do was not going to get done today. Jasmine had an attitude and I suddenly didn't feel like being bothered.

"I'm about to take you home," I told her before I turned up my music to avoid any conversation. I dropped her home and left the day with Jasmine where it was.

Jasmine

I was so angry at MyKing. I didn't really expect for him to react the way he did. I didn't even realize my question would be difficult to answer until he refused to. I really wanted to know, I just didn't know what else to ask to get it out of him. But his lifestyle didn't match with the place we were in. I could tell something was wrong. MyKing didn't seem to want for anything, all while living in a low-income apartment complex, going to a public neighborhood school, in a predominantly poverty-stricken area. It had me completely confused. I didn't want to press so I didn't ask him anything else. But my mind wondered the entire ride home. He didn't offer an explanation. He handed me my bag with the shoes after walking me to my doorstep and literally walked away without even saying goodbye. It really messed me up and I sat in my room puzzled until my phone started ringing. I answered it when I realized it was Candice.

"What you doing?" she asked joyfully.

"Nothing really just sitting here thinking," I responded.

"Bitch, about what? A suspension is for relaxing. Let's do something!" she stated.

"Like what?" I asked.

"Idk. Let's go get our eyebrows waxed. I'm looking like Frida Rivera by the face." She said before she burst out laughing.

"Why are you so stupid?" I giggled.

"Girl because I do! Come on. It's only like twelve dollars apiece. I got twenty. Let's run to the nail shop." She begged.

"Okay, I'll be down in just a moment," I told her before I hung up. I switched my blouse to a regular white fitted top and pulled some socks on so I could wear my new sneakers. They were cute. I got to the elevator and after standing there for over five minutes I realized it wasn't coming. I frowned before turning to the smelly stairwell. I hated taking the stairs! It was way too creepy to be safe. The lights were dim and always flickering. It smelled like mildew, mothballs, and urine. Not to mention there was no air circulation and it was hot and suffocating. I skipped stairs trying to hurriedly get out of the staircase and unto Candice floor. I knocked on her door so she'd come on.

I was greeted immediately with a smile before she locked her door and we were off to the bus stop. We waited for our bus a while before she noticed my sneakers.

"Bitch! Are those the new 11s?" she asked excitedly.

"Umm, I guess. I don't know. My King picked these. I just thought they were cute." I stated.

"Hmm. Must be nice." She said almost sarcastically.

"Well it was a nice gesture but I didn't actually want the shoe. To be honest I couldn't afford them. I told him not to buy them but he didn't listen and he even got upset with me for asking him where he worked." I told her expecting for her to understand where I was coming from. She started laughing the moment I said it.

"Jas...you are fucking hilarious. The man hustles. I told you that." She said.

"Yeah but evidently I don't know what that means. I thought

you were saying he works really hard on his job." I stated.

"Jasmine what do you think MyKing does?" she asked me.

"I have no idea. I've never seen him wear a uniform or even mention having to work. I mean he hasn't been with me in days. I just don't have a clue where he's going...but he doesn't seem to have a shortage of cash with the way he throws money around. I mean I appreciate it but it's definitely not necessary." I told her.

"Girl, imma just keep it gutter with you because you my bitch and that's the type of friend I am. Don't ever complain about him doing for you if he wants. You will lose good privilege's doing that because it almost seems like you're ungrateful or you think your shit don't stink. And I've known MyKing forever and I've never known him to trick. It's something about you that got him wide open. I say let the man buy you whatever he wants." She stated.

"Well, he doesn't have to try and trick me. I really like him. He shouldn't have to hide anything from me. We're best friends!" I stated.

"Jasmine...trick means to spend money on" she burst into laughter.

"Oh...well, that still doesn't explain where he's getting the money. We ain't exactly in the best financial region." I mentioned.

"Does that really even matter to you?" She asked confused.

"I guess I just want to know and for whatever reason, he won't tell me."

"What would it change? Would you still want to be with him if he didn't actually have a job and was illegally getting the money?" She asked.

"Illegally? Well yes, it would matter in that case. I mean there are jobs available everywhere. I don't personally understand why anyone needs to illegally obtain money with all this employment available." I stated seriously.

"Jasmine when I talk to you it really helps me put things in perspective. I never knew someone so smart can be so dense. And when I say that I don't mean any offense. You are so naïve and you see everything one way. You're so blinded by the way you were raised and taught you can't see shit for what it really is. Kind of reminds me of SpongeBob." She said.

"SpongeBob...really?" I asked. I couldn't piece her analogy with MyKing or his lifestyle as it relates to mine.

"Yes. A good person. Pure-hearted and he can see the good in everything and everyone. He's so positive and kind that he can't see that his neighbor is mean and does not like him, his best friend is stupid as fuck, and his boss blatantly rips him off every chance he gets. It's all right in his face but he's so...him. He can't even see it." She explained.

"Well...I guess I just don't know what it is I'm supposed to be looking for." I offered.

"Doesn't matter. Open your mind and your eyes. If you simply pay attention all of the answers are right in your face. You really don't need MyKing to tell you shit. It's right in your face and I know you done peeped game because something in you has you asking questions. You are in the wild now. The rules are different. The law doesn't protect us here so we don't respect it. Illegal activity keeps a roof over a lot of people heads. And to be honest. Rich muthafuckas do illegal shit too. The only difference is it's a little easier for them to get away with it." She said easily as we boarded the bus. I thought hard after that conversation. Especially since my own father was accused of doing something illegal. I felt guilty because now a part of me didn't care how MyKing made the money. What was more apparent is that he cared enough for me to willingly give me anything I needed. I could respect that any way you put it. I was just afraid of what would happen if he was into something illegal though.

We got our brows arched and stopped for something to eat and we returned home. I texted MyKing when I got home but I didn't get a response. I felt bad about our disagreement but in the back of my mind, I was trying to figure out what I'd gotten myself into with him. He was seemingly the man of my dreams and realistically I didn't want us to end. Regardless of that troubling feeling I had in the pit of my stomach about us, the butterflies always seemed to overpower that. I decided I'd take Candice's advice. I would let MyKing do what he wanted with his money and keep my mouth shut about whatever it was he did to get it. I had no worries and I slept well-knowing someone had my back. However, I made the decision then to start saving for a rainy day. Just in case things went left. Before I could doze off MyKing had come knocking at my door and I gladly let him in.

"I'm sorry bae. Look, I want to be honest with you. I want you to know everything about me but there will be a time for that. I couldn't honestly answer your question so I didn't respond and I'm sorry I reacted like that. I just don't wanna bring no smoke into what we have." He started.

"MyKing it's alright. I'm sure you'll tell me when the time is right. But what is it that we have? I mean what are we doing?" I asked almost immediately.

"We chilling. I'm getting to know you and you getting to know me. You have a problem with that?" He asked with his hand under my chin with a questioning glare.

"No. I was just wondering." I stated. I wasn't very honest then but I didn't know how he'd respond if I told him how I really felt, so I left it be. Figured we'd be official eventually. After all, he didn't seem to want to be with anyone else.

CHAPTER TEN: CLOUT

Jasmine

I turned to MyKing before preparing to exit his truck. My eyebrows were raised high and I was almost sure he could feel the heat coming off my body. My palms were sweaty as hell. He started laughing.

"Jas, I don't know why you act like you scared. You gone have to do a lot of things without me. Just go in there with your head high. After that ass whupping you put on them hoes in that bathroom, I promise ain't nobody gone fuck with you. And any nigga that do all you have to do is call and I'll be here." He smiled.

"But I'm going to miss you!" I whined poking out my bottom lip.

"I'm gone be here to pick you up as soon as school let out though. We won't be apart that long. He said.

"So! But I'm still going to miss you." I told him with a smile.

"Imma miss you too. Gimme a kiss before you go." He smirked before he leaned in closer to me with his lips poked out. The butterflies started fluttering hard in my belly as I leaned in to quickly peck his lips with mine. The moment I pulled back he starts laughing.

"What?" I asked nervously. He shook his head with his dimples on full display.

"Nothing, have a great day at school." He said.

"Thank you and you have a great day," I told him before I opened the door and hopped out his truck. I walked towards the front door dreading the day. But the moment I got into the door, I knew something had changed.

"Hey, Jas." Some random girl spoke as we made our way through the detectors.

"Umm hi," I said oddly before grabbing my bag and heading to my locker. I went to pull my book out of my locker and a smaller book fell from the top shelf. I jumped back and bumped my locker neighbor in the process. I've always been a bit clumsy at times and was immediately embarrassed but before I could apologize to her she spoke.

"I am so sorry Jasmine. I didn't even see you girl." She said. I looked at her confused.

"No, that was definitely my fault. I apologize. I'm a clumsy mess at times." I said before I picked up my things to leave.

"I feel you. Me too girl." She replied and I shook my head at how crazy that went. I walked into first period and sat in my usual seat but instead of MyKing being to my right Candice sat in his place with her feet resting in the seat in front of her.

"Wassup bitch!" she said excitedly.

"Hey girl!" I laughed as I sat down. Our teacher entered soon after and class went on as usual. Only suddenly people actually spoke. The girls who mean mugged me before mysteriously decided to fix their faces when I was looking. When lunch rolled around me and Candice sat down at my regular table. I didn't see why she wouldn't sit with me now since we were friends. I never cared where she sat before.

"Girl is it me or is everybody suddenly friendly here," I asked looking around nervously. She started laughing immediately.

"Bitch that's clout!" she smiled widely.

"What? I don't get it." I said looking at her crazy.

"It's clout. The entire time we were gone we were the talk of the school. You are no longer just that pretty dark skin girl with My-King. It ain't no secret Jasmine Davis got them hands. It's the last day of school which means the rules don't mean shit. It's about to be a dozen fights when school let out and don't nobody want to be on the other side of your fist! It's great, right?" she asked excitedly.

"Uh no! I don't want people to think I'm some mean bitch who likes to fight. I'm not even that type of person. To be honest I was scared half to death before that girl spit in my face! I wouldn't dare start a fight!" I explained.

"Yeah, but they don't know that. It really doesn't even matter. Just enjoy not being fucked with. It's a relief for me. I never got along with none of these bitches and all you had to do was break a bitch nose and all my problems were solved. I'd rather it be because they think you crazy than MyKing be the reason they try you." She admitted.

"Yeah well let's just hope don't nobody feel like testing that ridiculous theory. I'm not even in a fighting mood. The fact that everybody is so damn hostile is alarming though. What is the big deal here, Jesus!" Candice laughed as I picked over my food.

"Girl, I know you ain't from around here but in this neighborhood, everybody fighting for something twenty-four seven. Nobody has the luxury of just living unless you hustle and even then, you risk your freedom to live a little. And from what I hear, it's a whole lot of fighting with that too." She tried to explain.

"Hustling how though?" I had to ask. She started busting up laughing. I just stared at her. I was going to wait till she stopped laughing and answered my question but there were tears running down her cheek before two people approached us. One guy and a girl. The girl was pretty to me. She had hazel eyes, mocha skin, and a perfectly styled short haircut. She reminded me of

Meagan good. Her wardrobe was perfect, and I'd recognized the designer right away. I noticed the diamond earrings and matching bracelet she wore. And her make-up was applied flawlessly. The guy surprisingly was even more attractive than her. He had big dark brown eyes, the perfect face, and a head full of thick dark curly hair. I'd noticed both of them at some point before, but they seemed hard to get close to.

"Hey Wassup." The guy spoke and there was literally nothing at all masculine about him. I just knew he was a guy.

"Hi," I replied. "Wassup." Candice recovered from her near-death chuckle.

"Candice, we having the end of the year kickback Saturday at Val house if you and Jasmine wanna come." He stated easily.

"Okay what time it start?" She asked seemingly interested.

"It starts at ten." the pretty brown skin girl spoke.

"Okay cool. We'll swing by." She smiled before they nodded and walked off.

"Umm who are they?" I asked as soon as they got out of ear range.

"Girl that's Pumpkin and Val. They live in P-town. They throw the best parties and every year they throw a kickback to celebrate the end of the year. It's invite only and they will embarrass your ass if you just show up. Lamont Richards is Pumpkin's real name. He mixed with Puerto Rican and black. Ole pretty ass nigga who can pull a straight man if he wants to. He can dance his ass off and despite how he looks the nigga hands is nasty. Believe it or not, he's the man of the house. He has nine sisters and he protects them all. Niggas do not fuck with him because most can't beat his ass. He sweeter than sweet N low but ain't shit sweet about that man hands. He will beat a nigga ass quick. And Valarie Nelson is his best friend. She real bougie, only fuck with a nigga with money, and her attitude is nasty as fuck. But the bitch pretty. She always rocking the hottest shit, she keeps her hair and nails done at all times, loves to be that bitch." She explained.

"Dang....so what they want with us?" I asked trying to figure out why suddenly I wasn't invisible to these people.

"Val ain't never said more than two words to me. Her nose usually too high in the air to even think about fucking with a bitch from the projects. But Pumpkin a cool ass muthafucka and he ain't the type to bring no drama to anyone. He don't mess with people like that. I've never been invited to any of their parties. All I can think is maybe your name been ringing bells. They didn't have a choice but to see who you were. Pumpkin cool and all but I know that bitch Val up to something. You gotta keep your eye on her bougie ass. I know she ain't suddenly tryna be my friend." She explained.

"She doesn't seem that bad. She is pretty. You make her sound like Regina George." I joked.

"Bitch who?" She asked confused.

"You know... the movie Mean Girls! She was this really popular pretty girl who..." I started to explain before she cut me off.

"Bitch stop! I can't take it no more." She said seriously before the bell rang and we headed out of the lunchroom and up the stairs to our next class.

"What? You've never seen mean girls?" I asked confused.

"Yeah but this is nothing like that. Bitch look around you. You ain't in Hollywood! This is the Ghetto. Food stamps, gunshots, and dirt! It is not anything like that movie or where you're from. You are on the southside of Chicago! The closest thing to that is Beverly and you gotta be making some money to live in that area. You are just so lost. I never met anyone like you in my life." She said seemingly aggravated. I was offended and I sat in class for the entire period without muttering a word. The next period without Candice just made me think about what she said. I was upset. Not at her but at my life. I come from a place just like "Hollywood". The movie was set in Evanston, IL. That's only like 45 minutes away from Chicago. I didn't understand how it could be much different beyond the economic aspect. I'm completely out of my element. I thought.

◆ ◆ ◆

Candice

Jasmine is so irritating. Like, I think she's nice and all but ain't no way she that damn dense. Like "Mean girls?" Really? I thought as I sat in my seat. I was definitely thankful for the period I had without her. But by the time I got out of biology 2, I felt bad. Jasmine was my friend so I went to find her in sixth period. I sat right next to her in class.

"Girl I'm sorry, I ain't mean to make you mad or nothing, I'm just not used to someone who is so lost. But I was wrong for how I came at you and I'm sorry. I'm just your friend and I'm not no fake bitch so if I feel some type of way I'm gone speak on it. I know you don't wanna be here but since you are imma put you up on game. You don't need me to protect you because you can fight for yourself and plus you got MyKing. But I will help you understand how shit really is here…Maybe show you some realistic movies…" I said with a smile before bumping her arm with my elbow. She couldn't hold her frown that long and before long we were back talking again. Before the final bell, at least four fights had broken out. But I knew that was gone happen anyway.

"So, what you wearing to the kickback?" I asked her as we walked towards the exit.

"Girl I don't think I want to go. I don't have anything to wear anyway!" She shook her head back and forth.

"Girl we are going. I know you have something and even if you don't you're with MyKing. That nigga ain't broke." I told her.

"Girl I'm not asking him for his money!" she said seriously.

"Bitch you crazy! I mean I can't lie. I was scared as fuck to ask Kevin for money but after seeing how easy it was for you to get MyKing in line I knew I had to try. I'm definitely about to call Kevin and get me some outfit, hair, and nail money. And he is fucking me, so it shouldn't be a problem." I told her easily.

"Well...I'm a virgin. I'm not having sex with him." She said hunching her shoulders.

"But he's your man though. The man will do anything you tell him to do. I don't know why you're scared. But don't trip imma handle it." I told her before MyKing pulled up in front of the school. We both hopped in his truck and I immediately texted Kevin. As soon as he told me he would give me some money, I started.

"So, Jas I'm going to the mall to find my outfit today for the kick-back. You want to come with?" I asked her as MyKing eyed me from the rearview.

"Yeah sure, I'll help you pick something." She stated plainly. She didn't catch on to my play at all and I smiled just laughing at her in my head.

"Do you have an idea of what you want to wear? Or how you wanna get your hair?" I asked her.

"No..I don't really have going out clothes. I've never even been to a kickback." She told me as she turned to me to look at me. She looked confused, but I smiled so she'd know the conversation was intentional.

"What kickback?" MyKing asked.

"Val and Pumpkin invited me and Jasmine to they kickback."

"Val...in P-town?" he asked knowingly. His face scrunched up like I'd just said something foul.

"Yeah, we told her and Pumpkin we would slide through," I

stated before he cut his eyes at me in the rearview. He stopped suddenly as if it was a car in front of him. Me and Jas both grabbed ahold of something to brace for an accident.

"Fuck nah she ain't going to no kick back in P-town. You can go but that shit dead. You knew better to even try that Candice and I'm about to put you out my truck. I don't even like Lamont bitch ass like that! You sound crazy." He spat.

Me and Jasmine both looked at each other with identical faces. Neither of us said anything before people start blowing because the light was green, and he'd stopped in the middle of the street.

"MyKing...we just got invited. I mean she didn't know...I thought it would be fun...or at least an experience. It's not like I'm doing anything..." Jasmine tried to smooth it over before he mashed the gas hard and we took off.

"You not going in P-town with no fucking faggot! I don't fuck with nobody over there and Candice knows that shit. I can't protect you over there and you ain't going. You can find you something else to do but that shit dead." He said through gritted teeth.

"MyKing you aren't my father! I don't need your protection. I can handle myself. I don't understand why you're angry at me wanting to go hang out. You've been out a whole week and didn't bother to give me an explanation! And you don't have to curse me like I've done something to you. I'll get out of the car if you want to be disrespectful. It's just not caused for." She said seriously.

His whole face changed. Mine did too because I ain't expect for her to have a comeback.

"Jas, I ain't say I was your father...I'm just not feeling you going to no kickback with niggas around I don't fuck with." He attempted to explain.

"It's alright. We aren't even in a relationship, so I don't feel like I need to ask your permission to hang with my friend. You are very disrespectful. She said as she grabbed her bookbag in her hand. "Let me out." She said and my whole face dropped.

"Jas don't be like that," he said dreadfully.

"Stop the car, MyKing." She said sharply, and he did. She looked back at me before opening her door. "Come on Candice." She ordered before she got out and shut the door before walking towards the sidewalk away from his truck.

"Bitch get yo goof' ass the fuck out like she said." MyKing spat angrily. I didn't say a word. I jumped out of the back seat and got on the sidewalk as quickly as possible. He pulled off angrily and I looked at Jasmine trying to process what had just happened.

"Girl my bad. I ain't know he was gone flip like that." I started.

"Me either but I guess everyone shows their true colors eventually." She said.

"Yeah well, you want to walk or catch the bus?" I asked her. We only had two blocks to walk.

"Girl its only two blocks. We can walk." She declared, and we walked until we got to the buildings. We got on the elevator and pressed our floors.

"You still want to go? Because I will help you get a cute outfit. We can just split the money I get to find something to wear." I told her.

"Okay sure. Just let me ask my mom and I'll call you in a few minutes." She said before my floor came up.

"Cool," I said before I exited the elevator and went straight into the house to change.

MyKing

I was fucking pissed! I did not like Candice. I knew she was gone be trouble the moment I saw her with Jasmine. I went into my house mad. My reasoning was real simple. I was from Slater Mills. I grew up under the old heads that sold drugs in this area before me. My family was decided for me. I was plugged when I was a shorty and my protection has always been within this project. That is why me and Kevin were so mad at Tevin for going outside the box. The way that works is obvious. A set protects each area. Niggas that are not affiliated with your family is automatically an opponent. It is dangerous to walk your ass into someone else's house if you're a stranger or even worse, an enemy. We robbed the nigga to get on and it was risky to play in his territory. Jasmine is my bitch and that ain't no secret. The fact that she is about to waltz her ass into an area that considers me an Opp is dangerous. I cannot protect her in P-town. It's niggas over there that would snatch her up just because she mine. Problem is, Jasmine can't see shit for what it is. She is living safely in her own little world. And it's nearly impossible for me to show her without exposing her to my world. I like her, and I feel like the only way I can keep her close is to keep the blinders on her. But that bitch Candice was making it extremely difficult for me to protect her. I was mad as fuck. I stayed there for all of an hour before I was knocking at Jasmine door. I liked her too much to just let her go. I was mad, but I liked her. She opened the door and she didn't seem pleased to see me at all.

"What do you want?" she asked seriously.

"Jas, I wanna talk. Can you let me in, so we can just talk?" I asked her. She opened the door wide before walking away toward her room. She changed clothes and was fixing her hair in the mirror.

"Jasmine I was not trying to be disrespectful. I apologize. I just feel like Candice was purposefully trying to get a rise out of me. I don't have any friends in P-town. I don't care for Pumpkin and Val ain't even the type of female you'd get along with. I just don't want you to start that going out stuff. I can't protect you like that." I explained. I wasn't telling the truth but I wasn't lying.

"MyKing I am not your child...we're not even together. I never question or dictate what you do when you have to up and leave. When you hang with your friends I don't say anything because it's not my place. I feel like you're wrong for trying to mandate what I can and can't do. I have one parent and she said I could go. I want to go and I'm not going to let the fact you don't like it stop me. I don't need your protection MyKing." She said seriously. She'd put her shoes on as if she was ready to leave. I felt like she was putting me out and I wasn't having any luck with getting back in her good graces.

"Where are you going?" I asked.

"I am going to the mall with my friend to find something to wear." She said easily. I exhaled defeated. She wasn't trying to hear shit and it was obvious she planned to go to this kickback regardless of how I felt about it.

"Okay, Jasmine. Here." I said defeated. I reached into my pocket and handed her four hundred dollars. She looked at the money but wouldn't take it.

"I don't need your money MyKing. I'm alright."

"Jas just take it. I'm sorry, okay. Here." I pushed. I added another hundred thinking maybe the four wasn't enough. I didn't know. I just ain't like this shit.

"Fine. Thank you." She said before she took the money and walked away towards the front door. I felt like shit as I followed her out like a sad ass dog. She locked the door and walked towards the elevator.

"So, you just gone stay mad? You not gone accept my apology?" I asked.

"You can't buy forgiveness MyKing." She said seriously.

"I'm not trying to. I just gave you the money so you can have some for the mall. I'm asking you to forgive me because I was wrong. I know I'm not your daddy and I can't tell you what to do. I just care, and I went about it the wrong way. I was disrespectful and I'm sorry. Can you please forgive me?" I asked her seriously. I ain't sorry often but I hated the thought of her not fucking with me. We ain't together but she knows I care. I've shown that much.

"I forgive you MyKing." She said easily before the elevator got to our floor.

"Okay, so can I get a hug?" I asked. She smiled, and I was relieved when she walked away from the elevator with open arms. I pulled her into me and wrapped my arms around her. She smelled so good I didn't want to let her go but I did when she pulled away. I was stressed when she got into the elevator, but she was right about one thing I couldn't do shit.

CHAPTER ELEVEN: KICKBACK

Candice

O nce me and Jasmine got to the bus stop I started to explain the look I was going for. I figured we'd go to Ford City Mall because it would be easy for us to both get cute outfits from Charlotte Russe or Wetseal with enough money left to get our hair and nails done. It wouldn't be on any level with the brand's Val wore but we'd still be cute.

"MyKing gave me some money so you don't have to split your money with me." She stated.

"Really? Okay cool. How much he give you?" I asked as the bus approached us.

"About five hundred." She stated casually.

"What?! Bitch you lying! That nigga ain't never peel you off like that! Bitch, you gotta be giving some head or something." I burst into laughter.

"Are you referring to oral sex?" she asked with her mouth wide open. I just laughed and hopped onto the bus. We made our way to the back to sit down before our conversation continued.

"Shit we can go downtown to shop since we got more than expected. I got three hundred, so it shouldn't be hard to find something real fly for the kickback. I'm so damn excited!" I told her after not being able to hold my smile.

"I kind of am too. But what about our hair. Shouldn't we make an appointment or something?" she asked.

"Nah. We going to the shop. It's off 59th and this lady named Ms. Tina own it. Everybody in there can do some hair. It's like the hottest salon on the Southside. You can just walk in though." I explained.

"Cool." She said as we looked through websites on our phones and exchanged ideas for our outfits. By the time we got downtown I'd already pictured my fit but what I realized, after only being in the store with Jasmine a few minutes, is the bitch could dress. She wasn't a stranger to expensive clothes and she had a sense of style I don't see often in the projects. I realized we would be able to keep up with Val because Jasmine was accustomed to the brands she wore. I let her dress me and some name brand shit I personally had never heard of and I end up spending just under the three hundred dollars I'd gotten from Kevin but I wasn't even mad. I was fly as fuck in the stores dressing room mirror. She ended up buying a cute blouse that hung off her dark skin like silk. The matching shoes complimented the top and added four inches to her tall frame. She stood six feet in the heels but no bitch could touch her. I smiled thinking to myself that she was gone to give Val a run for her money. I was completely here for it too. We gathered our bags and made our way home for the day after our shopping was done. The next day Jas fronted me the money to get my nails and hair done. We went to the nail shop first allowing the chinx to give us both pedicures and full sets. While I kept it short and simple, Jasmine preferred hers long and loud. But the pastel tangerine color she got complimented her skin nicely and went well with the blouse she picked out. Jasmine was completely foreign to this place, but I admired her style. That bitch was fly as hell.

Jasmine

We'd gotten our nails and toes done before catching the bus to the Salon Candice spoke so highly of. We were greeted before having to wait over an hour to even be serviced. But right after having my hair shampooed I saw Val walk into the salon. She spoke lazily before plopping down into the salon chair as if it were home to her. Coincidently the stylist that was servicing me had a booth directly next to hers.

"How you want it Val?" the lady asked before throwing a cape over her.

"Girl you already know what you doing." She replied with a slick smile before she noticed me. She looked me up and down before plastering a smile on her face.

"Hey, Jasmine girl. I didn't even realize that was you." She said.

"Hey, Valarie." I smiled back before crossing one of my legs over the other as the beautician sectioned my hair for a blowout and silk press.

"Damn...them the new mikes?" She asked me seemingly impressed. With a smile on her face and her eyebrows raised.

"Yeah, the 11s. They cute, right?" I asked.

"Yeah, those are nice. You make me want to go cop me some." She smiled before she was led to the shampoo bowl. I didn't know what it was about Valarie that made me feel anxious, but I knew this girl was something. She carried herself like she had the key to the city. She was classy and so unbothered it made me check myself. I admired her attitude and what Candice and MyKing had said about her yesterday, I couldn't apply. Felt like I could learn a lot from her about being classy and fly in a place where there was no class at all.

After she sat back in the chair she started talking to her stylist about her new "this" and her new "that". I listened but tried not to make it obvious. Right after her beautician molded her short hair she was sat under the dryer. Ms. Tina had blown my hair out before Val returned.

"So Jasmine, where are you from?" she asked me seemingly being friendly.

"Winnetka, IL," I answered.

"Wow, really? You're a long way from home huh?" she questioned.

"No. This is my home now." I explained.

"Shit, I feel you," she stated.

"So, are you from around here?" I asked already knowing the answer.

"Yes, girl. Raised right here on the Southside," she said proudly.

"Oh okay." I smiled not being able to come up with anything else to small talk about.

"Your nails look good. Where you get them done?" she asked.

"Oh me and Candice went to this shop not too far from here. Thanks." I smiled somewhat proud I'd impressed her. We sat there the remainder of our sit talking and getting to know each other. I'd been given so many compliments before she was done, I start to feel myself. She left before me because my hair was down my back and hers was short, but she promised to see me later at the kickback before she left. When Ms. Tina turned me towards the mirror so that I could see my hair, I could've cried. It never looked better. It was silky, straight, and shiny. She pulled her fingers through it as I examined the style.

"Jasmine girl you got my arms hurting with all this damn hair!" she smiled.

"Oh my God! Ms. Tina, it is beautiful! Thank you so much. You truly outdid yourself. It has never been this perfect. Not even back home!" I smiled admiring the bounce and fullness of the silk out.

"Oh, girl them white bitches don't know shit about no natural hair in Winnetka." she laughed before several people joined her in laughter.

"Well, I love it!" I said. I wasn't even going to mention that my previous beautician was black. I handed her the money and got out of her chair. Back home this style had cost me three times what Ms. Tina charged me and didn't even look half as good as it did now. I was highly satisfied. I went walking across the salon towards the dryer where Candice was just being finished.

"Damn! Okay, bitch! I see you coming through looking like Naomi Campbell." She laughed excitedly. She stood up out the chair to move her curls around in the mirror.

"You look great! Okay, Tyra!" I said before we both burst into laughter. I paid her stylist and we left feeling and looking like a million bucks.

I got home and couldn't keep the smile off of my face as I admired my hair in the bathroom mirror. I carefully wrapped my hair and threw on a shower cap before showering and putting on my clothes. I was almost finished with my look before MyKing came knocking on the door. When he saw me, he shook his head. I thought he'd love the way I looked but the disgust on his face proved not to be true.

"Damn...bae, I really think you should stay home with me." He said with his face balled up like he was mad. I cut him a look before rolling my eyes. He exhaled in defeat.

"You look beautiful Jasmine." He said before he pulled me into his arms. I smiled into his chest because he smelled so good.

"Thank you," I said with a smile. He really didn't want me to go but I did anyway promising him that I wouldn't be out too late.

Candice

I got dressed and couldn't wait to get there to stunt. My cousin dropped us off at Val's house and it was cracking by the time we got there. Everybody there had a cup in their hands and it seemed the music was live and everyone was getting along. Val immediately greeted me and Jas admiring both of our outfits and hair. I smiled but I peeped how she didn't bother to speak to me earlier at the shop after looking me dead in my face. I knew it was Jasmine she really liked and I just played along. Once she poured me and Jas a drink she continued to fake the funk with me until I couldn't stand sitting in her face anymore. I went into another room where Pumpkin had blunts in rotation and he and a bunch of other people were getting high. I sat to join the circle and we sat laughing and kicking it until his song came on and we all got up to dance. Jasmine had come into the living room to watch Pumpkin as she nursed the drink Val had given her pretending to like it.

I got high and danced around that house like it would be my last time. Jasmine sat with Val and some of her bougie ass friends and they sat pretty the entire time. I realized I didn't fit and my only reason for being here was because I stood up for a bitch I envied. That's irony for your ass. Jasmine was a beneficial friend. I was happy to be in the bathroom when it all went down and even though I wasn't a fan of Jasmine, in the beginning, I am her number one fan now. She has it all.

We both had a good time kicking it and me and Pumpkin exchanged numbers. After a few hours, me and Jas got a ride home.

CHAPTER TWELVE: WIFEY

MyKing

I was disappointed. I didn't want Jasmine to go to the kick-back at all especially looking as good as she did. I wasn't feeling that. I slid on Kevin for a minute before just going back in the house. The moment I got comfortable I dozed off. I woke up to Jasmine on top of me kissing me like she'd had too much to drink. I didn't even question how she'd gotten into my house because I wanted to fuck her so badly, I didn't give a fuck at that moment. She kissed me, and I returned the affection grabbing her ass in my hands and pressing my hard dick against the hot spot in her leggings.

"MyKingg...I'm ready." She moaned, and I was so turned on that I didn't hesitate to grab the top of her leggings to pull them over her ass. I pulled my boxers just past my ass and positioned myself at her entrance. She moaned into my ear that she loved me when I pushed myself into her. Right before I could respond I was awakened by my ringing cell phone. I was mad as fuck because my dick was standing straight up. I answered the phone and Mya spoke on the other line. She told me she wanted to come over and against my better judgement, I told her to slide through. I was horny, and Jasmine wasn't even home to know anything about me fucking Mya. After all, we ain't together and she reminded me of that every chance she got. I didn't think it would be a big issue at all. The door knocked as soon as I got out of the shower. I threw on my boxers and answered the door. The moment I let her in she was all over me. I shut the door before leading her to the room. She kissed my neck, wrapping her arms around me.

"MyKing, I missed you so much... I need you right now." She smiled before kissing my lips and rubbing my hard dick in her hands. I tensed up immediately because the shit felt good. I grabbed her ass in my hands prepared to give her exactly what she had come for. She sucked on my neck before pulling my penis out of my boxers and placing my head in her warm mouth. I was so turned on at the thought of nutting that I grabbed the back of her head and enjoyed every second of it. It felt so good I started to think about Jasmine. I start feeling weak in the gut before I told her to get up. She stopped but smiled at me anyway.

"What's wrong bae...you didn't miss me?" She fake frowned.

"Yeah, I did. I said as I sat on my bed with a hard penis. I was debating in my head rather or not this was a good idea and I decided I'd fuck her and put her out before Jasmine could get home. I turned on the music just loud enough for Mya's moans to be masked and let her suck and kiss all over my neck before I couldn't take the teasing anymore. I bent her over and fucked her like my life depended on it. In my head, Jasmine was who I was with and I nutted quick at the thought of being with Jasmine like that. The moment I busted the music stopped and my phone rang. Mya and I both looked towards the phone that was laying on my nightstand as "Wifey" flashed across the screen. I pulled out of her the moment I realized Jasmine was calling. I didn't pick up because I was sitting right in front of Mya and couldn't explain to Jasmine what I was doing.

"Who the fuck is "Wifey" King?" She asked with a serious frown on her face. I realized then I'd made a mistake, but I didn't know what to say. Before that moment I didn't even give a fuck.

"Come on Mya don't start," I said shaking my head.

"King that's fucked up. You got a new bitch, right? You really gone do me like that? Like you couldn't just tell me you had a girl before you fucked me?" she said getting up to put on her clothes. I could hear in her voice she was hurt and I had never had an issue with Mya. She was cool as hell and I really didn't mean to hurt her.

"It's not even like that. I wasn't tryna do you wrong or no shit like that." I tried explaining.

"Yeah what the fuck ever. I'm gone and you ain't never gotta worry about me fucking with you again. I hate you!" She said seriously.

"My bad Mya. It wasn't intentionally." I told her as she pushed past me and left the room. I shook my head before going to the washroom to clean up. I opened the bathroom door to return to my room wearing just my boxers and Jasmine was standing directly in front of me. The look on her face made my heart skip a beat. She had tears gathering in her eyes and I didn't know what to do. After standing there for a few moments longer she turned to leave.

"Wait, Jasmine, I can explain!" I started following her into the living room. She turned to me swiftly before stopping in her tracks. Her hair bounced around her head as she locked eyes with me.

"Ok, so you can explain to me why you were just in here having sex with that girl?" She asked as her voice quivered.

"Bae...It's not what you think." I told her. I was lying like a muthafucka. It was exactly what she thought. I was just convinced the fact we weren't together gave me an alibi. The shit was justified.

"Oh, save that. I don't even want to hear it." She spat before turning to leave. I grabbed her because I didn't want to lose her.

I have feelings for shorty and I know she special.

"Jas, don't leave, bae. Let's just talk about it." I said at my last attempt to make it right before she left.

"Let me go MyKing!" she said as tears slid down her cheeks. I felt like shit and I can't say I've ever experienced the feeling before. I can't remember a time where a girl genuinely cried over me before. Or when I actually gave a fuck. Shit made my chest feel heavy.

"Baby come on. Don't cry. I'm sorry if I hurt your feelings. I really don't want you to leave... Just talk to me." I told her as I pulled her closer and wiped her tears away with my hand. It felt like the moment she got in my arms everything was okay. My heart was racing like crazy. I ain't no soft ass nigga but I couldn't stomach losing her and I didn't know why. This was the chick I planned to marry. She gone raise my kids. Wasn't no pussy worth losing Jas. Plus I couldn't picture another nigga with her.

"I don't want to talk to you, MyKing." She said before more tears came rushing down.

"Okay, Jas just listen to me. I want you. I want to be with you. I swear I don't want nobody but you but we ain't together. I didn't do anything to betray your trust because we ain't together. But if you give me the chance to really be your man... I promise I will never do shit to hurt you again. That's my word but you have to trust me." I explained.

"MyKing...I want to be with you too but I can't compete with women who want to have sex. I am just not ready for that and..." I cut her off.

"Don't worry about that shit. I swear I won't cheat on you. From this moment, I am really your man, you're my girl, and we are together. I'm not gone fuck nobody else. Just give me a chance." I explained. She dropped her head as a few more tears fell down her face.

"You just gotta trust me," I told her. I was gone wife shorty.

Wasn't no way around it.

"MyKing, I do trust you, but I can't give you what she did. If that's what you want, we might as well not be together..." she said.

"Okay, I can wait until you ready. Let me prove that to you." I stated. I pulled her face closer to mine and the worry in her eyes bothered the hell out of me.

"Jasmine I only want you. Just tell me you want to be together and I promise I will do right by you." I said seriously.

"Okay..we can be together, just promise me you won't ever hurt me." She said as she looked into my eyes. I held my breath as dead silence filled the room. I wanted her. I had no intentions of hurting her, so I just went with it.

"I promise you that I won't," I told her before I pulled her lips to mine before we embraced. Then I heard the door shut and looked in that direction.

"Uh..what you doing?" My mama asked before she eyed Jasmine who wiped her face when she saw my mama. Before I could even introduce her, my mama had some fly shit to drop out her mouth.

"King you bet not have got that girl pregnant. I done told you about these lil hoes." She said with her mouth turned in disgust. Jasmine's mouth fell wide open.

"Wait, what?...oh no ma'am. I'm not pregnant. I am still a virgin." She stuttered in shock. I was so embarrassed, and I would've checked my mama if Jasmine wasn't standing here.

"So, what you over here crying for? Why you in here hugging up on him like you got some bad news?" she started.

"Ma, she ain't pregnant. This is my girl." I said wanting her to just go in her room and shut the fuck up.

"Girl?" she asked before she started to cackle.

"I'm just gonna go home. I'll talk to you later." She said before she turned to leave.

"Bae, you don't have to leave, it's okay," I told her.

"No, it's fine. I'm pretty tired. I'll talk to you in the morning." She said before she left out the door. The moment she was out the door I turned to look at my hoe ass mama with a clear mug on my face.

"Oh, you must really like that lil stuck up heffa huh?" she asked before she chuckled her way into her room. I was irritated but instead of responding I just went to take a shower.

CHAPTER THIRTEEN: BOSS BITCH

Jasmine

I'd come in from the kickback, took a shower, and got in bed. I called MyKing when I'd laid down, but he didn't answer. I figured he was already sleeping and I went to sleep myself. That was until I was awakened by MyKing's music. It shook my walls and once I was awake I couldn't get back to sleep. I grabbed my phone again to call him and he didn't answer. I shook my head before getting up to brush my teeth, wash my face and throw on some shoes. I made my way towards his apartment before the door opened and a familiar looking girl walked out with the meanest look on her face. She was really pretty and shapely and I got nervous the moment I saw her about to leave his apartment.

"Who are you?" I asked hoping my gut was all wrong.

"Oh, let me guess. You must be "Wifey?" She said before looking me up and down and shaking her head. "You ain't even his type.... then again, he doesn't have any standards." She said bitterly.

"Excuse me?" I asked not even understanding what she meant but I was offended.

"Don't even worry sweetie. I'm not ever fucking King again. You can have him." She said before she brushed passed me. It angered me to understand what she meant. I started to just go back home and never speak to him again, but my anger made me go into the apartment to confront him. However, the moment I looked into his eyes I felt my heart break because I really cared for him and I was hurt. I turned to leave to keep him from seeing me cry but when it was all said and done I forgave him and we decided to be together. And I was glad I'd made the choice to allow him to prove how much he cared. I had some deep feelings for him and I believed he felt the same about me. We made it official and after that night he treated me like he loved me. I started to believe He'd be the man I'd marry and looked forward to our future together. I even considered having sex with him because I knew we'd be married one day. I loved him, and I was convinced he loved me too. Everything was fine until I met his best friend Kevin.

One day I was sitting in the house kinda bored when he called me. You are my rock by Beyoncé played as my phone rang. I smiled at the thought of MyKing calling. He had been gone all day, out handling his business, and I was impatiently waiting home for him.

"Hello!" I answered excitedly as he greeted me and told me to come open the door. I must have had the Tv up too loud because I didn't even hear it. I got up to answer and jumped into his arms the moment I saw him. He held on to me and I looked up into the deep brown eyes of a dark, shorter man who was as equally attractive as MyKing. A chill went down my spine the moment our eyes met and I'd never forget the feeling as long as I lived. His features were strong, and he had a memorable mole on the left side of his cheek. When MyKing let go of me I stepped aside to let him and the guy in.

"Bae this is my brother, Kevin... Kevin this is my girl, Jasmine." He introduced us. I knew immediately this was the guy Candice was crazy about because she talked about him every chance she could.

"Hi. Nice to meet you." I said before reaching my hand out for him to shake it. He looked down at my extended hand and started to laugh. When I saw his straight white teeth, I understood why Candice was so into him. He was fine if nothing else, but I was really offended by the fact he left my hand in the air and refused to shake it. I looked towards MyKing before I dropped my hand. I thought that was disrespectful and I couldn't hide the displeasure on my face.

"Bro stop playing." MyKing pleaded seriously.

"King why the fuck you play so much?" he laughed some more.

"Kev, I'm not playing this ain't a joke. Jasmine is my girl for real." MyKing explained seriously before I decided to just walk away. I didn't care for Kevin from the beginning and I didn't even attempt to hide it. MyKing grabbed me and pulled me into his arms.

"Bae don't be like that. I'm sorry, okay?" He whispered in my ear before he kissed my neck. The tingles that went up my spine made me momentarily forget anyone else was in the room. I kissed him back before Kevin spoke again.

"Wait...yall serious?" he asked stupidly with a grin on his face.

"What are you talking about?" I asked annoyed by him. I didn't even understand why MyKing brought his ignorant ass over here.

"So yall are really together?" he asked another stupid question.

"Yeah nigga, I told..." I eyed MyKing about that word and he stopped mid-sentence to correct himself.

"I mean yeah bro, I told you I was serious. This my baby, Jasmine." He said.

"Oh damn...my bad sweetheart. I really thought MyKing was trying to prank me or something. My Bad." He chuckled before he extended his hand for me to shake this time. I shook his hand, but I didn't understand why he would've even thought that. We are a little too old to be playing like that. I thought to myself.

Once we sat down and got comfortable in the living room I realized Kevin and MyKing were two peas in a pod. They were just alike. He turned out to be a really cool laid-back type of guy and he was funny. He completely changed my first impression of him and I got real comfortable with him in the short time he was in my apartment.

"So, you talk to my friend Candice, right?" The moment I said it he cut his eyes at MyKing. MyKing start laughing and Kevin started right behind him. I didn't understand what was so funny and I thought they were trying to be funny about my friend.

"Uh what's so funny, Iman?" I asked before MyKing stopped laughing and cut his eyes at me for calling him by his middle name. I started to laugh.

"What she just call you?" Kevin asked confused.

"Nothing." MyKing lied before telling me to watch my mouth.

"I mean, I only asked because she seems to really like you and I wanted to know if maybe you felt the same way about her?... I mean I get you younger men don't like to get into relationships but if you really care about someone I don't see what would be the hold-up, you know?" I asked before he looked at MyKing again before turning back to me.

"How old are you?" he asked.

"Sixteen," I responded.

"Well, I'm older than you." He said smartly.

"And I'm taller than you." I shot right back before MyKing burst into laughter.

"Okay, you win. I like shorty, she's cool. That's it." He responded.

"So, you're saying you don't want to be with her?" I asked.

"I ain't say that." He said before he got quiet. I didn't press him with any more questions.

"Yall hungry?" I asked.

"Why you think I came over here?" MyKing joked.

"Welp! You better go get us some Harold's or something." I laughed before he pulled me on top of him and started tickling me. We laughed until he started kissing me and I kissed him right back. I loved making out with him.

"Damn I missed you." He said.

"I missed you too." I smiled before I glanced at Kevin who could barely contain his laughter.

"Bro, yall just a little too "lovey-dovey" for me. Jasmine, you got my boy over here soft as fuck. Thought I'd never see the day." He laughed.

"Shut up!" MyKing said before we all made the decision to go get something to eat.

◆ ◆ ◆

MyKing

I dropped Jas back home after we grabbed some food so me and Kevin could make a few more runs. Since Tevin had been locked up our plate had been real heavy. I'm spending more time working than sleeping because the nigga increased the product with the intention of expanding our territory and the shit was harder to move. Especially since neither I or Kevin wanted to expand. It just wasn't safe, so we stayed within the box with more shit than necessary. However, we managed, and the money was still coming in.

"Bro where did you even find shorty? She bad as fuck but I can tell she not from around here. Don't even seem like your type." Kev started.

"She ain't. She moved here a few months back from Winnetka." I started.

"Where?" he asked confused.

"It's in the suburbs. Ole rich ass city people with them ends live. Some bad shit went down with her pops company and he killed himself. She and her mama moved here, and she works down at the hospital." I explained.

"Damn...so you in love for real or you fucking with me?" he laughed.

"Naw this legit might be my wife," I told him honestly.

"Wife? Nigga that bitch must have magic in her pussy. Ain't no way she got you open like that." He laughed. Although I didn't find shit funny.

"Bro, you tweaking. Don't call my girl out her name. That's disrespectful." I said seriously. He looked at me with his eyes bucked out of his head.

"Oh, my bad. I just never thought I'd see the day when somebody got your hoe ass straight." He smirked.

"She a virgin. I haven't hit." I admitted.

"Damn... nigga. I can't even believe that." He shook his head.

"What up with you and shorty for real though?" I asked changing the subject of conversation.

"Who Candice?" he asked.

"Yeah."

"I ain't gone lie. I fuck with her hard. She's cool and loyal and she can get anything out of me if she asked." He admitted.

"So why not just be with her like Jas said?" I asked curiously.

"I don't know. I just ain't tryna be in no relationship. Never even thought about it." He admitted.

"Okay well, that's on you bro," I told him as I focused my attention on the task at hand. Honestly, the lack of Tevin didn't make selling drugs harder for us. It made it easier. I have to admit the amount of product was the hardest thing to get over but Kev and I got shit done. We ran things calmly and smoothly and there were rarely ever any issues because we didn't leave room for error. That kept the police off of our asses. We always agreed on how we did things and even though our shipment had increased we were able to move it efficiently while staying within our territory. It just took longer to move. . Nobody had to die because of the increase. We always handled what we needed to. That was all that mattered to me. And Kevin wore them big boy draws when it came to moving the weight. The amount of money I was touching had me feeling like the man. I was counting tens of thousands at seventeen. At the time I didn't think we could do better. While Kevin was tryna be that nigga I had plans of getting away and going to college. Having Jasmine only made it seem possible. That's my real attraction to her. She makes the worse part of me want to be better.

The rest of the summer went by with ease. Business was smooth, and Jasmine and I were good. The school years started up again and I went into my last year with a positive attitude and good energy. For the first time in my life, I was comfortable with the way shit was. Well, that was until I saw some shit I knew was going to change everything. A few weeks after school started shit start going left. Jasmine and I had just got home from the movies and I came into the house with her. We got in and walked past her mother who was in a deep nod at the kitchen table.

"Hey, ma!" Jasmine spoke before making her way into the bathroom to urinate. I stopped in my tracks when she didn't respond. I walked over to her at the table watching her nod and when I realized what was happening I grabbed her arm to check for tracks. When I saw the rows of puncture holes in her brown skin I wanted to slap her ass.

"Bae come here!" Jasmine yelled from the bathroom. I jumped afraid that she'd see her mama like this.

"Fuck!" I gritted before I muffed her mother across her head out of frustration. That nearly knocked her out the chair and I hurriedly got to the bathroom to keep her from coming out.

"Can you hand me a pad from that bag on my bed, please. She asked. I went into her room and grabbed the whole pack of sanitary napkins and handed her the package through the crack in the bathroom door. Instead of closing it to handle her business she decided she wanted to have a full conversation.

"So, I've been thinking about prom since we've started our senior year. What do you think about a deep fuchsia? I mean I know you don't like pink but it will be kind of hot if you would think about wearing it.

"That's fine," I stated aggravated at the thought of knowing Jasmine's mama was in the kitchen high as fuck, nodding like a dope fiend. I didn't give a damn about the color she wanted to wear to prom at that moment. I knew how bad this was. That was the first sign that I was gone have one helluva winter.

"MyKing what's wrong?" she asked when I didn't respond.

"Nothing. We'll see what it looks like. I said but I couldn't hide the displeasure in my voice.

"Well… we can just talk about it later. No need to be so bothered by a color." She said concerned.

"I'm straight," I said dismissively as she came out of the bathroom.

"MyKing, what's wrong? I can look at you and tell you are bothered. I know you." She said before she looked me in my eyes. My heart was pounding against my chest and I was trying to figure out what things were going to be like from now on. Jasmine's mama is a hype. I don't have any doubt about it. That meant a lot of things. She won't be able to keep a job, she won't be able to pay the bills, and she can no longer be trusted. Then, when it was all said at some point Jasmine is going to have to experience what it feels like to have a hype as a parent. That ain't so uncommon here but it won't be pleasant if I don't do anything. Fuck! I thought.

"Jasmine, I'm good. Just hungry." I lied.

"Okay well I'll go start on dinner," she said before she walked towards the kitchen.

"No, it's gone take to long for the food to cook. I'd rather go out. Wanna go to your favorite restaurant?" I asked her plastering a fake smile on my face.

"The grand lux?" she asked with a smile.

"Yeah, that's fine," I said baiting her.

"Well yeah, ok cool. Just let me change first." She said easily as she turned in the opposite direction towards her bedroom. I exhaled deeply. I was just trying to keep her from seeing her mother high.

"Okay. Imma run next door for a second to grab something" I lied.

"Okay." She said before she went looking in her closet.

"I closed the door of her bedroom behind me before I went back to the kitchen. I grabbed her mother to help her out of the chair.

"She jumped before placing her hands in front of her in defense. I'm sorry please don't hit me again! I don't have any more money. Here…" She offered before she reached around her neck and snatched the gold chain off of her body. She placed it in my hand.

"That's all I have. Just take it." She said before she started scratching her neck and arms. I stood there completely mortified trying to figure out how long she been on that shit. She never even looked me in my face. I looked down into my hand and it was coincidentally the necklace I'd bought for Jasmine for her mother. I shook my head before I grabbed her again; forcing her wandering eyes to meet mine. Her pupils were tiny and darting back and forth like she was trying to watch two things in opposite directions.

"Mrs. Davis," I said slowly. She focused her eyes on me before she smiled.

"Hello, MyKing. How are you?" She said as if she'd just saw me. I shook my head as she scratched randomly in front of me.

"Look, just go in your room so Jasmine don't see you. I'm gonna get you some help. Just go in the room right now okay." I gritted trying my best to get through to her.

"I'm fine honey. I don't need help." She said before trying to fix her thinning hair. I shook my head at her sad attempt to convince me.

"Mrs. Davis just go in your room. I will handle the rest." I told her as I led her towards her bedroom. Once she was inside I shut the door and not even ten seconds later Jasmine opened her room door fully clothed.

"Okay bae, I'm ready just gonna tell my mommy bye."

"Nah she said she was gonna lay down because she had a headache. Told me to bring her something back to eat." I lied.

"Oh okay. I guess she called off." She said more to herself than me.

"Ok well let's go," I told her before walking her right out the front door with a thousand things going on in my head. One being I doubt she even had a job. I knew I would have to protect Jasmine and I planned to. That was my only concern.

Jasmine

"You know Jasmine, I like you. You got class. Your friend Candice could learn a lot from you." Val started as we took our time shopping downtown in Bloomingdales.

"Well thanks but honestly she is the one usually teaching me. I'm so lost when it comes down to being here." I admitted.

"Lost? I disagree. I think your ability to be quiet and observe gives you the advantage. Your style and class put you in a completely different category than Candice.

"Yeah well, I guess so." I partially agreed.

"I mean you have beauty, you seem really intelligent, and you're with a hustler. You already have what all them bitches in the projects want. Like a boss bitch. And I'm sure you mess with Candice the long way, but she can't teach you a damn thing about being a boss bitch." She stated seriously.

"Well, she talks to his best friend…" I added.

"Who Kevin? I mean he hustles too. I'm sure he got a few dollars but everybody knows King is the one moving the money." She said easily.

"Well I guess that would make me different, but still it's his money," I added. She laughed.

"You know I like the way he moves. He got the shit down to a science. He's quiet with his moves and he don't short step his business. Those are damn good qualities for a drug dealer. I mean I came from a hustler. I watched my daddy move my whole life. He was nothing like these young ass niggas today. Loud, arrogant, and stupid. I ain't never seen so many niggas that want everybody to know they sell drugs. The police ain't even gotta work no more. Niggas telling on themselves." She said easily.

"See my mother taught me everything there is to know about being a hustler's wife. I've never seen her sweat. Even when my daddy got locked up she handled shit like he would've. And when the feds came messing with her, she held her shit so tight they couldn't take a dime of my daddy's money because they couldn't prove it didn't belong to her. Girl, that ain't just his money. If it was, you wouldn't be in a luxury mall spending it. You definitely have the potential. All you have to do is realize who the fuck you are. See, I figured you were ready when you fucked them bitches up in that bathroom. I knew then you were a boss. Especially since ain't no bitch ever kept King attention long enough to be his girl." she explained.

"Yeah well, my mother wasn't much of a hustler's wife. But my father was a wealthy man. He had more money than someone could spend in a lifetime. He didn't want for nothing. But if my mother didn't teach me anything else, she did show me how to keep my man. It's real simple. Find out what gets his attention, then starve him." I explained.

She chuckled. "So, you mean to tell me you haven't fucked him?" she asked in shock.

"Evidently I don't have to," I replied before I gathered the few items I'd picked out and made my way towards the sales clerk.

"Oh see you know about this hustler's wife shit after all. Different field but the game ain't changed. I like that in you!" she laughed as we made our way to the next store. After shopping with Val, I felt completely different about my relationship with MyKing. The truth was I figured he was doing something illegal and she just confirmed it was drugs. Not only did I not care but it made me love him even more. He's a great boyfriend and I don't want for anything. Can't be mad at that.

Few days after the shopping trip I had with Val, MyKing was supposed to take me out only his phone rang while we were in route to the restaurant. He told me he had to make a move and he was taking me home. Only now that I understood what that meant I wanted to calm him about how he handled me.

"Bae, it's cool. Imma ride with you. Handle your business." I stated coolly as I let my seat back comfortably.

"Nah Jas, I can't do that ma." He looked on with uncertainty.

"Baby, if it can't wait until after dinner, it can't wait. Do your thing." I pushed confidently. He looked at me a while but he didn't respond. He turned the truck around but he didn't take me home. I sat quietly as I watched him and Kevin load what I presumed to be drugs in the trunk of his truck. Once he got back in the car he exhaled loudly as if he was nervous. He looked at me before he put the truck in drive and took off into the street. I'd say three blocks from that spot I had gotten tired of him constantly looking into the rear view.

"Pull over MyKing," I said sternly. He looked at me like I was crazy.

"Bae, chill." He said nervously.

"Pull the damn truck over, MyKing!" I told him seriously. He pulled over and looked at me. "Bae look, now ain't the time for this, ma. On some real shit. I need you to chill." He told me.

"I got you. Let me drive." I told him calmly as I unbuckled my seat belt.

"Fuck no! Jas this ain't the time!" He said seriously. I hopped out of the truck anyway and was on the driver's side before he could protest. He reluctantly got out the truck and we switched seats. I pulled into the streets and made my way using the directions he gave me as my guide. In my head, I was being the boss bitch I thought I was. It didn't dawn on me that maybe I was perpetrating until I had flashing blue lights in my rearview. The moment MyKing noticed he couldn't hold his anxiety.

"Fuck! Bae, do not say a fucking word. I swear on Ma grave, if you just tell them you don't know shit, they can't hold you." He said regretfully. I nodded my head and pulled the truck over. I was holding the urine that had crept into the finish line of my bladder. It was so quiet after I stopped the car I could hear his shallow breathing.

"MyKing, what's in the trunk?" I asked slowly.

"Trouble," he said before the officer came tapping on the window. I rolled it down and was nearly blinded by the flashlight he rudely flashed in my face.

"License and registration." He said while chewing a piece of peppermint gum.

"Sure, bae would you pass me my purse?" I turned to MyKing. He nodded before he grabbed my purse from the back seat and placed it into my lap. I'd gotten my license right after turning sixteen because my father wouldn't let me drive my truck off of our property without one. I quickly retrieved my license and MyKing handed me the registration for the truck.

"This is a fine automobile Ms...Davis." The officer said as he looked at my driver's license again.

"Thank you!" I smiled politely.

"Wait...Jasmine Davis from... Winnetka? Are you related to Mrs. Ella?" he asked inquiringly looking over me and MyKing. I smiled even brighter. Silently thanking God, I didn't get the chance to update my license to match my current address.

"Yes! She is my grandmother!" I assured him.

"Well, I grew up in Winnetka. I know your whole family. Real nice people! What are you doing way down here in Chicago? In this neighborhood?" he frowned.

"Oh, you know after daddy died my mother couldn't bear the grief of losing everything. She started nursing again at the University of Chicago and we relocated here. You know the loss of my father was hard on everybody but it's not so bad here." I lied.

"Yeah...I heard about that. I'm really sorry for your loss. I only stopped you because of the tints on your truck. They are a little dark and that is usually the first sign of trouble in this neighborhood." He stated before looking at MyKing.

"Oh no! You know I am well taken care of. I wouldn't dare cause any trouble. There is no trouble here. We are just on our way to dinner." I smiled as I glanced at MyKing.

"Yes ma'am, pardon me. I apologize for stopping you. I hope you have a good night and make sure you send my best regards to the family." He said respectfully.

"I sure will. Thank you, officer...Bates." I said peeping at his name badge." You have a wonderful rest of the night." I smiled before I put the truck in drive and proceeded into the street. It was quiet again.

"Is Ella really your grandma? "My King asked suddenly.

"Yeah, I can't stand that bitch." I chuckled. He started to laugh too. When I looked at him he was looking at me in at the moment I saw something in his eyes I had never seen before.

"That shit was sexy." He said.

"I know. I just want you to know I got you, bae." I smiled before we finally got to our destination. And instead of my man sleeping in somebody's jail cell, he slept laying right next to me. Now that's how a boss bitch does it!

CHAPTER FOURTEEN: A BAD OMEN

Kevin

"Shit bae!" I groaned as I wrapped my right hand around Candice's neck as I held on to her waist and pounded at her insides like I had something to prove. She loved for me to choke her ass while I was beating that thing down. It drove me crazy. She drove me crazy! It had gotten to the point where I really wanted her and I don't even know when the shit happened. She started to moan loudly, and she tightened herself around me. I pulled back slightly to keep from busting.

"No Kevin, go harder! I'm about to cum." She hissed. She pulled me back in by wrapping her hands around my waist. I hit it harder like she asked, and I knew I was gone nut. I busted all in her and for the first time, I didn't give a fuck.

"Kevin did you just do what I think you did?" she asked confused.

"Candice, you questioning me?" I asked her.

"You don't even want to be with me though." She started.

"Who told you that? Jasmine?" I asked her quizzingly.

"She ain't have to tell me shit. I been fucking with you for damn near two years? You make it perfectly clear you don't want to be in a relationship. You don't even want me sleeping in your crib, so I'm definitely not convinced you want me having your baby." She explained.

"I do want to be with you…" I started.

"But.." She spat and rolled her eyes like she knew I was gone hit her with some lines.

"But shit. You want to be my girl or not?" I asked her seriously. She attempted to look at me crazy, but she couldn't hide the smile on her face. I loved her smile.

"Yeah but I'm not ready to have no kids." She said with a smirk.

"You'll be ready when they get here." I smiled. She chuckled before she wrapped her arms around me and we laid in my bed just talking and shooting the shit.

"So, how's business since your brother been away. Yall good?" she asked suddenly.

"Yeah, shit been smooth as fuck with King. It ain't never no bull-shit, I sleep better at night." I admitted.

"His mean ass got a way to him." She chuckled.

"King ain't mean. He one of the easiest people to get along with." I told her.

"Your boy don't fuck with me at all. He ain't never liked me." She said.

"That's not true. He the one that told me I better lock you down before you move on." I admitted.

"What? King? I know you lying!" she laughed.

"I swear on my Og and you know I ain't finna lie on my mama," I told her.

"Yeah whatever!" she laughed as she gathered her things to leave.

"Wait, where are you going?" I asked her seriously.

"I'm going home." She said easily.

"Why won't you just stay here?" I asked her.

"Now all of a sudden you want me to stay with you?" she smirked.

"Candice stop fucking playing with me. You gone stay or what?" I asked her as if I didn't care. I did though, and I wanted her to. It was really hard for me to ignore all of those red flags but I didn't want her to leave. She stayed the night with me though.

MyKing

I checked Jennifer into rehab the moment I was able to get Jasmine away from her. She was occupied with her studies most days. Regardless of the time I spent doing what I thought had to be done, she kept me afloat too. Most nights she was the one doing my homework and taking my notes. I appreciated her and I didn't want her to know her mother was on the drugs I helped sell. She was being served right at home and that was my domain. After Jen left the rehab by checking her own self out, I had to send the word out to the lil niggas not to even serve her. Her money was no good in my territory as long as it concerned my girl. I started to foot the bills in Jasmine apartment to keep her from finding out about her mother. I came up with a bullshit story to account for her absence and I made sure it was always food in the house. I knew she had her suspicions because of the relationship she had with her mother. One minute they were surviving together and the next her mother had disappeared. But I took care of her so that she was good.

I and Kevin were around making moves in the trap one day when Jen came to me crying. It was starting to get cold out. She stunk and her clothes were dirty. Her teeth were starting to rot and she looked nothing like the woman I'd met when her and Jasmine first moved here. My heart felt heavy when I saw her and regardless of how many times she checked out of the rehab I'd put her in, I could never turn her away. I walked her inside the trap and we sat down on the raggedy furniture. I handed her the plate of food I had for me in my truck and let her eat. Once she was done we just sat. It was quiet and besides Kev, nobody else was there. It was rarely peaceful in the trap.

"Jen, what is it that I have to do for you to shake this shit?" I started. She scratched.

"My King please take care of my daughter. I ain't strong enough. I want to stop this shit. But I can't." She cried.

"You can't or you won't? What happened to you? I told you, I had you. Why did you go fucking with the drugs anyway? I took care of you! It wasn't that bad Jen." I exclaimed.

"You don't get it...I understand that. I've been miserable for a long time. I got this bad luck with me that I just can't lose. I grew up right here in Chicago. On the west side. That's where my family lived my whole life. My daddy was a drunk who beat my mama ass anytime he got the chance and my mother was a fool. My father lost his life gambling with the wrong muthafuckas. They stabbed him in the chest when they realized his drunk, shit talking, ass ain't have no money to put up. We were poor before he died but boy did I appreciate him when he was gone. Most times the only food I had was at school. My mama's family wasn't shit. I realized that when we had no choice but to move in with them. It was a dozen people living in one house, but nobody could protect me when my mama's brothers would snatch me up." She huffed.

"I hated it there. I hated everything about my life. When I was offered a scholarship to go to the university, I went and never looked back. I vowed to never go back to that place. I left for college and left my family behind. I went with a few rags and a plan to finish. By the time I'd graduated, I had caught the eye of my husband and even in rags, he saw the jewel that I was. That's what he said. So, he bought me diamonds and he made sure I was kept. He promised me he'd make sure I was always taken care of. Despite the fact his family despised our union he married me and he did what he promised. I never had to work, and I never needed to worry. I never even used the degree I'd earned. Until I had to and ended up dragging my child into the same shithole lifestyle I escaped from. I was miserable." She cried.

"So, you feel better now?" I asked her quickly. "I get your sob story but it's like a slap in the face to me. You in here dirty, hungry, and itching and you think that somehow shooting that bullshit in your arms was gone be better than just humping it out?" I exclaimed.

"I didn't say that! And you have your nerve. You are selling the shit to people just like me. What makes you better than me? You better get off of that high horse or it'll run you straight into the ground!" she spat.

"High horse! What? Did you think my funky ass mama was doing good? I been here all my life. Barely eating because the government only give you enough so that you can survive. That's what I've been doing. I work my ass off out here. I risk my life and freedom just to make sure I and the people around me are eating. I didn't do it to hurt nobody! I saw an opportunity and took it. I take care of your daughter because I love her. I'm tryna help you because I love her. I know she deserves better than this. I plan to give her better but I need you to get clean. Stop the bullshit excuses and get clean. I been trying to help you for her. And if it wasn't for that your funky ass wouldn't be sitting in my face right now." I said harshly. I had love for Jen and she knew it. I have been coming to her rescue since I found out she was on that shit.

"I want to get clean MyKing." She said seriously.

"No, you don't. You right. You ain't strong enough and I'm not about to keep wasting money trying to help you. Don't come back here until you tired of the streets and you really wanna get clean. I ain't finna let you ruin Jas because she deserves better than a hype for a mama." I said before I got up and opened the front door for her to leave. I was angry at the time and I figured if I gave her no choice but to straighten out, she'd come back better. I wanted her to want it for her and not because I was trying to make her. She stood from the couch and wiped the tears from her face.

"You take care of my daughter MyKing." She said before she walked out the door.

"You come back stronger," I said before I closed the door. I was agitated by the exchange, but I had faith in Jen. I did understand but I couldn't show her that because she'd think it was okay. But she came through like a bad omen and everything in me told me shit was about to get worse. Kevin and I sat in the trap going over numbers and my mind was everywhere. I knew I had to get home soon because I had school the next day and I was committed to finishing. Right before I got ready to leave my phone rung. I answered easily.

"Wassup," I answered after checking the caller I.D.

"Hey King, It's Mya." She said.

"I know, Wassup," I asked again. I was surprised she called at all considering she hadn't said shit to me in months.

"I got something I need to tell you." She said nervously.

"Okay Wassup?" I asked more irritated. I had asked her three times. I did feel bad about the way we ended because I knew I was wrong, but my patience was short and it wasn't shit I could've done about it now. I couldn't figure out why she was even calling me.

"I'm Pregnant," She said clearly.

"What?" I asked raising out the seat across from Kevin.

"MyKing, I'm pregnant and you already know I don't play games. I'm not calling to ask you for anything. I just thought you'd like to know you have a baby on the way." She said. I couldn't hide the displeasure on my face and Kev looked at me crazily, anticipating for me to tell him what was going on. I start trying to think about the last time we fucked and all I could remember is Jasmine catching me afterward. We'd been official damn near four months. I knew it was a possibility.

"How far?" I asked hoping she'd say anything that would give me an alibi.

"Going on 16 weeks." She said easily. I sighed because I knew damn well that was my baby. My attraction to Mya is the fact she was always cool as hell. She wasn't about the bullshit and I couldn't stunt like I wasn't gone be there.

"Okay cool. You know I got you. Just keep me posted. Imma be there." I told her.

"Okay...I can do that. Thank you, I'll talk to you later." She said before she hung up.

"FUCK!" I exclaimed as soon as she did. I buried my face in my hands to try to settle my racing heart.

"Bro, what's up?" Kevin asked concerned.

"Jasmine bout to leave my ass. I'm bout to lose her for real." I said seriously.

"What the fuck did you do King?" he asked shaking his head.

"I fucked around and got Mya pregnant?" I told him.

"That was her calling you? Damn, she keeping it?" he asked.

"Yeah, she four months already," I told him miserably.

"So what you gone do?" He asked.

"I know Jasmine gone be hurt. Telling her will break her heart.

She gone stop fucking with me." I told him.

"Damn bro, that's heavy but if I was you I would go ahead and tell Jas. The shit ain't gone go away." He said seriously.

"Nigga, didn't you just hear me tell you she gone leave me if I tell her that shit?" I spat.

"So, what you gone do, not tell her?" He asked. I sighed.

"Nah, imma tell her when the time is right," I told him.

"You bullshitting, me and Jasmine cool. I'll tell her if you want me to." He offered.

"Nah, I'm gone tell her myself," I told him.

"Fine, that's on you. I just hope you don't wait until she don't need you to tell her." He said.

"Bro I just said imma tell her! Stop sweating me and worry about paying that fucking lawyer so you can get your brother out of jail." I spat angrily.

"I already paid him. I got this. But congrats on the baby my dude." He chuckled before I got up and left. I got into the house, took a shower and went next door to get in bed with my girl. I wrapped my arms around her and went to sleep.

CHAPTER FIFTEEN: IT'S OUR ANNIVERSARY

MyKing

It had been two months since Mya told me she was pregnant. Even though I was uncomfortable with the situation at first, I did what I felt I was supposed to do. I took care of Mya because she was carrying my child and I made sure she didn't need anything. I made all of her appointments and I supported her. We had a cordial relationship. I didn't feel like what I was doing was wrong considering I could've made her do the shit alone. I pulled up to her apartment and knocked on the door. She opened it and stood big and pregnant in the doorway. The smile on her face made my chest feel light and I thought she looked beautiful pregnant. She held out her arms for a hug and I stepped forward wrapping my arms around her neck. I kissed her forehead.

"How you feel? You aight?" I asked her.

"Yeah this lil girl wouldn't let me sleep last night and my feet are killing me but I'm alright. She said easily.

"I'll rub them for you, don't trip," I told her.

"For real?" She asked surprised.

"Yeah, I got you," I told her before I directed all of my attention to her protruding belly.

"Hey, daddy baby! You okay in there." I asked excited at the thought of holding her. It didn't take me long to adapt. I already loved my seed and regardless of the situation, I couldn't be more excited. She gives me the opportunity to be better. My overall goal is to be better.

I sat at the edge of the bed with a bottle of vanilla smelling lotion from Victoria secret as Bad girls club played on the Tv in front of us. I grabbed her feet in my hands and rubbed them like I'd promised.

"Thank you...you gone be a good father." She started.

"Oh...you musta been worried." I chuckled.

"My King you aren't exactly an ideal guy. You made it clear you just wanted to fuck. I never woulda thought the day we met you would be my baby daddy." She chuckled.

"Yeah well, I couldn't imagine that either, but shit happens. I ain't never claimed to be the perfect guy and I did want to fuck. I wasn't on no relationship shit then. Damn sure wasn't tryna start no family. I just felt like I was too young for all that serious shit. Just on some get money shit. That makes me a bad guy?" I asked.

"Nah but the way you handle bitches do. You sling dick and don't seem to give a fuck about nobody feelings." She said.

"I care about yours though," I argued.

"I'm having your baby." She laughed.

"So, I could still be that nigga but I'm not. I'm tryna do the right thing for my shorty." I said as I finished rubbing the lotion into her skin. I glanced into her eyes momentarily. The chemistry between us was still strong.

"Thank you, baby daddy." She smiled before she repositioned herself on the bed and placed her lips on mine. I accepted briefly before I remembered I was with Jasmine. I pulled away, but it killed me to have to. Mya was sexy as fuck to me and it took everything in me to keep from touching her when we were together. Especially when she wanted me to.

"No Kinggg, I am so horny. Come here." She moaned as she pulled me towards her and kissed me again. I tried to get up from the bed so I pulled her arms from around me. I was not about to get caught up and I knew if I'd stayed here a second longer I was gone give her what she wanted.

"What's wrong...you haven't touched me since the day I got pregnant. I don't look good to you anymore? Is it because I'm bigger?" she asked carefully like she was ashamed.

"Nah..it ain't nothing like that. I think you look beautiful. I just don't want to do the wrong thing and fuck up nothing." I said referring to my relationship with Jasmine.

"I need you though. You won't hurt me." She said as she pulled at my shirt and placed her lips on mine again. I didn't pull away this time and we tongue locked as I positioned myself between her legs. I kissed her deeply and she pulled me to let me know she really needed me. I grabbed at the panties she had on and she helped me take them off. I pulled away for a second.

"This ain't gone hurt my daughter, right?" I asked quizzingly.

She chuckled. "No King, the doctor said it was healthy and it will help me during labor. I'll tell you if it hurt." She smiled as she undid the buckle on my jeans. She leaned forward and kissed me again and I worked on getting in between her thighs. I felt like I was obligated to keep Mya happy and I couldn't picture another nigga hitting my baby mama while she carried my shorty. Mya wouldn't even do that disrespectful shit.

"Shittt." She hissed as she gripped my back as I worked my way into her.

"You okay?" I asked to make sure.

"Yes...damn, I missed you, King." She moaned as I deepened my stroke.

"I missed you too, baby," I told her as I tried my best to control my nut. It had been so long since I had sex I forgot how good it felt. I had real love for Mya and I gave her exactly what she needed. When it was all over I spent a lil more time with her and before she could get me started on another round I opted to leave.

"I'm sorry baby, but I gotta go handle some business." I kissed her forehead and proceeded to leave.

"Can you come back tonight? I want you to stay the night." She pouted.

"Nah, I'm probably gone be out real late. I'll see you tomorrow." I told her.

"Bae, I need you to come back tonight." She whined as she walked up on me and pressed her belly against me. I smiled because she made me happy even though the situation was fucked up, our relationship was good. Nothing about it felt wrong to me. I convinced myself that I would be a deadbeat if I didn't keep Mya satisfied while she carried my baby.

"Aight, I'll come back later. Just let me make these runs." I smiled. She kissed me on the lips and I made my way towards the door.

"Good and can you bring me ice cream!" She chuckled.

"Yeah, I got you," I told her.

"I love you!" she said, and my heart dropped to my shoes. I loved my child and that was the only real reason I was here. I was in love with Jasmine and she was the only girl I truly felt for but because Mya was the one carrying my child. I lied.

"Love you too," I said easily as I walked out of her apartment.

I got to the trap to meet with Kevin and by then shit had gotten real. We had no choice but to extend the box. The money moved but not fast enough. Kevin thought we should do it slowly to give the niggas over there time to adjust. Unfortunately, you can't stomp in nobody else yard nicely. The only way we were getting a piece of P-town was to go in and take it. I knew it was gone be ugly and I knew it was gone cost. Tevin fucked up our spot the moment he upped the shipment. It had to be this way and even though I knew it wasn't safe. I strapped anyway.

"Move on that block. If you run into any complications, handle it. Shoot first ask questions later." I said seriously trying to plan for the move. I sat on the couch across from him with an Italian beef sitting in front of me on the table.

"What? You sound crazy! You talking like Tevin! "Kevin exclaimed in disagreement. He shook his head as he snatched one of my fries off my plate.

"Kevin, you got the money to pay that man today? Because if you do I got you. I can run him his shit and we ain't gotta move past the grounds. But the money ain't coming fast enough. I been fronting the last few shipments with my own money to keep our load straight but I'm drowning. Either we extend the box or lower the shipment! Which one you wanna do?" I asked seriously.

"Fuck! We extend this box and we got a war....but I ain't tryna cut my pocket." He said as he pondered the idea. He pulled out his phone and seemingly returned a text message.

"Exactly, I got a baby on the way. I can't afford a cut either and I want all the money I put in back. I haven't made a profit since Tev upped our count so either you take that shit into P-town or you lose some of your money." I explained.

"Hell naw, I can't go back to that lil shit. Fuck it, we running through that bitch." He said easily.

"That's what the fuck I thought," I said as I shoved the empty food container back into the plastic bag and picked up the duffel bag he had in the closet. I dropped the heavy bag onto the couch and pulled one of the guns from the bag and stuck it in my pants. I wasn't no killer but I wasn't planning to die. If my mama ain't teach me shit else, she taught me how to survive. I hoped I would never have to use the gun but If the time came, I wouldn't hesitate.

Jasmine

I and Val were in Victoria Secret trying to find something special for me to wear for me and MyKing's six-month anniversary. It was really a big deal for me and I was certain that I was in love with MyKing. The fact he hadn't mentioned we'd been together six months let me know my surprise would catch him off guard. We had the perfect relationship and I knew he'd be the man I would spend the rest of my life with. I decided with that in mind that I should give him my virginity. I felt like I was ready and the heat that rises between my legs when we kiss or when he touches me was getting hard to ignore. I wanted to do it for our anniversary, so I asked Val to help me get ready. Now I was standing half naked in the dressing room trying on lingerie.

"Dammmmnnn Jas, bitch I ain't no lesbian or no shit like that but he is getting you pregnant if you wear that one." She said in awe.

"Oh no, honey! I cannot get this one then because I am not ready to be anyone's mother. I want to go to college and collect my coins before I have a baby. Besides, MyKing isn't ready for no kids either. We're going to college!" I told her matter of factly. She gave a quick side eye and smirk. I peeped it, but I couldn't figure out if she was being shady or I really looked that good.

"What? If you have something to say just say it." I said as I took my eyes off of my body in the mirror and eyeballed her.

"I ain't saying shit. I just think you look good enough to be his baby mama." She chuckled lightly.

"Well, I want to be his wife. And he won't be putting any babies in me until we are married. I'm not baby mama material." I stated.

"Yeah well, what you won't do another bitch will." She added.

"MyKing is not about to cheat on me. That's why I feel like I should just go ahead and give him the cat. He deserves it." I said as I gave myself another look over. I decided I would buy the set I'd tried on and go through with losing my virginity.

"Well if you're sure about that do what you see fit." She said knowingly. Her whole demeanor seemed genuinely happy for me. I wouldn't have doubted her encouragement a second. After we left the mall, I went to get my hair done and went straight home to cook. When I got in, I sat my bag on the living room couch and headed towards my bedroom to which had been rummaged through. When I saw my mother going through my things, it caught me by surprise. She kneeled at the bottom of my closet with an old coach purse in her hands.

"Hey, ma…what are you doing? What are you looking for?" I asked confused. Her hair was all over her head and her skin was sweating. She looked up at me and smiled with noticeably rotten teeth. I'd never seen my mother look worse than she had at that moment. She was the complete opposite of what I remembered about her.

"Oh..hey Jazzy…I was just looking for something to wear. All my clothes just hang off me since I've lost weight." She stated before she giggled oddly. She stood to her feet from the bottom of my closet and my mouth dropped.

She stood before me skin and bones in a dirty T-shirt and shorts. They hung off of her body like they were soiled and three sizes too big. Her knees were ashy and scarred and she'd lost everything that made her my mother. She popped and scratched at her skin like bugs were on her. Her eyes were dark and tired. Her skin was dull and blotchy. She looked sick. My eyes watered when she came towards me and I got a whiff of the pungent body odor coming from her.

"Mommy...what did you do? What happened?" I asked full of concern. This wasn't my mother...it couldn't be. I thought as tears filled my eyes.

"Oh, jazzy I'm alright. Just need a quick shower and I'll go on about my night." She said easily as she walked past me and towards the washroom. I was completely baffled. I didn't know what to even say. I knew she was ill and even though I couldn't pin point the problem I was certain it wasn't anything good. I grabbed my phone and immediately called MyKing. I hadn't heard from him since he dropped me at home from school and he had been M.I.A the entire rest of the day. I tried not to nag him about it but it was our anniversary and my mother being here would ruin my plans. His phone rang but he didn't answer. I figured he'd call me back when he saw the call and I got comfortable by changing my clothes. When I came out of my room to go start dinner, I realized my mother was out of the bathroom. I wasn't convinced she'd washed anything from the short time she was in there.

"Mom!" I called for her making my way around the tiny apartment looking for her. After a short tour, I realized she'd gone. I was confused until I saw all of the items that were in my purse spewed out onto the couch. It didn't register to me that my mother was on drugs until I picked up my wallet and every dime I had in it was gone. I dropped to the floor and cried my eyes out. Wasn't just about the money but the idea that my mother was officially a druggie that messed me up. I couldn't believe she'd steal from her own daughter. I didn't feel like cooking anymore and when I got off the floor I just got in my bed. I called MyKing until his phone starts going straight to voicemail. I was hurt, angry, and confused and I put all the blame on the only drug dealer I knew. My boyfriend. My plans didn't even matter to me anymore. MyKing didn't come home that night anyway.

CHAPTER SIXTEEN: CAUGHT UP

MyKing

I was anxious to get home. My stomach was turning flips like I had weight in the car. When I turned my phone back on after spending the night with Mya my notifications were going off. I had already told Kevin I was dipping off so the money was cool. Jasmine was another story altogether and I knew by the text messages, she was mad. Our anniversary completely slipped my mind. Shit, I'd never had a real girlfriend to celebrate an anniversary before. Didn't know the first thing about one but I knew I made her feel like she ain't matter. That wasn't cool so to make up for it I was planning to just give her some money. I got to the crib and showered before going next door to see Jas. She was mad at me and I just wanted to calm her down so we can enjoy the rest of our weekend. I knocked on the door and waited momentarily for her to open it. When she did the look on her face told it all.

"Bae...I already know you mad. I was out hustling late last night. I'm sorry I missed our anniversary, but we can celebrate all weekend to make up for it." I started.

"You sold drugs to my mother!" she hissed.

"What?!" I looked at her crazy before I stepped in and slammed the door behind me.

"My mom came in last night and took all the money I had in my wallet. She stunk, she's skin and bones and she looks sick. I know its drugs! You sold that shit to my mother!" she snapped as tears filled her eyes.

"I swear to God I ain't sell your mama shit. Bae, I wouldn't do you like that. You know that." I told her.

"MyKing I don't know anything! I didn't know that my mother was a drug addict. I don't know how that happened. I don't know what I'm supposed to do. She is all I have" She cried. Evidentially, I didn't do the best job trying to keep that away from her. That's what I regretted at that moment.

"Bae, you got me. I ain't gone leave you. I'm sorry about your mother but I swear it wasn't me." I assured her as I pulled her into my arms.

"You have to help her! She can't be a druggie." She cried into my chest. I felt bad as fuck. I knew months ago her mama was on that shit and lying about it just makes me feel worse. But I knew she was gone blame me because of how I made my money so I ain't say shit.

"Look we can try and put your mama in rehab or something. I'll make sure she don't get served around here and we probably need to change the locks to keep her from taking anything else," I told her.

"MyKing, what about bills? What about me having a parent? I was living in a four million dollar estate last year. How'd I go from having the perfect life to no father and a drug addict mother within a year! Like what the hell kind of crap is that!" she snapped. I was offended the moment she said that. I'd been busting my ass to make her comfortable and she just disregarded everything I'd done.

"Jasmine you don't need for shit and anything you want I get for you. I can't bring your rich daddy back and I can only try to help your mama kick that shit. But I make sure you're good and you never have to question that much. If it makes you feel any better my daddy was dead before I was even born. The way my mama chase dick you'd swear she was an addict too. We in the same boat and we got each other. If that ain't good enough for you, I can't help." I spat.

"My...that's not what I meant...I just. We're still kids. I don't expect you to take on the responsibility of a parent at seventeen. We need them." She stammered.

"Nah I don't. I been taking care of my mama, not the other way around. I grew the fuck up a long time ago. I realized that nobody is going to give me a way out. I had to make one and I have. You got me and I can handle whatever you need. I can't be your daddy, but I know how to handle my shit. You are with me, so you gone be good regardless. I got you, Jas." I told her seriously.

She looked up at me with teary eyes, but she didn't speak. I wondered what she was thinking but I didn't speak on that either. I wiped her tears away and did my best to settle her feelings

Jasmine

"Hey, bitch!" Candice walked up to my locker excitedly.

"Hey, somebodies happy this morning. What were you up to this weekend?" I asked as I pulled my history book from my locker.

"Girl, you show wasn't tryna kick it. I called you a hundred times." She told me.

"I was not in the mood. I stayed in all weekend. MyKing spent most of it with Kevin doing what they do and I was just in the house.

"He was with Kevin?" she asked confused.

"Yeah, you know how they are. I shook my head. She stared at me crazily like I'd said something foul.

"What?" I asked before I chuckled at her facial expression.

"Girl...Kevin been with me...." she stopped talking when Val walked up. Candice rolled her eyes.

"Hey Jas, wassup Candice." She said with a smile.

"Shit, I'll catch you in first period, G," Candice said before she walked away.

"What's her problem?" Val asked nonchalantly.

"I don't even know." I lied. The truth was neither of them liked one another for real. I was the common factor and I just wanted to keep the peace.

"Whatever, so did you do it?" she asked attentively.

"Do what?" I asked confused.

"Did you and MyKing fuck for yall anniversary?" she asked.

"Oh...no we didn't," I told her easily.

"hmmm, why? You had your mind made up Friday. What happened?"

"I changed my mind," I told her. MyKing walked up and mugged her so hard she decided to go to class suddenly. I couldn't figure out why he didn't like her either. It seemed nobody really did. People just liked her clout so they dealt with her. I liked Val because she understood me. We never disagreed and from what I could tell she always had my back. So, when it came down to it that was my friend. I never doubted that.

Candice

The week was longer than ever. I was so tired of school I ain't know what to do. I was ready to graduate and in a few months, it would all be over. When Friday came, we were released for winter break and I was relieved. I caught a ride with Jasmine and King and took my ass to my nigga house. All I ever wanted to do was be with him these days and I he spent most nights with me. That's why I was confused about some shit Jasmine be talking. I mean I know niggas be lying but Jasmine trust King with her life. If I tell her that nigga lying I have to have some solid evidence. So, I figured Kevin would tell me the truth.

"Hey, bae wassup?" I asked him when I waltz my ass into his apartment.

"Not shit! Been waiting for you to come give me some pussy." He chuckled.

"Damn nigga, I'm glad that's all you want," I said fake mad. I wanted some dick too.

"Bae you know I'm just fucking with you." He said as he pulled me into his arms and kissed my neck.

"I don't believe you. I need some convincing" I teased as I walked towards his bed with the biggest smile on my face. One thing I loved about our relationship is him always being willing to please me. When he decided I was really who he wanted, I got the perfect guy. I felt like I'd won and in comparison, Kevin was better than King. I never worried about him cheating on me because he made the effort to make me feel as though I was the only bitch for him. He was always respectful, and I loved him. He made his money and did whatever he needed to do to make sure we were good. My momma had a few negative things to say about how he made his money, but she never complained when he gave me cash for groceries after we ran out of Link or when she was short on the rent. I knew I'd be with Kevin for the rest of my life. In the future, we'll get away from Slater and build a future together. I wanted the same thing for Jas, but I knew King wasn't that nigga. I wondered how long it would take for him to go right back to being a hoe. I was sure he was cheating on Jas and I planned to warn my girl. So, after I made Kevin nut I started with my questions.

"So, you know King told Jasmine he was with you last night, right?" I asked on the sly.

"Okay so?" He asked carelessly.

"And he was with you all weekend long," I stated.

"Okay and... what's your point?" he asked.

"How was he with you when you were with me? How that work? I was with you all night and all weekend, so I know he lying." I stated.

"I was with King yesterday." He said easily.

"Yeah, and you were with me last night. So where was your boy?" I asked him.

"Minding his fucking business. Why you all on his dick Candice?" He asked.

"Cause yo lying ass brother cheating on my friend," I said matter factly.

"Aye watch your fucking mouth. Mind your own business you ain't got shit to do with that and I don't wanna hear shit else you gotta say about my brother. That's the easiest way to fuck up with me." He said agitatedly.

"Kevin that's my friend though. How am I supposed to just be quiet why she out here getting played?" I asked.

"You mind your own fucking business. I'm telling you to stay out of that shit." He said seriously before he read a text message and quickly decided he was finna go. I grabbed my coat to leave and I was mad as hell. I knew Kevin was right though. I didn't want no problems with my man so instead of telling Jasmine I decided to keep the shit to myself.

"You told me you were taking me to the mall." I pouted before getting ready to leave.

"I gotta make a run. I will give you some money and drop you off." He offered.

"So, I'm supposed to go by myself?" I asked with a full mug on my face.

"Naw, ask Jas to go with you. Just hurry up so I can make this move." He told me.

"Okay, we'll meet you downstairs." I told him as I left his apartment. I called Jasmine as I walked towards our building.

Jasmine

I was laying across the bed with an attitude. MyKing hadn't picked up the phone since he dropped me off and I was sick of that shit. I understand what he does is time-consuming and dangerous but him blowing me off certainly don't make me feel better about it. He's out all night and I'm stuck in the house worried he's gotten arrested or killed. My phone rung in my hand and I thought it was him. I was disappointed when Candice name flashed across the screen, but I answered anyway.

"Hey, girl," I answered.

"Wassup. What you doing? Let's go to the mall. I got a few more gifts to buy." She said excitedly.

"Naw its cold as hell outside and I ain't getting on the bus today. I don't even feel like it." I told her.

"Bitch put on your coat! Kevin gone drop us off and pick us up. I'm coming up now." She told me. I frowned but got up anyway. I was bored and needed something to take my mind off MyKing for a while. Besides, I always enjoyed Christmas shopping with my parents. Maybe that would cheer me up some. I got up and put on my coat and boots and met her at the door.

The ride to the mall was long. It seemed Candice and Kevin's relationship was going well. I had to watch them cake it the whole ride. They laughed and talked like I wasn't even there. I wasn't jealous, but it only reminded me of how distant MyKing had become lately. For a moment I thought maybe it's because we aren't having sex. Then I settled that thought in my head because I knew he loved me. We practically lived together now. Maybe I'm tripping. I thought as I looked out the window at all the Christmas decorations and lights. I thought about the big deal light competition my dad had with the neighbors every year and my eyes watered some. Everything that made me happy just makes me sad now. Even though I loved being with MyKing, I missed my old life sometimes.

When we pulled up to the mall I cheered up a bit. I loved to shop, and I needed this lil girl time with my friend. Maybe talking about how I felt would help. We got out and Kevin promised to come back and get us. We made our way into Ford City mall prepared for some retail therapy. I needed to do some Christmas shopping anyway. Now Ford City was one of the city malls that everyone went to. It wasn't too far from the hood but just far enough away. I had grown to love everything about the mall once I started visiting regularly with MyKing and Candice. It's where I and MyKing met, and I've been a fan ever since. It was the holidays, and everyone was out and about catching up on all the sales. Candice and I moved from store to store picking up items to give to our people for Christmas. I didn't expect my mom to show but I bought her a few things too. I didn't want Candice to know how down I was about my mother's drug habit. I was embarrassed, and I kept the fact to myself. So, I paraded around the store as if everything was cool. Even though it was hard to think about my mother doing drugs in a dirty, strange, cold place. What about her love for art and beauty? Her career as a nurse? What about me? I thought silently as I held the earrings she'd probably pawn. Her life has been reduced to itching and stealing all for drugs. The shit was unreal to me. Before my father died, I'd never seen my mother out of place. She slept in diamonds and walked around in slippers and satin robes. I just couldn't believe that woman is a druggie. I pushed the thought to the back of my mind and continued shopping with my friend.

The shopping really did lighten my mood though. I had really started to relax once I got me a pretzel from Aunt Annie's. So, I was all for going into one of my favorite stores to try on clothes and act a fool in the dressing room. It was something me and Candice always did and we enjoyed doing. When we walked into Sassy's, the store was packed. It always was but I loved it! We'd try on something and walk clean through the store like it was a runway. I always purchased something because they allowed us to have our fun without complaining or calling security on us. I was completely for the fun today! We picked a few outfits and got into the dressing rooms to start our little show. Candice picked this little black dress with the back out and the stiletto boots to match. I grabbed this badass pair of Seven jeans with the matching fitted top. The outfit went perfectly with the new mikes I'd just gotten. We opened the dressing room door and walked through the store like Americas next top models. I laughed at the poses Candice hit every time somebody looked her way. And I enjoyed the attention I got from a few onlookers who watched. Right before I got ready to switch my way back into the dressing room I locked eyes with a very familiar face. Realization set into her face when I stopped short to do a double take. She had her hair curly pulled into a sloppy ponytail on top of her head and her skin glowed brightly against her chubby face. For some reason, I went deaf and my legs moved without my permission. As I walked towards her, I saw that she was sitting into her coat where she had pulled it off. She instinctively rubbed her swollen belly as I got closer to her. Every step closer to her my heart broke a little more. I'd had my eyes fixed on a neat pair of dreads kneeling before her as he assisted her with her shoe. I looked back at her big, round, pregnant belly again before I stood directly in front of her. My eyes had started to water. The moment my feet stopped moving MyKing turned around towards me. The look of shock and guilt ran across his face before he spoke.

"Jasmine..." He started as I looked back and forth between him and the pregnant girl. I didn't speak as I waited for him to explain.

"King, what's up?" She asked confusingly. He looked to her for a moment then back at me. Even though nothing was said everybody looked on knowingly.

"Just tell me it ain't what it looks like." I spat as hot tears fell from my eyes. He looked at me seriously.

"I can't." He said regretfully as he dropped his head. The heat that ran over my body made it feel like I was going to suffocate. My head had gotten so stuffed up with tears I couldn't breathe through my nose. I felt like I was the color of the Santa suit the man was wearing in the center of the mall. I felt like a complete fool and I was embarrassed. I could hear the whispers and see the pitiful looks on some of the other shopper's faces. I couldn't begin to explain the type of pain I'd felt as I looked into his face. I was hot. So hot that I could no longer stand in that spot anymore. Before I could even think about it, I took off running out of the store. Honestly, I didn't have a destination but thought maybe I could go into the washroom and cry my eyes out. The moment I got past the door the alarms started blaring and it only put fire on my ass. I ran away as if someone was chasing me. The tears on my face cooled once the wind I made running hit me. I spotted the sign for the washroom and got right to the opening before I was tackled hard to the ground by mall security. It caught me completely off guard and before I could ask why I was snatched up onto my feet. He aggressively pulled me towards him.

"The police are on their way." The security guard barked angrily. I was confused about what I'd done and could only guess he was angry because he was out of breath.

"But what didn't I do?" I cried as the image of that girl's belly ran over and over in my head. My vision blurred from the thick tears invading my eyes. The officers walked through the double doors closest to us. I saw MyKing a second later and attempted to move in the opposite direction. I didn't want to see him at all and I didn't want him to see me as hurt as I was. The security guard gripped me tighter and the Chicago Police felt they needed to help him. Before I could even open my mouth, I was placed in handcuffs and escorted out of the building. They read me my Miranda rights and pushed me towards their vehicle. The cold air hit my wet face and I felt like I'd been slapped. But I still couldn't stop crying. They threw me into the back of the police car and the seat was hard. The cuffs around my wrist were extremely tight and uncomfortable. When they slammed the door behind me I immediately looked out the window where MyKing stood looking stupid as they hauled me away.

CHAPTER SEVENTEEN:
IT'S OVER

MyKing

I dropped Jasmine and Candice off back home as soon as school let out because Mya had a doctor's appointment. Seem like the closer she got to her due date the more appointments she had. I made it a priority to be at every one of them. So, I told Jasmine I had some business to tend to and went to pick up Mya. We got to the doctors and once they checked all they needed to, we left. I figured since it was the end of the week it would be a good time to go ahead and pick up the car seat and a few other things she ain't get at the baby shower we had last month. Even though I didn't want to participate, it turned out all right. And more importantly, it never got back to Jasmine.
I wasn't sure how long I was gone wait to tell her about the baby but I didn't intend to wait this long. Shit just got complicated when I started fucking Mya again. Things were good between me and the both of them and I ain't want to fuck it up.

When we got to the mall, I helped Mya out the car and let her shop for whatever she wanted our daughter to have. The Babies-R-Us there was the biggest in the city. After we got all she needed I was ready to go. I missed Jas and I knew if I didn't get home soon she was gone be mad all weekend. Mya convinced me to go further into the mall to buy the baby some more clothes. I was hell-bent against that because this was Jasmine's spot. But against my better judgement, I let Mya talk me into it. I texted Jas to see where she was to make sure she wouldn't end up seeing me with Mya, but she didn't respond. We bought a few of those baby Jordan packs from the kid's footlocker and stopped by a few other stores before Mya convinced me to take her in this chick store. I believe she got a kick out of me never telling her no. I'd been a sucka since I found out she was pregnant. No matter how many times I told her no I always end up doing whatever she asks. Honestly, I just wanted her to be happy so my seed will be healthy. That was my only concern. I hadn't thought about how it would all work once Jasmine found out, but I didn't plan for it to happen today.

The store was packed, and I had a bad feeling about it when I saw how many people seemed to be in it. One of my biggest concerns was somebody seeing me with Mya and running back to tell Jasmine. The only thing I had in my favor is the fact nobody fucked with Jas. Before it was because nobody liked her. They thought she was stuck up because of the way she talked and carried herself. She reminded everybody of a bougie ass Val. But when she put them hands-on Rashiya and her crew, the hoes just steered clear to keep the peace. That made all the difference. Either way, I had to make sure she didn't find out until I could tell her. I thought to just give Mya the money and let her get what she wanted but she didn't like that idea, so I went into the store with her and let her do her thing. She ends up picking up a pair of shoes she just had to have.

"Bae, these cute ain't they?" She asked me.

"Yeah, they nice. You should get them." I said easily. I just wanted her to get what she wanted so we could leave.

"Imma try them on to make sure they're comfortable. I'd hate for you to waste your money on shoes I ain't gone even wear." She said before she asked a sales associate to get her size. We waited for her to get them and I squatted before her to help her put them on. She had gotten so far along she could not even see her feet. That said, I had to help her.

"Aww, I feel like Cinderella." She cooed. I laughed and shook my head.

"So, who that make me? Prince Charming?" I asked before I chuckled. She didn't respond, and this strange ass silence happened. I had an ill feeling about it because it seemed like the whole store got quiet. I looked up at Mya who had her eyes fixed on something behind me. She nervously rubbed her stomach and I could swear it was a nigga standing behind me with his piece out based on her facial expression. I turned around and saw Jasmine standing there and my heart dropped to my Timbs. I think I'd have rather saw a pistol in my face than for Jasmine to be there.

"Jasmine...I started as I stood. But the look on her face kept me from saying anything else. I didn't know what to say anyway. I just looked back at Mya and down at the floor. What I didn't realize is that I had to explain this shit to two people because I never told Mya I was still with Jas either.

"King, what's up?" Mya asked confused. I looked up at her and I couldn't think of shit to say. The disappointment was written all over her face.

"Just tell me it ain't what it looks like." Jasmine cried, and I knew I had fucked up real bad and I couldn't tell her that.

"I can't," I told her before she took off running. Right after the alarm went off, Candice walked towards me.

"You are a trifling muthafucka!" She spat to me as she mean mugged the hell out of Mya. "Bitch, you knew he had a girlfriend." She said angrily.

"I thought I was his girlfriend," Mya responded miserably as she got up to put the shoes back. "Imma just go." She said as she slid back into her boots. Candice looked up at me like she hated my guts and walked away back towards the dressing room. The commotion had every bitch in there looking at me like that.

"Nah, I'm gone take you home. Just give me a second" I said as I walked out of the store to find Jasmine. When I saw CPD put her in cuffs I knew the night was only gone get worse. I watched as they put her in the back and drove off and I knew it was my fault.

Mya had pulled her coat back on and met me at the door with all the bags in her hands. I took them, and she started walking towards my truck. I followed her with a million and one thoughts running through my head. I unlocked the truck and placed the bags on the back seat before trying to help her in, but she pushed me away.

"Please don't even touch me." She said as her voice quivered. She grabbed the handle and pulled herself in the truck without my help. I stood there trying to figure out what to say to her. She didn't seem to even want an explanation. I closed the door once she had gotten in and made my way around to the passenger's side and got in. I started up the car because it was cold as fuck. I sat there a minute while the car warmed.

"Look I know you mad at me, but I'm still gone be there for my baby," I told her.

"We don't need you. You can take me home and be with that bitch for all I care." She said seriously.

"You know better than that. We don't have to be together for me to be a father to my child." I argued.

"King just take me home." She said angrily. I exhaled loudly and pulled off into the street trying to figure out how imma fix this. I quickly got back to Mya's apartment. She hopped out of the car swiftly and I followed her with all the stuff I'd bought for the baby.

"You can keep that shit." She said when she realized I was behind her.

"Mya stop fucking playing with me," I said angrily as I unloaded my truck and put everything in her apartment like I intended to. She didn't say anything else as she watched me. When I got done, I looked up at her trying to find the words.

"I can do it without you." She said before she burst into tears.

"Why, when you ain't got to. I'm here. I been here since day one. I ain't tell you about Jasmine because she doesn't change shit. I'm still gone be a good father to my daughter and make sure yall good." I exclaimed.

"I wanted to be a family, King. Would you want your daughter to be with a nigga like you?" She asked seriously.

"Nah, but I ain't no deadbeat, sourpuss ass nigga. I have done what I was supposed to when it comes down to making sure you had everything you needed. I ain't the perfect man and that's something I can only work on. I will do my best to make sure my daughter has me in her life though." I told her.

"She don't need you in her life." She said as she went into her bedroom and closed the door. I did attempt to talk to her, but she locked the door on me and wouldn't open it. I just said fuck it and left. I wasn't gone let her keep me out my daughter's life anyway it went.

Jasmine

I didn't get the chance to ask the officers why I'd been arrested because all I could think about was MyKing and the girl he got pregnant. So, I cried loudly as the sirens masked the sheer pain I let out. I felt worthless the whole way. I doubted he was faithful sometimes, but I never thought it would come to this. I had so many questions. That was the same bitch I caught him with before and he promised he wouldn't do this shit to me. I cried like I'd been shot because that's truly how I felt. When the car and sirens stopped, the officers both looked confused. They simply instructed me to cooperate as they pulled me out of the car. The lady pulled me by the arm making the cuffs tighter. But it was cool because I'd went numb a few minutes after we pulled off. It was a cold walk until we got to the front doors of the station. Wasn't until then that I realized I didn't have my coat on. I was grateful for the heat that met me when we got to the station. Before then I'd only ever seen one on Tv. I was sat in a hard plastic chair and told I was waiting to be processed. The male partner walked away and found him something else to do. The female cop stayed with me. I dropped my head into my lap and cried about the fact I thought we had a good relationship. I only felt stupid for not seeing this sooner. That girl was huge! She's been pregnant for months.

"Why did he do this to me?" I asked miserably. The question caught the attention of the pretty lady officer that brought me in.

"Because you were stealing." She said easily.

"What? I have never stolen a thing in my life." I cried.

"You stole that outfit out of the store, Chica. That's why security contained you. You didn't make it better by trying to run. It's the holiday, they have us on call specifically for thieves." She said seriously.

"No, I was running from my boyfriend because he cheated on me and got another girl pregnant and she was in the store. I was just trying the outfit on. I was planning to buy it before I saw them in the store. I was just going to the bathroom by the door. I forgot I even had the outfit on." I explained. I didn't look like a thief. My nails and hair were done. My shoes were expensive and despite the fact I was wearing tags I didn't look like I needed for anything. Realization registered on her face.

"Oh wow…you have the money for that outfit?" she asked quiz-zingly.

"Yes. It's in my wallet. Where is my purse?" I asked her seriously.

"Umm, you didn't have a purse. You didn't have anything when I got to you." She stated plainly.

"Dang, I must've left it in the store. It's a brown coach bag. I have the money for this. I didn't know why he attacked me. Like I said, I forgot I even had the outfit on. I guess I did look like a thief, but I was just ashamed." I said as I shook my head in disbe-lief. This day was getting worse by the second. She listened at-tentively, and the look of understanding crossed her face.

"Okay look. I'll take you out of the cuffs and put you in the cell. You just have to call someone to bring me the money and I will let you go. This seemed to be a misunderstanding and I can understand the situation and why you were running now. Honestly, I might've run too or proceeded to whup his ass. I'll see what I can do about the charges. Just call your people and sit tight." She said genuinely. I nodded my head gratefully as she removed the cuffs from my wrist. They were raw and sore when she removed them. I momentarily stopped crying and wiped my face before she allowed me to my feet.

She led me to the phone on top of a desk and allowed me to call someone. I sped dialed Candice praying she'd pick up from an unknown number.

"Hello?" She answered, and I sighed in relief.

"It's Jas…please tell me you got my purse and coat out that dressing room?" I asked nervously.

"Yes, bitch! Where the fuck they take you? I had Kevin pick me up right after I saw you get knocked.

"I'm at the station on 63rd St. Bring me my purse and they'll let me go. They think I stole this outfit!" I exclaimed.

"Okay don't trip we on our way." She said and hurriedly disconnected the phone. I exhaled deeply at the thought of going home to cry in peace. However, the situation required me to be strong for a little while longer. I wiped my face really good and sucked up all the tears I had left to let out. The thought of being rescued was enough to calm me internally. The lady officer approached me again with a smile.

"Were you able to reach your people?" she asked as if she cared.

"Yes, my friend was able to get my purse from the dressing room so I can give you the money as soon as she gets here. Thank you so much for trying to help me. I know how crazy I must look right now." I chuckled lightly.

"Trust me I understand. Anything I could do to help." She said easily as she led me down the walkway of the noisy station. It was police officers everywhere. They all seemed to be busy and I was literally nobody compared to some of the rough looking faces I saw. I focused my attention back towards the young lady cop who was short and serious. She looked to be Hispanic and had a quick tongue and the perfect eyebrows. She was a real bad-ass and I could tell that the moment we met. The male officer seemed to follow her lead and I could respect that.

"I'm officer Perez, just ask for me if you need anything." She said nicely. Her demeanor had changed, and I started to feel protected as she led me to the cell. I had a million questions about how she had become an officer and why. I liked her fearless attitude. She was right, I should've busted MyKing's head in that store. I thought angrily as we stopped in front of a cell with people in it. She proceeded to open the large heavy gate that secured it and I was confused. I was too emotional to be nervous, but I was anxious to leave. I thought I'd be placed in a cell alone, not with actual criminals. However, I was instructed to walk into the cell with three other attendees. I glanced at the first one I saw who was a big burly bitch that looked like the meanest stud in Chicago. She had a medium brown skin complexion and a permanent frown on her face. She reminded me of a Pitbull dog that had been detained. I didn't have the slightest clue what she was in for, but I was sure she'd done it. Not only had she done it but she ain't give a damn either. I quickly diverted my attention away from her because I didn't want any problems. Next face I saw was of an older white lady. She smiled when I caught her attention. All her teeth were rotten and I shivered at the thought of getting too close to her. Her smile reminded me of the Grinch. Her stringy blond hair sat flimsily on her head and her eyes darted back and forth in her head. I knew she had to have been on some serious drugs. Then my mother clouded my thoughts as I walked toward the little bench to sit. There was a younger lady sitting calmly with her legs crossed picking at her nails. She was really pretty. She wore a tight fitted dress that showed off her nice figure. She was slim and much shorter than me but still had curves of a woman. The parts that were uncovered by the outfit were covered in tattoos. She had them everywhere. She had on a sexy pair of black stiletto boots to match her dress. She was extremely attractive. Her makeup was cute, and her hair was cut in a really pretty asymmetrical style where it was long on one side and cut short on the other. I'd saw Meagan Good rocking hers the same way lately. Only hers was a bright honey blond that matched her honey brown skin complexion easily. When I sat down she looked up at me with a smirk.

"Why you come over here by me?" She asked nastily.

"Because you can't beat my ass," I stated aggressively before she burst into laughter. I had every intention to keep the mug I had displayed on my face, but I started laughing too. We looked at each other easily sharing the same thoughts about the encounter.

"I'm Bianca, everybody calls me Bebe." She smiled before she reached out her hand to me. I grabbed it and shook her hand.

"Jasmine, nice to meet you." I chuckled.

"I was just fucking with you. I saw how you peeped big bertha and that raggedy white woman over there." She whispered before she laughed again.

"Yeah." I chuckled.

"So, what they get you for?" She asked easily.

"Girl, they thought I was tryna steal but the whole time I was trying to get away from my cheating boyfriend," I told her honestly. I figured I'd never see her again, so I didn't care that she knew.

"Why are you here?" I asked. I figured she was on her way out to the club or something judging by the way she was dressed.

"Solicitation of prostitution." She said smartly as she chuckled at my facial expression.

"Girl, were you really selling your body?" I whispered in shock. She didn't look like a prostitute to me. Maybe a stripper but not a whore.

"What color is your money?" she asked with a smirk.

"It's green...but what does that mean?" I asked completely missing her point.

"Means it's the same stuff I use. I bet it spend all the same too." She said coolly.

"How old are you?" I asked curiously.

"Nineteen. You?" she asked.

"Sixteen," I stated. I momentarily went off in my own thoughts about how she ended up being a prostitute. I thought to ask her before she spoke.

"I been dealt a fucked up hand. Just doing what I got to do to live. It's not so bad." She smiled.

"So, how are you gone get out?" I asked her seriously. For some reason, I cared.

"Honestly, I'm probably gone be stuck here all weekend. And imma get my ass kicked for the money I'm losing sitting here. I got enough to make bail but if I don't take at least four hundred to Cash for the day he gone beat my ass anyway. Might as well sit here and relax my feet. I'm getting my ass beat with any move I make. I ain't in no rush for that." She said seriously. I felt for her and I could only imagine how hard her life had to be to take an ass whooping.

"You'll be alright," I stated trying to match her positive outlook on things.

Officer Perez walked up to the gate and called for me. I turned and said my goodbye's to Bebe and followed her back to the front of the station.

"Your friend has come for you. I just need you to sign a release statement and you can go, " she said with a smile. I nodded my head in agreement and I was relieved until I walked towards my "friend" and MyKing stood to pick me up. Anger resumed itself if my body and I stopped in my tracks.

"Jasmine…you can go." The officer started. I could tell my sudden halt confused her.

"Hell no, I'm not going anywhere with him," I stated angrily. MyKing looked towards me pitifully.

"Bae…come on. Just come home and we can work on everything else later." He said. His voice full of regret.

"Fuck you!" I spat as I turned my back on him and walked back towards the cell I'd come from. I didn't want to see his lying ass face.

"Lock me back the fuck up," I said as I waited for the officer to put me back in the cell. I wasn't going anywhere with his cheating ass.

She hunched her shoulders and walked me back to the cell. She looked at me knowingly before she unlocked it.

"That must be your boyfriend huh?" she asked.

"Ex-boyfriend. I didn't even call him, so I'll wait for my friend to come and get me. Her name is Candice." I told her.

"Is she eighteen or older?" she asked.

"No. But neither is he." I stated disappointed.

"Look he paid the fee for you to leave. You've already signed the paperwork to leave….but because he's underage I can't release you anyway." She informed me.
"I don't care if he'd paid a million dollars to get me out of a burning building, I still wouldn't have gone anywhere with him," I stated as a matter of fact.

"Okay, Chica well you need to call someone else over eighteen to pick you up." She chuckled.

"No need. My friend's boyfriend is with her. He's old enough to sign for me. They shouldn't be much longer. I'll just wait in here until they come." I said easily.

"Alright," she said as she opened the cell and let me back in. I went and sat right back next to Bebe.

"I thought somebody came for you. Why are you back?" she asked with a smile. Didn't seem to mind my return though.

"Nah, nobody I knew came," I stated easily as I thought about the look on his face when I refused to leave with him.

"Damn, that's messed up. Before long, you gone be stuck all weekend just like me. I know Cash won't send nobody for me tonight." She stated.

"You don't have any family to come to get you?" I asked her.

"Family? Yeah, I got plenty of family." She said sarcastically before she laughed. Officer Perez came back to the iron bars insisting I come to her. I stood up again prepared to put the night behind me. She walked me to the front where Candice and Kevin stood waiting to pick me up. I couldn't be happier to see them together. It's ironic considering their union made me nauseous earlier. Now it all made sense. I grabbed my purse from Candice and proceeded to get my wallet.

"Jasmine…the young man already paid your fee. You can go Chica." She smiled.

"Yeah…this is for Bianca. I'll pay her way. She's over eighteen so she should be able to just go right?" I asked. She raised her eyebrows and chuckled.

"I suppose she could after she signs her paperwork. But you do know you're wasting your money. It's not her first walk in the park and it won't be her last…" She stated.

"Yeah maybe but it'll save her an ass-whupping either way," I explained before I handed her four hundred dollars.

"Okay. Wait right here." She said to me before she fetched Bianca from the cell.

"Damn bitch, you made some friends?" Candice asked before Kevin burst into laughter.

"Yeah…I'll meet yall in the car. Just give me five minutes." I told them as I waited for her to bring Bebe to the front. She walked towards the desk like Americas next top model. I smiled because she had style. Much better than any whore I'd met.

"Thanks for the assist. Here." She slid her hand in her bra and produced money. I chuckled at the look on Officer Perez face.

"Nah, that was on me. You just too cute to get your ass beat tonight. Just be more careful next time." I said before I turned to leave.

"Hey, if you ever wanna link up come down 79th street and ask for me." She said coolly. I honestly couldn't imagine what we'd have in common, but the gesture was kind.

I tore the piece of paper the officer handed me and scribbled my number on it.

"Here, you call me when you get the chance," I told her as we said our goodbyes. I thanked officer Perez and walked out of the station. The cool air hit my body like a ton of bricks, but I was grateful to finally be free. I walked towards Kevin's car feeling better than I did when I got to the station. I grabbed the handle to the back door and opened it. Soon as I got ready to get in I felt a hand grab me from behind. I turned quickly because I was startled. When I saw it was MyKing my body warmed all over again.

"Don't touch me." I spat as I proceeded to get in the car.

"Jasmine...just talk to me." He said as if he expected me to after what he'd done. If he had any sense he'd be trying to rush home and get his shit out of my house before I got there and put it out. I ignored the shit out of his request and he stood in the doorway blocking me from closing the door on him.

"Nigga if you don't back the fuck up off me! We don't have shit to talk about. It's fucking over! I want you to stay the fuck away from me. I don't want anything else to do with you. Have a good life and congrats on the baby." I spat as he backed up just enough for me to slam the car door in his face.

Kevin and Candice looked on but said nothing. I didn't feel like going over it again anyway. When Kevin put the car in drive I didn't even look to see if MyKing was still standing there. I just hoped he stayed his cheating ass away like I'd asked.

When we got back to the buildings I thanked them and swiftly got upstairs. I didn't have the energy for any more crap tonight. I was tired and I felt like I'd been hit by a bus. I opened my door and went straight to my bedroom where MyKing had brought his game and clothes. I grabbed a big garbage bag and proceeded to throw all of his shit in it. I was debating in my head if I was going to put it next door or throw it down the garbage shoot. Right after I'd gathered everything and drug it to the front door he opened it.

"Really Jasmine?" he asked seriously.

"Nigga, I ain't got the energy for no more of your bullshit tonight. Get your shit and get the fuck out. I will do whatever I have to do to pay the bills. Just go." I said disgustedly. I frowned at the thought of having him in my space a second longer.

"Jasmine imma leave because I know I fucked up, but I'm still gone take care of you because I love you. We can talk whenever you get ready." He said seriously.

"You love me?" I asked before I laughed hysterically. "If that's love please, please don't do shit else for me. I will gladly get a job. Just please get your ass out of my face and out of my life." I laughed.

"I do love you." He said.

"Um huh, I bet you do. I hate you, bye!" I said before he picked up the bag and walked out of the apartment with his head held low. I reached back and slammed the door as hard as I could behind him. I walked back towards my bedroom like Angela Basset in waiting to exhale after she set her husband's car on fire. I pulled off my stolen outfit and tossed it right in the trash. I never wanted to see it again after the night I had. I turned on the water to get in the shower and once the hot water calmed my adrenaline I broke into a full, ugly, and loud ass cry. My heart broke into a million pieces and I couldn't believe what a nightmare my life had become. I cried myself to sleep.

CHAPTER EIGHTEEN: WINDY CITY

Jasmine

I applied to several places in the area, but I got hired at the McDonalds a few blocks off. I took the bus back and forth to work every day and because of the holiday, I was able to get the hours I needed to make decent money fast. Having a job was a liberating experience for me. I hated going to work most days but when I got my first check, I was satisfied. It was easy for me to put everything I had into making the money and before then I'd never had my own. We were still out for Christmas break and I hadn't quite figured out how I'd make my work schedule and school schedule fit but the important part is that I had some form of income coming in that didn't involve MyKing. It had been close to two weeks since I found out he cheated and I had been ignoring the shit out of him. I never responded to his text or answered his calls. I would've blocked him if I didn't enjoy watching him beg so much. I had no intention of taking him back and I didn't feel like I needed him. I thought he'd get the idea one day. I did still stupidly have feelings for him and I cried sometimes when I thought about what we had. Or at least what I thought we had. Most times I only felt like I wasn't good enough and I reflect on how dumb I must have looked to not have seen it coming. Candice tried her best to convince me that he kept Mya a secret, but I knew the truth. Val had been hinting towards his baby mama for the longest and it never made sense until I saw it. Even MyKing's mama mentioned a baby on the elevator when her rude ass was trying to make me mad. I thought she was just saying anything to cause conflict because she never liked me. His constant disappearing acts and distance should've been a red flag, but it never was. I was just stupid. And when everything came out I realized I was the only dumb ass that didn't know. I questioned rather or not Candice knew because I was certain Kevin did. That made me keep my distance from everybody after that. Candice was my friend and I trusted her to a certain extent, but I chose not to hang with her like I had before I found out about MyKing.

When Bianca, the girl from the police station, finally called me, I wasn't so disappointed with her contacting me. Although I was skeptical about what we'd have in common, I decided to give her a chance anyway. We arranged to meet up and I kicked it with her a few times over the holiday. We never did anything extravagant, but I liked just being away from home and being able to talk to somebody who wasn't biased about my situation. Plus, I never had to worry about my business being spread around because she ain't live nowhere near Slater. So Bebe end up being my friend and I confided in her and she did the same with me. I valued the friendship we were building, and she was who I preferred to kick it with when I didn't have to work.

One day after I had gotten off I walked towards the bus stop. It was cold as fuck outside as the Chicago wind blew around me. It had stopped snowing the day after Christmas, but the salt was still present in the air. I was fully covered with a hat, gloves, and a scarf to match the full bubble pea coat I'd gotten right before it had gotten cold. I had a solid black windbreaker underneath that matched my uniform because my boss wouldn't allow us to wear our coats at work. I stood at the bus stop before I locked eyes on the figure across the street. She didn't have a coat just a light rain jacket and a beret that barely covered her head. She had on a pair of cloth boots not made for the snow and she shivered past me like she had somewhere to be. I recognized her walk the moment I looked up.

"Mommy!" I hollered across the street towards her. She turned around and ran towards me happily. She crossed the street without paying any attention to the traffic. Cars beeped as she dodged being hit. You'd think she'd run in the opposite direction considering the last time I saw her she stole my money, but she greeted me like she had no recollection of that.

"Hey Jazzy! I missed you she said as she threw her musty arms around me. She looked worse than she had the last time I'd saw her.

"Hey mom...where are you going?" Where is your coat?" I asked her.

"I was umm...finna go get me some food...but I don't have enough money." She started. I knew where this was going but I shook my head and gave her a few dollars anyway. Right before she walked away happily I stopped her. I removed my coat, scarf, and gloves and handed them to her to put on. She happily accepted them before giving me another hug and running off. I stood a few more minutes at the bus stop with my hands jammed in my pocket freezing. I had talked myself into controlling my tears because I was sure if I had tried to cry they would freeze on my face. I was grateful when the bus finally came, and I thought about the chance she might pawn the coat I spent two hundred dollars on. I swallowed the big lump in my throat and pushed the thought to the back of mind. I got off the bus at my stop and walked swiftly towards my building scrunched up and cold. I got to my floor and got off the elevator to see MyKing make his way out of his apartment. Seeing me caught him off guard because I dodge him most of the time. He had on his dark leather Pelle Pelle jacket with his brown Timbs and I could smell his cologne from where I stood. He looked good, but I didn't keep eye contact with him long. I was still freezing and just wanted to get into my apartment.

"Hey, Jasmine." He said as a sad attempt to start a conversation. I didn't say a word. I pulled out my key, opened, and closed the door without giving him a second of my attention. Fuck him, I thought as I got comfortable and got ready for bed. I worked nights because I figured once school started back up it would fit my schedule. I slept late and didn't leave the house until it was time for me to go to work. The next day when I opened my front door to leave, a big box sat on the doorstep. I wasn't expecting it, so I picked it up and carried it back into my apartment. I knew it could only be from MyKing because nobody else cared enough to buy me something. I sat it on the couch and pulled the top of the box open. In there was a folded brown faux fur leather pea coat. It had this thick, soft fur in the inside and had these pretty brown buttons to match.

I pulled it out of the box to expose the matching gloves, hat, and scarf. When I pulled the coat on I saw the Overland Sheep Company tag and my eyes bucked out of my head. The price of the coat was a little over twelve hundred dollars.

"Shit...that nigga real sorry." I laughed, still with no intention of talking to him. But I loved everything about this coat and planned to wear it for the rest of the winter. So, I walked to the bus stop happily in my very warm coat. I didn't plan to even tell his ass thank you.

MyKing

The money had started to pour in when we extended into P-town. Tevin had that part right, but running in that area was like playing Russian roulette. Everybody fucking with us had to stay strapped because shit went left every now and again. The money was straight though, and I had started putting my shit up. I saved more than I spent and put all my energy into making sure when the time was right, I could walk away from the hood and put some other ideas into play. I knew I was finished with the shit after I graduated. The type of shit I was doing wasn't long term. I had to wash my hands before the police put them in cuffs. I wasn't going to jail for the rest of my life for no amount of money. I was hoping Kevin and Tev followed suit. Tevin's lawyer said he was supposed to be getting out soon and I hoped he would be able to because we needed him. In the meantime, Kevin and I made it happen as best we could. Between trying to get the money and trying to get it right with the women in my life, I was spent.

I made up with my baby mama on Christmas day. That morning, I woke up prepared to give all the gifts I'd bought for the people I got them for. I bought my mama what she wanted and didn't expect anything in return because she stopped getting me Christmas presents years ago. Surprisingly, she bought me a new pair of brown Timbs this year. It was more than likely with money I gave her but none the less she got them. So, I was in a good mood from the start. I pulled the white box from the closet that Jasmine had bought weeks prior for Christmas. She told me that I couldn't open it until Christmas day and even though she hadn't talked to me since the day at the mall, I kept my promise. When I opened the box and saw the Pelle Jacket I wanted, I could've cried. I missed the shit out my girl and seeing the jacket only reminded me how bad I had fucked up. I wasn't sure what it would take to make it right but I woulda done anything. I got up motivated to fix what I had messed up. I figured I had to start with Mya. She had been ignoring me since she found out I was still with Jasmine. I never stopped trying to reach out to her because she carried my child but I stopped popping up just to be left outside her door looking dumb. I got dressed and went to her apartment and I expected for her to give me a hard time about letting me in because that's what she did every time

I tried. I knocked on the door and waited for her response. I was gone keep knocking until she answered. She realized it was me and opened the door to let me in without saying anything. I gladly entered with several bags in my hands hoping that my gifts would make her feel better about me.

"Hey…I just came to bring your gifts and shit to you and see how you were." I started.

"Thanks," she said as she sat comfortably on the couch to continue watching Tv. She attempted to ignore me as I watched her from across the room. I figured she wouldn't have let me in if she didn't want to be bothered with me.

"How do you feel?" I asked her.

"I'm alright. Just tired of being pregnant." She told me.

"You need anything?" I asked her.

"Nope." She said as she focused her attention back on the television. I stared at her a few minutes trying to make her talk to me but when she didn't I figured I'd leave her alone.

"Aight…well I'm finna just go. I'll come back to check on you later." I said as I got up to leave. She started laughing.

"You just can't do it huh?" she asked me with a full plastered grin on her face.

"Do what? You won't even talk to me." I stated.

"Apologize! I have waited over a week for an apology and no matter what comes out of your mouth, you won't say it. Are you even sorry that you got caught the fuck up? Does it matter to you that you may lose the chance to be in your daughter's life?" She asked seriously. I knew those questions were rhetorical because there was no way I was going to let her keep my child away from me. I'd probably kill her first.

"Okay you're right, I'm sorry. I didn't mean to hurt you or jeopardize my relationship with my baby. I just didn't know how to tell you that I was still with Jasmine. My intention wasn't to start fucking with you again, but I did to make sure you were taken care of. The shit was selfish, and I apologize for that. I want to be in my child's life and I promise I can do that without fucking up." I said easily. I knew it was something she needed, and I meant it wholeheartedly.

"So, what about your lil girlfriend?" she asked.

"I love her. She ain't trying to talk to me right now but it won't change the fact that that's who I want to be with. I knew I wanted to be with her before I got you pregnant and that's why I let you go so easily after we fucked. I shoulda told you but I ain't think we'd have anything else to talk about until you called and told me about the baby. Jasmine is who I want to be with though. That's on some real shit. I would be lying to you if I told you anything else and we wouldn't be happy as long as I want her." I explained.

"Well, I guess I don't have a choice but to accept that. Thanks for being honest." She said before silence filled the living room again.

"So, we cool?" I asked her hopefully.

"Yeah just do what you're supposed to do for this baby you want so bad." She smiled.

"I will. Now, look what I bought her for Christmas." I smiled as I grabbed one of the bags.

"Damn I thought the gifts were for me." She smirked as she grabbed the bag from my hand.

"I might've got you a lil something. I laughed as we sorted through all the stuff I bought. After that, Mya an I were cool. I saw her every day and I spent time with her. I ignored the sexual attraction I had for her and focused solely on being cordial. I knew I had to make that very clear if I wanted Jasmine back.

I had to sacrifice what I felt for Mya to get my girl back in my life. Most days, I watched Jasmine come and go as if she had forgotten about me. She had gotten a lil job and did her thing. She never replied to me when I tried to contact her. She didn't even accept the Christmas gift I sent to her through Candice. She just wasn't fucking with me. I couldn't even blame her. I knew I'd hurt her and I felt bad. I made sure to still pay her phone bill and planned to pay her rent for January too. Even though she wasn't fucking with me I was still gone look out for her because I loved her. It took me to lose her to realize how much I cared.

One night I was on my way to pick something up from Kev, it was late, so I just threw on my Jacket and hit the door. It was cold as fuck outside when I was out earlier, so I knew it would be even cooler. The temperature always dropped at night. I locked my door and the elevator opened on my floor. I walked swiftly to catch it and only slowed down because Jasmine got off. Just seeing her made my heart stop for a second. This anxious feeling ran through my body. She was balled up in a lil black jacket like she was freezing. She didn't have on a scarf and when she removed her hands from her pockets to open the door she didn't have on gloves either. I spoke to her hoping she would say something to me, but she purposefully kept her mouth closed. I was defeated when she went in and shut the door like she didn't even see me. I supposed that was better than her waking me up blasting some song about busting my windows out like she'd done the first week we broke up. I was nervous every day that week because I thought she would actually bust all the windows out my truck. I shook my head and left the building feeling low. When the cold air hit my face, it felt like I'd been slapped. I hurriedly ran to Kev's building with a mental note to get Jasmine a coat. It was too cold outside for her to be wearing that lil ass jacket.

I couldn't even sleep that night just thinking about her and what I could do to apologize. I made a mistake and I regretted it. I got up early that morning and went downtown to the coat factory.

I found her the warmest, most fashionable ladies coat they had. At least that's what the sales associate who helped me called it. I didn't even blink when she told me the price. I just wanted my girl back. I had it boxed real nice and waited until just before she usually left out for work and sat it there. I slid into my apartment and listened as she opened the door and pulled the box inside. I smiled and shut my door satisfied that she accepted my gift. She knew it was from me and she took it anyway.

Candice

Right after New Year's, I start feeling real sick and nauseous. At first, I thought it was the fact I got drunk as hell at my cousin's party. But the shit ain't go away after a few days. I was laying down at Kevin's apartment waiting for him to come back with our food. Soon as he got back and I smelled the Italian beef he bought, I threw up all over the floor. He jumped back and looked at me like I was crazy.

"Ugh! What the fuck Candice?" he frowned angrily. I caught my breath and immediately went to the bathroom. I could hear him cursing me from the room and I shook my head as I ran water over my face. It didn't dawn on me that I might've been pregnant until after I start cleaning the shit up off the floor. I called Kevin back to the room and he stormed back angrily chewing a big bite of his sandwich.

"What?" he asked like he was disgusted. Although the sight certainly didn't ruin his appetite.

"I think I'm pregnant." I said as I looked up at him.

"Say what?" he smiled forgetting all about being mad. I chuckled.

"Yeah…think that's why I feel so sick." I told him.

"Damn, you pregnant?" he asked like it was good news to him.

"I don't know for sure, but I think..." I said as I got up the last of my mess.

"Well, you need to go find out. Go buy a test so we will know for sure." He suggested.

"What if I am, though?" I asked before nervousness crept into my whole being. I was only seventeen years old. I was just about to graduate high school and still lived with my mother. I knew this was a bad idea but I didn't think about it until I'd been faced with the possibility.

"What you mean? Imma be happy. You don't think I'll be a good daddy or something?" He asked jokingly.

"No..I just ain't ready to be nobody mama," I told him honestly. I didn't even try to hide the nervousness I felt. If I was gone be scared around anybody it was gone be him.

"You'll be aight. I'm gone be here regardless. Just go get a test. Imma sit right here and take it with you." He said before he kissed me and slapped my behind. I laughed and pulled my coat on to go to the store. I never passed up the chance to drive his car around. I loved Kevin with all my heart and no matter what situation came up he was always easy going. I knew I could depend on him and he'd have my back because that was the type of man he was. I wanted to spend the rest of my life with him and he made me feel like that was our plan.

When I got back to the house I went into the washroom to take the test. He came into the bathroom and sat at the edge of the tub as we waited for the results.

"Don't be scared, Candice. You know I won't ever leave you alone with my kid. I never did shit for you not to trust me. Don't start tripping on me now." He said before he chuckled.

"Kevin it's not even you. I just don't think I'll be a good mother. I don't doubt you at all." I said truthfully.

"Candice if I thought for one second you wouldn't be a good mother you wouldn't even be here. Regardless of what the test says I'm rocking with you the long way.

"So you plan to be with me for the long haul?" I asked seriously.

"You ain't even gotta ask. You gone be mine forever," he said before he leaned forward and kissed me on the lips.

I think the scariest moment of my life was reading that pregnancy test. A part of me hoped like hell it would be negative because I knew I wasn't ready, but I'd never forget the disappointed look on Kevin's face when the test read negative. For a few moments, I wished that I could give him the satisfaction of having a positive test. Then, I shook it off grateful that it wasn't my time to be anybody's mama.

Later that day I called Jasmine to see what she was up too. The last time I talked to her was New year's eve when she declined my invitation to my cousin's party. We hadn't talked much since the whole mall incident. I knew she was hurt and embarrassed after MyKing did her so bogus but I ain't see why she wasn't talking to me. I didn't know he had gotten that girl pregnant and regardless of how Kevin felt about it, I woulda told her if I'd known. But whenever I tried to link up and kick it she was never interested. She got her a job at the McDonalds in P-town and I rarely saw her. I missed my friend and I tried my best to support her. I was surprised when she answered the phone and we talked a while like old times. I was glad we were still cool despite her break up. To be honest, I was worried. I loved Jasmine like a sister, and I'd hate for MyKing to ruin our friendship. With his dog ass. I thought.

CHAPTER NINETEEN: WEAK

Jasmine

I had enjoyed my few weeks of winter break while I got use to my new job. But the return to school was unavoidable. There were five months left of school before graduation and I couldn't wait for this part of my life to be over. I had not only planned to leave and go to college, but I was going to Spellman which seemed to be a thousand miles from Chicago and Slater Mills. I took the bus to school and held my head high as I entered its doors. I had already prepared myself for the whispers and questions I was sure to get from people when they saw me. I'm sure the news about MyKing and his baby mama had spread like wildfire. I knew when I saw Rashiya and a few other bitches who hated me, they all knew what had transpired. The smirks on their faces were supposed to have me sick but I smiled instead. I wasn't a weak bitch and I didn't see anything attractive about a man who couldn't be faithful. MyKing might have been fine as hell but what I felt for him went away when I realized I wasn't the only person he was giving his love to. My mama always told me that a cheating man is a weak man. She explained to me what it meant to be with a cheating man. It's a reflection of who you are as a woman. If I took him back after he lied and cheated on me then I became a weak woman. I made it okay for him to fool around with other women because he figured I'd take him back. I loved MyKing, but I couldn't be that woman. So, any one of these jealous bitches who broke their necks just to cackle in my face could have him. I wasn't a weak woman on no day. Besides, I figured he would've made up with the mother of his unborn child by now. I'd ignored him for weeks and nothing was going to change about that. I got to my locker and rearranged a few books I was using before Val walked up on me.

"Hey girl, I ain't heard from you the whole break. Why you ignoring me?" she asked playfully. I screwed her nastily before I responded to her phony ass.

"Bitch, I was being nice by ignoring you. I was trying to keep from cursing your phony ass out. You knew that girl was pregnant the whole time and ain't bother telling me." I retorted.

"Well excuse the fuck outta me. I was just minding my business. That ain't have shit to do with me. I don't see how me telling you was gone change anything." She responded.

"You were supposed to be my friend. You coulda saved me the embarrassment of having to see the shit." I responded.

"Nah you woulda looked dumb either way. That nigga a hustler. Bitches come with the territory and I was friendly enough to tell you that much. The best thing for you to do is act like it don't faze you so bitches won't think you hurt." She said easily as Candice approached my locker rolling her eyes.

"You weren't no friend to me knowing my man had me out here looking dumb. And I am nothing like you, the shit does hurt but it doesn't even matter now. I'm done with him and his baby mama drama and I'm done with yo phony ass." I spat as I slammed my locker closed.

"Fine, whatever. Just don't fuck up my order when I come through the drive through next time." She said before she walked off.

"How about she fuck up your face instead, bitch," Candice said smartly before she turned back towards me.

"You aight G? she asked seriously.

"Fuck her," I said as I walked towards my first class. I remained quiet and kept to myself. I wasn't in the mood for people and I no longer cared to be here. I was counting down the days until graduation. I saw MyKing in just about every class and ignored him like I'd been doing for weeks. I made sure I didn't make eye contact with him and I never bothered to look his way when I heard his voice. He could've been on another planet for all I cared. After school everyday, I rode the bus home or got a ride with Candice. I usually washed up and put on my uniform to go to work when I got home. I realized how difficult working was after the first week of school. I was tired as hell by the weekend and that's usually when I worked double shifts. By Saturday night I had the nastiest attitude. It seemed like we were extra busy, I was cramping so bad, and Latrice, one of my coworkers, was getting on my last fucking nerves. She was one of the loudest people I'd ever met. On top of being loud, she was fat, ghetto, and nosy. I was counting down the time before I could leave. I silently prayed for God to send me a ride. I would've called Candice, but I didn't feel like waiting for her to get there. Right before it was time for me to clock out, I'd ordered me something to eat. I hadn't cooked in ages and I wasn't about to start back tonight. My cycle had me craving everything on the menu. I clocked out as soon as my food was ready. And dreaded the walk I had to the bus stop. My feet were killing me and I just wanted to get in my bed. I walked towards the door before big loud mouth Latrice bid me farewell. I smiled politely and said goodbye before rolling my eyes and walking out the door. My attitude worsened when the cold air hit me in my face. I kicked my boots and made my way out of the parking lot before I heard my name.

"Jasmine..." he called. I knew who it was right away and the only reason I stopped to give him the time of day is because of my attitude. I was in the mood to be real ugly and I was about to let some foul shit fly out my mouth. He'd hesitate the next time he tried to talk to me. I turned in his direction and he got out his truck to approach me. I stood still standing in the middle of the lot with a nasty frown on my face. My back, thighs, and vagina were kicking my ass and I didn't feel like this right now.

"Hey, Jas...Let me give you a ride." MyKing offered before he looked down at his feet. I chuckled to myself at his sudden bashfulness. The person I knew was more confident than anyone could stand. Suddenly he acts like he was scared to speak up. I couldn't wait to tell him hell no and to kiss my ass. The thought of it made me smile in anticipation. I was going to burst into laughter when the disappointed and pitiful look crossed his face. But before I could answer, he smiled and his big beautiful dimples made my heart skip a beat. I actually thought about taking the ride I had just asked the Lord for a half an hour before. MyKing stood in front of me just as fine as he was the day I met him. My eyes teared up when he looked at me. His gaze was deep, and I could see his heart.

"I swear to God I'm sorry. Just let me give you a ride tonight." He said as I fought with all my might not to cry in front of him. I knew I'd be a fool to get in the car with the man after what he had done to me but tonight I didn't have the patience to wait on the bus. I didn't even respond. I just walked away from where he stood and let myself into his truck. I got in strapped the seatbelt and pulled my food out of my bag to eat it. I was planning to eat it on the bus anyway.

He got in right after me and started the car. The heat blasted in my face just how I liked it and I was grateful. He was talking, and I heard his voice, but I wasn't paying attention to shit he said. I nodded as I counted every fry I put in my mouth. I gave him an "um huh, that's crazy" every few fries to keep him satisfied. Everything was good until he mashed the breaks real hard.

"Jasmine, I'm trying to fucking talk to you. You ain't gotta be like that. Just talk to me." He exclaimed. The anger I'd been holding for weeks combined with the cramps brewing in my uterus made me snap my head towards him to regulate.

"The nerve of your ignorant, black, cheating ass. I don't give a fuck about you wanting to talk, muthafucka. You ain't got a bitch ass thing to talk to me about nigga! When you had the chance to talk to me and let me know what you were doing behind my back, you made the decision to be quiet. Got me looking like a fucking fool while you paraded your slut ass side bitch around town carrying your child. Fuck you MyKing! I don't care about shit you have to say. Either shut the fuck up and drive this truck or let me the fuck out and I'll walk!" I spat as hot angry tears ran my face. I wasn't even hurt no more. Just mad as hell. I couldn't really look at him after that because the thought of what he did just came rushing back. He mashed the gas pedal and the car moved again but he was silent. He didn't say another word all the way back to the building. I wiped my face and hopped out the truck with no intention of ever talking to him again. I hated him. I thought.

He followed me into the elevator and I wouldn't dare look his way. When the elevator stopped on our floor, I got my key out to open the door. He stopped right behind me. The hair on the back of my neck stood because for a split second I thought he'd hurt me. I turned to look at him before he spoke.

"I fucked up real bad. I made a mistake about not telling you, I had gotten Mya pregnant before we got together. I didn't find out until she was about four months and I just ain't have the heart to tell you then. I never wanted to be with her and you can quote me on that. I can't say I didn't cheat because we both know I'd be lying but I apologize with everything I got in me. I will do whatever it will take for you to be mine again. I fucked up, Jas. I am sorry, bae. I know that I want to be with you though and it was not my intention to hurt you the way that I did.

That shit eating me alive. But I ain't perfect and I'm gone fuck up sometimes because I'm human but when I tell you I love the shit out of you, and I'm sorry, you know I'm being honest." He said as he lifted my chin up to look at him. His hands were warm on my face despite the cold weather. I looked into his eyes and my lips quivered. The tears fell from my face so easily and they only thickened when his eyes got watery too. I knew then he was sorry. All of my feelings came rushing back and my head was about to explode from all my reckless emotions. He moved his face closer to mine and crashed his lips against mine. All the anger and pain I had held melted away and my stomach became full with butterflies. My heartbeat was loud in my ears and I only felt one way as he held me in his arms. Weak.

MyKing

I loved Jasmine more than I ever loved another woman. After a few weeks with her ignoring me, I couldn't take it a day longer. When I thought about my future I saw her in it and that didn't make me feel like a bitch ass nigga. Before I met her, I couldn't have imagined the man I'd try to become. I learned a lot about myself when I changed for her. I did make a mistake with Mya and I made my peace with it. My goal was to get her to understand I'd never make that mistake again. I promised myself that if I ever got her back, I would never cheat on her again. I didn't make that promise to her because I didn't know if I could keep it but I would try. Jasmine wasn't somebody I felt like I could live without and that was enough for me to try to straighten up. I didn't throw around a bunch of promises to bait her. I didn't bother begging. I gave her the truth she deserved and apologized as sincerely as I could. After we kissed, it only confirmed what I already knew about Jasmine. She is meant to be my wife. I mean, I wasn't ready to walk down the aisle at that moment, but I wouldn't do the shit with anybody else. That night she let me stay with her and I held her in my arms like I'd never let her go. Before she drifted to sleep she looked up at me with those big pretty baby doll eyes.

"You forgive me?" I asked seriously.

"Yeah...but I can't compete with your baby mama. I don't want to be second in your life. I can't compete with her." She said.

"I'm gone put my child first because my mother never did that with me but in comparison you being second will only mean I'm doing what I'm supposed to do as a man. Mya isn't a problem and I can prove that to you if you give me the chance." I told her.

"MyKing...she's the mother of your child. I know at some point you're going to put her before me. I can't deal with that." She said seriously.

"You just gotta trust me, bae. I can't promise you I'm gone be the perfect man because I'll fall short but give me the chance to make it right and I won't disappoint you again.

"Okay," she said before I kissed her forehead and she went to sleep. That night I slept like a rock. I woke up refreshed and confident. I got up ready to work.

I spent all day trying to plan the perfect evening. And when it came, I was nervous as fuck. I sat at the restaurant with Jasmine sitting across from me just as beautiful as the day I met her.

"MyKing...what are we doing? You made me call off work for dinner just for you to be quiet the whole time?" She asked seriously. I was so nervous I just didn't know what to say. I'm not really the romantic type.

"You don't have to work Jas. I got you." I told her seriously.

"No, I want to work. I gotta have my own money. I can't depend on you to do everything. Especially with a baby on the way. I have to make sure I'm good if you decide you want to be with her." She said hesitantly. I looked at her for a while after that but I smiled at my attempt to make it right.

"Aight cool." I agreed only because I knew what I was about to do would change her mind.

Not long after that Mya was escorted to our table big and pregnant but also beautiful. I got up to pull out her chair and this awkward silence filled the space. Jasmine's expression wasn't pleasant but she didn't get up and leave. I figured that was a start.

"Jasmine this is Mya and Mya this is Jasmine." I introduced the two nervously.

"Hi," Mya spoke first.

"Hello," Jasmine responded politely and I started to speak.

"I brought yall here to make sure that we can all get on the same page. I know that I hurt you both by not telling you what I was up to the last few months. I realize that shit was wrong and I'm trying to fix it. So, I want to start by saying I apologize again for what I did. Both of you mean something to me and I want to be in both of your lives." I stated plainly. I didn't want any misunderstandings and I only had one shot to clear it all up.

"Mya, you having my baby means the world to me. I didn't intend for it to happen but I'm not mad it did. I want to be in my daughter's life and I will do anything to make sure I can be. We're cool now and I'm glad co-parenting is an option for us." I started, pausing briefly to see if she would respond but she just looked at me and nodded. I could tell she wasn't comfortable with the arrangement because that meant losing what we had. But I had already let her know the shit was dead between us. I mean I would still be down to fuck Mya but that would only complicate things between the three of us and I ain't need no more problems.

"Jasmine, I love you. I know that I want to be with you and Mya knows that too. I just had to show you that I'm serious about us and I'm willing to do whatever to show you." I told her. She didn't say anything either. But the look on her face was clear. She was salty. The waitress came to take our orders and walked away. It was quiet as fuck. They both just sat there staring at me.

"Yall ain't making this easy." I stated as I shook my head and chuckled at their attitudes.

"I mean... I understand what you're trying to do and all but you cheated on me with this bitch and got her pregnant. Now she sitting in my face and I just gotta deal with her." Jasmine spat. I whipped my head towards her so fast my neck cracked.

"Bitch, I ain't know shit about you. I been fucking with him for over two years. You just popped the fuck up. I didn't know shit about you being with him. I ain't no side bitch lil girl. I don't even want your young ass around my baby." Mya retorted. Jasmine's face screwed like she was about to go the fuck off. Mya was sitting on the edge of her seat and I knew this dinner was gone end real bad.

"Whoa...hold up! Chill....chill. I ain't bring yall here for this shit." I started.

"Then why the hell you bring us here? To sing kumbaya?" Jasmine asked smartly and I cut my eyes at her real quick. Her mouth had become real flip lately and I was trying to figure out where she developed this nasty ass attitude. You'd swear she'd been in the Ps since birth. She just had a proper dialect that set her apart. She enunciated every word but that didn't lessen its sting. She had me ready to choke the fuck out her though.

"Jas, what else you want me to do? I apologized, I done introduced yall and I'm tryna clarify whatever plan we have. If you ain't willing to let what I did go, we are never gone work." I said seriously. I didn't have the patience for them to be going back and forth in this restaurant embarrassing me for nothing. My phone rang and when I saw it was Kev, I answered.

"Bro where you at?" He asked seriously.

"I'm out, Wassup?" I asked as Mya and Jasmine looked at me like I was crazy.

"JT just got killed. I need you here now." He said seriously.

"Fuck, aight. I'm on my way." I told him before I got up and disconnected the call.

"Imma be back to get yall. Don't leave." I told them as I threw on my coat.

"MyKing where the hell you going?" Jasmine asked smartly. It pissed me off because she never questioned me before and I wasn't feeling that shit.

"Aye, what the fuck I just say?" I asked her seriously. I dared her to have a rebuttal. I wasn't gone touch her but I would embarrass the fuck out of the both of them in this restaurant. She looked at me but didn't say anything.

"I love you." I told her before I walked away from the table and left them there hoping they wouldn't get into it.

Jasmine

I sat at the table quietly waiting for my food. I was happy to see it once the waitress sat it in front of my face. I ain't even want to be here and damn sure not with her. I momentarily questioned my love for MyKing. That nigga is trouble and even though I knew it, I couldn't leave him alone. Something about him just drew me in and I forgot all of my sense when I let him in.

"Okay, let's just get it out there. My patience has become real short and I'm sick of beating around the bush. Say how you feel so we can resolve this issue. Because I'm not feeling this bullshit." She stated seriously.

"You are my issue. You fucked my man and I gotta act like everything is cool. I want him but I don't want no parts of you." I told her honestly.

"Well honestly I don't want to deal with your silly ass either and If I wanted to be petty I'd.." she started.

"No, let me stop you right there honey. I am not one of these ignorant ass project bitches you are use too. If you'd done your research you would've heard. I don't have time for pettiness. This is my livelihood and quite frankly MyKing is not worth it. I love him but I will not belittle myself or my beliefs to come down to your level. Keep all that petty shit for whoever got time for it." I stated.

"Look, I don't like you and I'm not about to sit here and pretend I do. MyKing wants you in his life. I don't have to deal with you're stuck up ass. I just need you to understand my daughter is the priority now." She said.

"I understand, now would you shut the fuck up talking to me?" I asked her nastily.

"Cut the shit white girl. I know you ain't about that life." She retorted.

"As black as I am? Really? You just better be lucky you're pregnant and I just got my nails done because I would properly bust yo ass if I could." I told her seriously.

"Look, I'm only gone be pregnant another month and a half. After I have my baby we can meet up and scrap if you want. I will gladly teach your siddity ass a lesson about "Project Bitches". Until then, let's tuck the beef and be civil. Deal?" she asked.

"Deal." I agreed looking forward to an all-out brawl. But after that agreement, Mya wasn't a problem for me anymore.

CHAPTER TWENTY: BAD LUCK

Tevin

When I heard that gate shut behind me I wanted to take off running. I was so sick of being locked up I couldn't stay in that bitch a day longer if I had to. I had been stuck in that musty ass cell for eight months and I was finally free to get right back to the money. I couldn't be happier to see my brother's Camaro parked in front of me. I hopped in with the biggest smile on my face, but he didn't look as happy to see me.

"Wassup bitch, fresh out that muthafucka! What's the move and where the hoes?" I laughed hitting him in his arm like I always did. He didn't even react as he pulled his car out into traffic.

"Aye wassup? Why you acting like you ain't happy to see me?" I asked him looking upside his shit.

"We are at war with them niggas in P-town. JT, Dre, Rashawn, and Brody got murked. The lil niggas getting hit too. We making the money but losing our guns." He said seriously. That instantly pissed me off. Being locked up kept me from protecting my people and I knew them hits were on me. Moving into P-town was my move and I fucked up by getting knocked. I had to make up for that shit and because I felt guilty I wouldn't hesitate.

"Nah don't even worry about that. Get me to the spot. Imma clear all this shit up." I told him seriously.

"Aye, don't get out here and start acting a fool in that nigga shit. We done lost too many niggas to keep up with that beef bullshit. Just secure our land and leave the bullshit for the birds. I want to make money. I don't plan to attend another funeral no time soon. Just focus on the Cash, Tev." He said seriously. Whole time I was just sitting there brewing. The fact them lil niggas thought we was some goofies just pissed me off more. I stopped talking to think about the type of damage I was gone do when I caught them niggas slipping. I ain't agree or listen to shit Kevin said. I wasn't no bitch ass nigga and wasn't nobody finna play me as one.

Although I can tell everybody was a lil stressed out, King seemed to be happy to see me back. He greeted me with the hug I expected from Kevin.

"Wassup nigga, how you living?" I asked him like I always did.

"Just living, you ready to get back to it?" he asked coolly.

"I been ready. Waiting on yall to show me the layout." I told him as we sat down over some fried lemon pepper wings and a bunch of pistols. I was ready to become a real problem for Quan and all the lil niggas in P-Town. I didn't think I'd get my opportunity so fast but a few days later, after my brother gave me a layout of the land, I was posted in the trap on the block and got a lil thirsty. My brother had just come to drop me some clothes and I grabbed his keys to ride to the gas station. I walked in the store daring a muthafucka to say anything to me. I had been itching to use the pistol King had strapped me with days before. I go in the store and buy me some hot crunchy curls, and a fruit punch and go on about my business. I walk out to a group of niggas standing by the door. Now, I did peep this one nigga there when I went in, but I got an uneasy ass feeling when six niggas stood there on my way out. I screwed my face and carried my ass right past them hoping I wouldn't have to light this gas station up. Not a second after that thought, I heard a nigga say, "Yeah that's one of them Slater niggas." Now, I shoulda kept walking but I turned around to make sure it wasn't no problems. And I was ready for a muthafucka to have one with me.

"Come again?" I asked trying to see if somebody would address me directly.

"Nigga, ain't nobody say shit to yo bitch ass." One of the niggas said. Before I could respond, another nigga shifted in his pants and I saw the butt of his gun. I dropped my drink and grabbed my pistol from my waist and squeezed towards the nigga I saw with the gun.

"Oh shit!" I heard before gunshots start happening all around me. I squeezed until I backed my way into Kevin's car. I jumped in and peeled the fuck out the lot like it was fire on my ass. My heart was beating fast as hell as I tried to catch my breath. I kept tryna feel to make sure I wasn't hit. I couldn't figure out how I made it out without getting hit once. I quickly made my way back to the trap. I parked the whip and flew up the porch like it was people chasing me.

"Man, what the fuck wrong with you?" Kevin asked as I burst through the door. I couldn't even tell the nigga what had just happened because I was too excited. I sat down on the couch and closed my eyes to try and control my breathing. The whole time Kevin was standing over me asking a million questions. He left when I didn't answer him right away. I didn't think nothing of it.

Kevin

Candice and I were just getting back from a movie. I was tired as hell and just wanted to lay down when I got back in the house. I had smoked me a blunt and got comfortable before Candice came in the room tryna unbuckle my belt. I took my attention off the Tv to look at her. I had mad love for her pretty ass. She smiled when I let her take my dick out my pants.

"Now what you finna do with that?" I asked her as she let it hang out and pulled her shirt over her head. I sat up to help her remove her clothes and we went at it. I loved everything about being with shorty and when I let go of that doubt I had about her in the beginning, I realized what a dime Candice really was. After we finished, I got a call from my dumb ass brother asking me to bring him some clothes. Truth was Tevin had been getting on my last nerve. That nigga just be doing fly off the handle dumb shit. He never thinks about the consequences and never apologizes. Shit was so much easier when he was locked up and I was mad at him for the heat he caused by upping the shipment. King and I been busting our asses trying to make it work and that extra stress is because of Tevin. Crazy thing is, he hadn't seen the bullshit he caused. I wanted him to get out of jail but I knew that meant shit would get worse. I didn't feel like leaving my crib and I almost said fuck him and stayed home but I didn't.

"Bae, I'm finna slide and drop something to my brother. You can stay here till I get back." I told her as I threw my jeans on and got ready to go.

"Damn, King can't take it to him? I don't want you to leave." She wined.

"Imma be right back shorty. I promise I'll only be a minute." I assured her.

"Okay, bring me back something to eat." She said before she kissed me.

"Damn..now I don't wanna leave." I chuckled as I grabbed her by the ass and kissed her back.

"I love you." She said easily.

"I love you too," I told her honestly as I smacked her booty and headed out the door. I couldn't wait to get back home to just be with her. I drove all the way into P-town to drop him some clothes. King called me while I was in route.

"Aye, I'm on my way to the hospital. Mya water broke." He stated quickly.

"Damn, for real! My nigga finna be a daddy today!" I laughed geeked up about him being a father. I couldn't wait for my girl to get pregnant cause I wanted a son myself.

"Yeah, it's about that time. I need you to make sure Jasmine good when she get off though. I just don't want her to feel no type of way about me being gone." He said.

"Yeah, I feel you, you know I got you, bro. Congrats." I told him as I pulled up to the spot.

"Thanks, bro. I preciate you." He said before we hung up the phone and I got out to give Tevin his shit. It was dark and I was tired. I just wanted to give him his shit and get back home. I grabbed the bag out my trunk and went in. I had to pee.

"Aye, let me see your keys, I'm thirsty as fuck. Imma run to the gas station right quick." He said easily. I shook my head because the nigga was stupid. Tevin had money just like me and King but he hadn't bothered to get him a car since he had gotten out. The one he had was impounded when he got arrested. So, I said yeah because he was my brother, but I wasn't feeling the idea. I wasn't no petty nigga though, so I threw him the keys and went in the bathroom.

I sat on the couch for a moment and fell asleep. I didn't know how long I went out but when Tevin burst through the door like somebody was chasing him I jumped up off the couch and pulled the pistol from my waist.

"What the fuck wrong with you?" I asked him. He looked like he was about to pass out. He couldn't even talk. He just sat down on the couch and closed his eyes. I questioned him a good ten minutes before I thought about my car. I snatched the keys off the table and ran outside to look at the damage I knew his dumb ass had done. He had barely parked it. The ass of the car was sticking out into the street and when I got close enough I could see bullet holes. I got pissed off immediately. I turned back around about to go knock Tevin's head clear off his body when a truck mashed the gas towards me. I could only see the color of the black truck. I couldn't comprehend the style or the year. I just turned to run and heard a loud gunshot. It was close enough to ring my eardrums. I lost my hearing after that, but I felt the bullet hit me in the back and come straight through my chest. Ripped straight through my Pelle. Then another and another after that. Maybe they had come all at once. It wasn't clear. I lost the feeling in my legs and fell face first to the pavement. My vision got blurry as the truck speed past me. The concrete was cold and salty. It felt like an elephant was sitting on my back and the ringing in my ears was consistent. I knew I'd die in the street and I knew it was because of Tevin. But I wasn't upset anymore because I could no longer feel the pain. I could only think about the love I had for Candice and the saxophone. I thought of my favorite song and the birth of my brother's daughter. My eyelids had started to feel heavy and I was tired.

"Kev! Broo...come on...bro breathe. The ambulance coming bro. Just don't die on me...I'm sorry...I'm sorry!" Tevin cried as he pulled me into him and looked me in my face. I didn't try to talk. I had no last words. Just thoughts about all my favorite things. I didn't see my whole life flash before my eyes or nothing like that. I felt like I'd done the right things by the people in my life. I was a good person and I believed everyone knew that about me. I just lost my will to fight the pleasure of a good sleep. I didn't want to die but at the brink of death, I was grateful for the relief. I forgave Tevin in my heart and I closed my eyes. I could hear my mother's voice as Boney James blew the Sax in the background. I fell into a peaceful sleep.

Jasmine

I walked on the block Candice sent the address for and it was empty. This strange feeling came over me when I got on the block. I was afraid that whoever killed Kevin might return. I called Candice again, but she didn't answer. I stuck my phone in my pocket and zipped it up. My gut told me to turn around and walk back towards the main street, but I figured with all the commotion that had transpired she probably just went inside the house. So, I kept walking down the block towards the house she'd given me the address for. I walked in the middle of the street towards the street lights until I saw the red tape the police left wrapped from one tree to another. My heart dropped into my shoes because seeing it only made it more real. Right under the street light was a pool of blood that confirmed Kevin had died in that spot. It was a large dark stain and it was sealed off like it was a piece of art or something. The lump in my throat got thick as I thought about Kevin. I walked towards the stain in the street and squatted near the curb and I cried. I didn't know who would do this and I didn't understand why. I was hurt to have lost someone so close to home. I trembled at the thought of him dying right here on the cold streets. Like a dog. "God why?" I asked as I looked up from the blood spot at the figure standing in my peripheral. When I locked eyes with him, I lost all the air in my lungs. He staggered towards me like a zombie. My mouth fell open and I stumbled to my feet. I knew some supernatural freaky shit was going on and I couldn't believe my eyes. I thought about every horror movie I'd ever seen and realized what I had walked into was the perfect surrounding to be attacked by someone who was presumed dead. He staggered towards me with nothing but his wife beater on that was covered in dark blood. I didn't hesitate to take off running in the direction opposite him. I ran between the walkway of two houses and hauled ass towards the alley. I ran as quickly as I could and as soon as I stepped foot into the alley I was snatched backward by my hair. I squealed before I was thrown against the wall like a rag doll. He wrapped his cold hands around my neck and I start swinging wildly towards his face.

"You bitches fucked up....you bitches done shot the wrong muthafucka!" he spat in my face. I was terrified. His breath reeked of alcohol and his eyes were bloodshot red. He banged my head against the brick wall behind me and it made me dizzy. I lost my vision and I felt vomit rise from my stomach, but it wouldn't come out because of the grip he had on my neck. I scratched at his wrist to loosen his grip and spit out what I could of the vomit before he tightened his grip again.

"You nasty bitch! You dirty, slut, bitch...you spit on me! Imma kill you bitch. Imma kill all of you!" he cried as he choked me out. I moved my body back and forth trying to break away from his grip. I used my legs to free myself by trying to kick him in between his legs. I couldn't see anything but darkness. It seemed like I was fighting a shadow. I used my hands to try and grab between his legs and as soon as I felt the inside of his thigh he knocked my head against the wall again. I cried but I felt like the tears were falling inside my head. I could no longer inhale, and I could just barely hear him. My limbs felt like noodles as he pinned my arms across my body like a straitjacket.

"That's what you want bitch? Imma give you what you want!" he said angrily as he snatched at my pants. I felt like I'd been nailed to the side of the building and the world around me moved in circles. I couldn't even fight. My vision was distorted and all I could see were shadows in front of me. They swirled around like they were chasing one another. It wasn't until the cold air hit my bare ass that I realized my pants were off. I bucked up against the wall and I attempted to scream. I felt like I was trapped inside myself with no way out. I screamed no a thousand times and I cried stop. I begged please but I couldn't figure out if it was all inside my head or not. He had strength I couldn't explain but I remember feeling relief when the pressure around my neck ceased. I pulled in as much air as I could when my legs were pulled apart. I felt the cold building against my ass before a sharp pain ripped through my vagina. It was the most horrible feeling I'd ever felt. I knew I was going to die at that moment and I screeched in pain. It felt like someone had taken a hot knife inside me as he pushed himself into me. The force behind each stroke just made me want to pass out. I felt like I was being torn apart. Like he was angry with me and he hated me. I could feel hot wet liquid falling onto my face and I didn't know which of us cried harder. He held my arms down with one hand and my legs apart with the other as he pushed himself deeper inside me. I gave up fighting when I realized the deranged animal of top of me would kill me. I prayed that my death would come soon, and it would be quick. It felt like someone had rung a big bell inside my skull and it hadn't stopped ringing yet. I was expecting a white light and for my whole life to flash before my eyes but that didn't happen. And despite the torture of having my virginity taken away, I couldn't pass out either. My vision cleared just enough to look at one of the shadows in his dark eyes.

"Kevin...pleassse stop." I cried. I heard my voice inside my head and it sounded like I was so far away. And the shadow's eyes bucked out of his head as if he had just seen me. He pulled out of me and warm liquid ran down my inner thighs. He jumped back away from me like I was diseased with his pants and boxers dropped around his knees. I remember hearing the train not far off when I hit the ground. My legs were numb when I tried standing. He threw up right next to me and I jumped up onto my feet with everything I had in me and took off running towards the street. My pants were only hanging on one leg and I'd lost one of my shoes, but I ran up that street like Flo joe and I didn't stop until I couldn't breathe. I was terrified, and I waited until I was on the main street to throw my leg into the pants and pull them back up across my butt. I shook my head back and forth as my ears popped.

"God help me...please help me." I said out loud trying to figure out what to do. I searched my pockets looking for my phone and came up short until I remembered where I zipped it. Only the screen had been cracked in so many places I couldn't see it clearly enough to dial 911. I just mashed the screen until the phone starts ringing and I held the phone up to my head praying anyone would answer. The back of my head was so tender it throbbed endlessly.

"Hey..bae imma call you back! Mya in labor..." he answered.

"MyKing!" I cried into the phone. I could not have been happier to hear his voice. I needed him more than I'd ever needed him before. But the phone disconnected and no matter how hard I tried I couldn't get him back. I knew one day he'd put Mya before me and I was devastated it had to be the moment I needed him to choose me. I cried and kept mashing the screen and the phone rang again and I put it up to my ear and prayed MyKing would answer.

"Hey, Jasmine...wassup." I heard a voice whisper on the other side. I couldn't immediately figure out whose voice it was but I was relieved they knew my name.

"I need help. I just got raped I need help." I cried into the phone.

"What...Oh my god where are you? I'll come, where you at?" she asked on the other line. I looked around but I didn't have a clue. I couldn't read the street signs and I was afraid to knock on someone's door and ask. It was late and I just wanted to lay down.

"I don't know. I have no idea where I am. I can't see. He hit me in the head. I can't see!" I tried explaining.

"Can you walk? Are you away from him?" she asked seriously.

"Yes..I ran away. I lost my shoe..I don't know where I am though." I cried.

"Look just go to the next house and ask for help. Just go knock and ask for help." She told me. I looked back and forth as the circles started again. It seemed like whenever I stopped moving my vision got screwy. I saw the shadows of a dozen houses and

I ran towards the one with the Christmas lights still up. I loved Christmas! I stumbled up the stairs and mashed at the sides of the door because I thought I saw a bell in one of the shadows. I heard it ring and I cried out for God to help me. I banged at the door and when it opened I fell inside and everything went black.

I woke up with the worse headache of my life. My neck and throat felt like I had swallowed glass. I tried to open my eyes but the light just made me cringe. I felt like I'd been hit by a car.
"Turn off the lights." I moaned. There was shuffling in the room before the lights went down. Something in my nose was blocking me from breathing so I snatched it off. I heard voices and when I opened my eyes Bianca stood over me.

"What the hell?" I asked confused as I looked around the hospital room.

"You're okay chick. Everything is gone be ok. Imma go get the doctor." She said, and I shook my head no. I thought it had all been some sick ass dream. I needed time to process where I was and why.

"Jasmine, they need to examine your pussy. They couldn't touch you there because you were passed out. You have a concussion…. That man coulda had anything. Let them look." She said seriously before I grabbed her arm.

"Wait…I am sixteen. My mother is on drugs and I live on my own…If they examine anything child protective services will be here….this won't end well if I stay here. Just help me get out of here and I'll get checked later. I whispered. She looked at me a while as she processed what I'd just said.

"You know who did it, right." she said knowingly. I nodded my head yes. She looked at me seriously for a second before she agreed.

"Okay..put your clothes back on and wait till I come back." She said before she left the room. I got off the bed and I was extremely sore. My vagina felt agitated and I felt nasty. I couldn't even begin to accept what had happened to me and I didn't understand. I was too tired to try at the moment. When she returned she tiptoed back in and we slid our asses right out that hospital. I didn't even look back.

CHAPTER TWENTY-ONE: REST IN PEACE

MyKing

I didn't know how to feel. Today I lost my brother and watched my daughter come into this world. I didn't know how to be happy and sad. I cried after I saw her little pink face and I didn't know if it was because she was beautiful, or Kevin would never see her. I just felt and I didn't hide it from Mya at that moment. I had her back the way I promised her, and I didn't leave her. In return, she had mine by being considerate. I knew she wasn't gone like the name I picked for our daughter but when I told her she didn't even blink. I guess she felt too. And I needed her to feel for me.

I signed the birth certificate paperwork and held my daughter until her mother insisted I put her down. After I made sure they were comfortable, I left to figure out the damage. I saw the red tape as I stepped into the trap. I had to swallow the tears attempting to come out. Tevin was passed out on the couch when I walked in. His pistol was on the table in front of him along with a knocked over bottle of Remy and all kinds of other shit. I've never known Tevin to do drugs so I was shocked at the trail of white lines in front of him. I shook my head as I checked the house to see if things were still in place. One of our guys Vonte came out of the bathroom and greeted me.

"Bruh shit was crazy last night." He held his head sadly.

"Yeah… I know." I shook my head. I didn't want to even talk about it but I needed to know what happened.

"Tevin ran through this bitch last night zooted. He been out on bullshit all night. It's bodies everywhere" he said seriously as he nodded towards the gun on the table. I caught his eye and grabbed a towel to wrap the gun.

"Are we leaving P-town now?" He asked seriously.

"Nah, we gone take it," I told him with enough rage in me to go through with it. This was bigger than money now and I and Tevin would paint the city red until this was our shit. I woke Tevin up to figure out what had happened. Kevin was fine on his way here and now he was dead. I knew Tevin had everything to do with it. The cocaine on the table did nothing to settle my thoughts.

Jasmine

Bebe and I hopped a cab that drove us to the entrance of Slater. She paid the man and helped me up the walkway. It was well after three in the morning and I was in so much pain. I just pushed myself into the building to get to my apartment. Unfortunately, the elevator was out of order and I had to drag my body up the nasty stairwell. I held on to Bebe for support, but I was crying before I could get on my floor. It felt like I'd been run over by a truck and I was sore and miserable.

"G, its gone be okay. We gone put this night behind us. You will be okay." She said as we made it to my door. She took my key and unlocked it and I stumbled into the apartment. I was exhausted but went into the bathroom to bathe anyway. I had so many thoughts running through my head I couldn't function. I peeled off my clothes and stepped into the tub as the hot water ran over my body. I turned it up as hot as I could get it. I moved the washcloth around my sore neck and down my body lathering soap along the way. The only thing I could hear was the water and my loud heartbeat. I thought I would die tonight and I kept telling myself "You're alive." But I still felt dead. I couldn't put in words what had happened to me. I couldn't process what I'd gone through and I didn't want anyone to know. I was ashamed, and I felt dirty. I washed between my legs anxiously. I wanted to clean away anything that would remind me that I was violated. And even though I was in my own home and washing, I could somehow still smell the alcohol on his breath. The water burned at my skin, but it didn't out way the pain in my heart. I was damaged, and I didn't think I'd ever be whole again. My head ached and my thoughts suffocated me. I couldn't consider anyone's feelings but my own and I just felt like I died. I stepped out of the tub and wiped the foggy mirror to look at myself. My reflection was blurry but I could see my dark skin and my wild hair. I looked into my red puffy eyes.

"You're Alive," I said out loud before I wrapped the towel around myself and opened the door. Bebe sat on my bed where she had laid out a shirt and a pair of shorts for me.

"You good?" she asked concerned.

"I'm alive. I owe you." I told her as I dropped the towel and pulled on my clothes in front of her.

"Nah, you don't owe me shit. You had my back and I wouldn't hesitate to have yours. You need to rest and don't wait too long to go get checked out. I'll go with you when you're ready." She said. I appreciated that support because I needed it. She came through like a sister and I needed a sister. I thought about Candice but I was too exhausted to check in on her then. Besides, her man raped me and she is the last person I wanted to be around now.

"I will. Thank you." I said as she stood to leave.

"I'm gone get going so I can get in this house before my curfew. I'm coming back to check on you." She said easily.

"You got enough to check in?" I asked.

"Nah but you were worth it." She said as she walked towards the door.

"Hold up," I told her as I went towards my closet and into the shoebox MyKing always dropped his pocket money and peeled four hundred off the roll. I walked towards her to hand her the money.

"Jas I'm good. Like I said, you don't owe me shit." She said seriously.

"I know but I ain't gone let you take an ass whupping for nothing. Thanks for coming through for me." I told her as I placed the bills in her hand. She grabbed the money and pulled me into her arms for a hug. I embraced her back and we held on to each other until she pulled away.

"I'll be back to check on you." She said before she left. As soon as I locked the door behind her, I got in the bed and cried myself to sleep.

I woke up after the sun arose the later feeling worse than I had before. I threw the alarm clock across the room when it woke me up and my head starts hurting again. I got up to urinate and was reminded of the trauma when I wiped myself. I had washed and still felt disgusting. I reached into the medicine cabinet before I took two ibuprofen and got back in the bed. I didn't plan to go to school and didn't care to ever return. I went right back to sleep and didn't know how long I'd slept when I was awoken. I jumped to the head of the bed when I heard the door hit the back of the wall. I looked up at MyKing standing in the doorway like a deer caught in headlights.

"Bae, what the fuck wrong with you? I have been calling you all day." He said as he looked at me crazily.

"I was sleep and my phone broke," I said as I tried calming my beating heart. I couldn't even look him in his eyes when I thought about what had happened. I hadn't done anything but I still felt guilty.

"What's wrong? You sick or something?" he asked as he came closer to examine me. When he touched my leg I felt uncomfortable.

"Nah, I'm good," I said quickly as I moved his hand away from my body. He noticed my rejection and the look on his face changed. I just didn't want him to look at me as disgusted as I felt.

"Jas...she was having my baby. I know you ain't mad at me. Its been a long twenty-four hours. Don't be like that. I told Kevin to make sure you were okay..." He said seriously.

"What?" I asked as tears filled my eyes.

"Bae, I love you and you know that. It's just been a long night. You know Kevin got killed and my head all fucked up right now. Just rock with me for a minute because I need you." He said. The thought of Kevin angered me, and it just made me want to fight.

"That nigga ain't dead." I spat as I moved further away from him. The idea that MyKing sent him after me kept running through my mind. He looked at me seriously unable to respond right away.

"Jasmine...he got killed in P-town last night. His body is at the morgue. I'm sure of that." He explained.

"That muthafucka ain't dead," I said bitterly as tears ran down my face. There was no way he could've died last night when he had me pent up against a brick building trying to kill me before day. That nasty nigga wasn't dead, and it was nothing anyone could've told me to convince me otherwise. I couldn't figure out what I'd done to deserve what I got from him. It just made me hate him. I cried angrily when I thought about what he'd done to me and I didn't feel like trying to hide how I felt. My-King looked at me like I was crazy, but he swallowed whatever he was going to say and pulled me into his arms instead. He held on to me and let me cry. After I cried all I could, he kissed my forehead.

"I love you, Jasmine." He told me.

"I love you too MyKing...but Kevin is not dead." I added. He exhaled loudly before he got up to leave. I laid back down trying to figure out if he'd believe me if I told him what really happened. But I quickly erased the thought. He would not want to be with me if I tell him what Kevin did. I was ashamed and that made me unworthy of love. I just couldn't picture a man wanting me after that. I couldn't tell him what happened because I didn't want to lose him. I just didn't see him taking my side and I wasn't going to give him the chance to turn on me. It's just best I keep the night between me and Bebe and pretend it never happened. I loved him, and I didn't want to lose him. So, I kept my mouth closed about it. He believed Kevin was dead anyway so if I'd ever seen him again, I'd kill him.

Candice

I was heartbroken. I got a phone call from my cousin saying my man had been shot. I got all the way into P-town and on the block just in time to watch those people put his body in the white unlabeled truck. The body bag made me feel nauseous. The police surrounding the area were assholes. They wouldn't let me near him. I tried to cross the red tape and they made me feel like they were simply taking out the trash. I'm sure it was something they did all too often because this was Chicago. This part was normal here. But the man in that bag was someone who was special, and it hurt me to my core they followed the same procedure with him. When they finally got him away from the scene I laid in the last spot he was and cried my eyes out. My cousins consoled me, and I could not even wrap my mind around the love of my life being gone. I wanted this to be a bad dream. I wanted this to be untrue but the blood in front of me was enough to wake me up. He was gone, and I just wanted him back. There was a big crowd surrounding the red tape and Tevin ran around crazily swearing he'd kill anyone responsible. Knowing that crazy nigga, I believed him. People eventually withdrew from the street and into their homes as it got later into the night. My phone rang off the hook as I sat at the scene trying to feel anything left of my man. The only call I answered was from Jas who promised she'd come to see about me when she got off. I told her exactly where I was and even though I wouldn't say it, I needed her here. I sat in that spot for hours crying and needing someone to give me what my man couldn't. I woulda sat in the street all night waiting for someone to hold me. I just couldn't get over what I'd lost. I expected Jasmine to come so I waited until my mother scooped me into her arms and carried me home.

"It's okay Michelle, mama got you. It's gone be okay because I got you." She said as I cried into her breast like a small child. She never would let me go. That night I slept in my mother's arms and that's when I realized she was the only friend I needed.

I didn't return to school any that week. I did all I could to help prepare Kevin's home going. MyKing was more supportive than anybody and he earned my respect within that week. Ironically his bitch just made me want to snap her fucking neck. She was supposed to be my friend but when it came to her being there for me she never would show up. It changed my whole perspective and just made me hate her. After all I'd gone through, her lack of support changed me. Jasmine was no friend of mine.

Tevin, MyKing and I made all of the arrangements and when the funeral rolled around I dreaded it. I had a whole week to get my mind right, but I still wasn't ready. I just wanted him back. My mother escorted me to the front of the church where Kevin's body lay peacefully in the silver casket. Jazz music played in the background as his brothers entered the church behind me. My-King's dreads swung as he pulled Tevin's drunk ass behind him. If this wasn't such a sad day I might've laughed. I noticed Mya behind him with the car seat and chuckled inside at the thought of Jasmine's absence. If she was still my friend, I might've warned her about losing her nigga but since I was about to bury mine, I didn't give a fuck. I sat right next to his baby mama and didn't think nothing of it.

The church was packed to capacity and there was a line of people standing up in the back of the church. They closed the casket after the viewing and proceeded along with the service. Someone sang a solo then the pastor got up to do the eulogy. I cried the whole time with my mother's arms wrapped around me. People cried, but for the most part the service was uplifting and positive until it was time for people to speak. This yellow bitch switches her pregnant ass to the mic with a face full of tears. I got an uneasy feeling the moment I saw her because I didn't know her.

"I just wanted to say…I enjoyed the time I spent with Kevin and I'm glad I'll always have a piece of him." She cried dramatically as she rubbed her swollen belly. I gasped as she insinuated Kevin was the father of her unborn child. Fire shot through my veins as I got up to beat the fuck out of shorty before she could sit down. Mya grabbed me to hold me back and the whispers after that just made me want to disappear. A guy got up after that and said some positive things, but my mind wouldn't let me forget the chick who'd gotten up and crushed my whole relationship in front of everyone. I was hurt, and I wanted to ask Kevin a thousand questions. I looked up at the silver casket and the fact I couldn't ask him only made me angry at him. I stood up as the soloist belted his eyes is on the sparrow and made my way towards the outside of the church. I opened the door and cried as the cold snowflakes hit my face. I needed to feel them because I was so hot with anger. Why the fuck would he do this to me?" I asked myself as I thought about the same thing happening to Jasmine.

"Aye," MyKing said as he walked up on me outside the church. I scolded him because I knew he knew about the bitch. I cried angrily.

"Don't do that g. You know Kev loved you. I know he did. Don't let some bitch who ain't mean shit to him fuck up your last chance to see him." He said seriously.

"You knew about this?" I asked angrily.

"Nah, she lying. He woulda told me if he had a baby on the way.

That bitch wasn't shit to him." He said easily.

"He fucked with her?" I had to know.

"Before you. He told me when he thought you were pregnant. I'm telling you that bitch a damn liar. Don't let that hoe fuck your head up. Kevin was better than me. That's not his baby and he woulda told me if it was. Don't do this to him. Fuck her. He loved you and that's all that matters. You gone regret it if you let her ruin this goodbye for you. He doesn't deserve this." He said seriously and although I had some doubts about the girl MyKing was right. It was my name in the obituary and it was understood I was his girl. MyKing walked me back into the church and I held my head up. I walked back towards the front of the church only stopping momentarily to slap the shit out the pregnant bitch. As soon as I did MyKing told her she had to leave, and the service resumed as it should of from the start. My last memory of Kevin was him laying in the silver casket on top of the most comfortable looking white pillow. He was dressed perfectly as his hands crossed in front of him. I touched his cold hands as my tears fell into the casket. "I love you, Kevin," I said out loud as My-King stood to my right with his hand pressed against my back. I didn't want to see him be placed into the ground, but I felt like he was at peace. He deserved that.

CHAPTER TWENTY-TWO: FROM BAD TO WORSE

Candice

It had been two weeks since my boyfriend's funeral. I was still devastated and my whole world was gloom. I felt like a part of me was buried when he was. I died the moment he did. I could no longer breathe. I wanted to be with him still. I felt like we'd just gotten to the point where we really loved each other. I had finally got him to act right after fucking with him for almost two years and now he was gone. The shit was so unfair. It still felt like it was a bad dream. Only I couldn't wake up. The bus stopped in front of the school and I got off dreading having to go. I walked into the building amongst others, but I just felt like I was by myself. After being missing from school since the day he was killed, I didn't even feel like I'd fit anymore. I still didn't want to go back but if I miss another day, I wouldn't graduate. There were only a few weeks left so I gathered myself and came to school. I went to my locker trying my best to focus on anything but Kevin and his blood in that street. He promised he'd come back and I'm still waiting on him to do what he said he would. I closed my locker and saw King. He smiled when he saw me.

"Wassup Candice. Why you ain't ride with me this morning? I know you saw me text you." He said before he gave me a hug. I needed it and I appreciated the support King had shown since the shit went down. He never seemed to like me before, but he had my back like nobody else. Throughout this whole nightmare, I have been able to lean on him for the motivation to even get out the bed. He texts and checks up on me every day to make sure I'm okay. I saw his text message, but I knew Jasmine was riding and I ain't want to be nowhere near her ass. I still ain't over how she completely abandoned me. She told me she was coming to me the night of Kevin's death but never showed up. And I hadn't heard from her since. She never even tried to get in touch with me to see how I was. Friends don't do that to friends and I quickly realized Jasmine was not my friend. All this time I believed she was capable. I've never been so wrong in my life.

"Yeah, I saw...just ain't wanna ride with Jasmine," I said aloud.

"Mann please tell me what's going on? She won't even talk to me...Lately, I just can't get through to her. What's up?" He asked seriously.

"That's your girl. That ain't got shit to do with me." I said easily. He shook his head in confusion.

"That's your best friend. What happened?" he asked.

"I thought she was...but she hadn't reached out to me since Kevin died. She doesn't give a damn about me." I told him.

"I think Kevin's death is what's got her tweaking though. She's in denial, she doesn't believe he's dead..." He said seriously as the warning bell rang.

"Well, he is..." I said before I walked away to go to class. He always walked her to class anyway. It was nothing he could say to convince me that she cared.

The day just aggravated me. I hated the looks of pity people gave me whenever I made eye contact. I didn't need them to feel sorry for me. I lost my man. I just needed him. I entered the lunch room with my head down. Things had changed. Food no longer had a taste…I wasn't interested in eating. I just wanted to be left alone. I glanced over at King for a second as he waved me over. Jasmine sat in front of him picking at her food. I shook my head no and sat at my table alone. I decided I didn't need her. I drifted off into my own thoughts before they were interrupted. "Wassup Candice?" she started before she smiled. He hair was laid like always and she smelled of Victoria secrets bombshell. Her hazel eyes glistened like she owned the world.

"Wassup. "I spoke even though I didn't like her bougie ass.

"Look, I know we don't see eye to eye all the time, but I just wanted to offer my deepest condolences for your loss. I know what it feels like to lose a boyfriend. I understand chick." She stated.

"Thanks…" I said as looked up at her quizzingly. I was trying to find her angle because she always had one. She wasn't the type to just feel for somebody else. When she sat down in front of me I got confused. I looked around to make sure I wasn't tripping. Surely my eyes were deceiving me. I caught Jasmine's eye and she wore a look of surprise when she realized Val was sitting across from me. It was the first reaction I'd gotten from the bitch since Kevin died. It sparked something in me that made me want to smile. Instead of telling Val to get her phony ass on, I decided to talk to her. I loved the fact Jasmine seemed bothered by the exchange. Val became a friend of mine at that moment because we had one thing in common. Neither of us liked Jasmine.

MyKing

I was angry about the death of my brother. They had taken my best friend away from me. I wanted to retaliate like everybody else, but Tevin took revenge to a whole nother level. A month had gone by and he laid down any nigga that repped P-Town. The heat started to draw our way so much we could barely operate out our spot. There was never a peaceful night as he assisted the city's murder rate increase. We met in our own territory to keep the bullshit to a minimum. Tevin was drunk talking shit as always. Lately, that's all he ever did. After Kevin's funeral, I realized it was a problem. He was unreliable when it came to business and that shit wasn't cool. Imagine me trying to run shit alone without any help. I wasn't feeling asking other niggas to step up, but I had no choice when I realized Tevin would get me killed. Our connect wasn't shit to play with and even though our weight was small compared to a lot of other niggas, I'm sure he'd check the both of us just the same. I didn't even have time to mourn Kevin with the bullshit that followed his murder. Tevin swore he'd killed everyone involved and I believed him. However, the drugs and alcohol were a problem. He ran around high as I kite most times. He would drink until he passed out. All I could see was him dying just like Kev. I knew if I ain't do something I'd go down with him.

"Tevin...bro you gotta stop this shit...you gone get yourself killed." I started as he stared at me drunkenly. He smiled before he spoke.

"Nigga shut the fuck up, I can handle myself." He laughed.

"Tev, what happened?" I asked hoping he'd slip up.

"Don't matter, I killed them, niggas." He slurred.

"You gotta stop the drugs and shit. It ain't gone bring him back." I said as I looked at him seriously. He stopped laughing and a frown replaced the smile.

"That's the only way I can sleep at night. Them was my bullets and he took them. I know they were mine." He scrunched his face as tears rolled down his cheeks.

"What the fuck did you do?" I asked again. The fact I didn't know made me question our brotherhood.

"I did a lot of fucked up shit that night. You wouldn't believe me if I told you." He said before he got up, tucked his pistol, and left me sitting there wondering how the shit happened. I dropped my head in my hands and took a deep breath. My world was falling to pieces around me. I didn't know what to do and the only people I knew could steer me in the right direction was dead. I got up and went towards home. Where Jasmine stayed locked in her room. Ever since Kevin got killed she had been a completely different girl. She quit her job. She doesn't fuck with Candice. And she won't talk to me. I felt like she ain't want me around her most times. Whenever I touched her, she either tweaked or came up with some bullshit excuse about why I shouldn't touch her. Things were not the same and the hardest part was not knowing what the problem was. I didn't know why Kevin died and I don't know why Jasmine is so upset about it. If I hadn't known my brother I would've sworn Kevin and Jasmine had some shit going on behind my back. That's how she was acting. I had to fight that theory every time it came to me.

I tried to do things we talked about before the bad shit happened but nothing I did helped. I even took her to buy her dream prom dress and even though she got exactly what she wanted she still wasn't herself. She never allowed our relationship to go back to the way it was. After that night, I'd been stuck with somebody I don't even know. I couldn't honestly say I wanted to be with her like this. But I loved the hell out of the girl I got to know before. That memory is the only thing keeping us together. I can only hope it won't fade away.

I pulled up to the building with a low heart. I was down and even though I had a little money I'd never felt so broke. I was tired of carrying everybody else's burdens. I was tired of being the good guy. I needed some peace and I was grateful I always had a person I could go to for it. Regardless of what was wrong and what I lacked, she could always see the good in me. And I knew she loved me. Every time I held her in my arms or heard her voice I knew she was my light. I didn't understand why she was created until after all this shit happened. I needed her and I made sure she was included in every decision I made. I knocked on the door and Mya opened it with a smile. I walked in and she hugged me after closing the door behind her.

"Hey, I'm so glad to see you! I need a break!" she said easily as she quickly gathered her things and headed towards the bathroom. I chuckled as Jasmya welled from her crib. She had strong lungs and I could tell she'd been at it for a while. I washed my hands and went towards the crib to pick her up.

"What's wrong with daddy baby? Why are you so upset?" I asked as she quickly went mute at the sound of my voice. I smiled because the moment I touched her that despair I was feeling went away. It was swallowed and replaced by a joy deeper than the dimples decorating her bright pink face. She stared at me quietly as I stared back in amazement. I placed kisses all over her and told her how much I loved her. I held her to my chest kissing the top of her head until she fell asleep.

"No, you put her little-spoiled ass back in that crib. I'm not about to sit up and hold her like that!" Mya told me seriously.

"All you gotta do is talk to her. She just wants some attention." I chuckled.

"No, she just be wanting her damn daddy and I'm about to start letting her go right on over there with you when she be hollering like I'm in here tryna kill her!" she stated smartly.

"Forreal?" I asked excitedly.

"Yeah but only after me and your lil girlfriend have us a talk." She said slyly.

"Man whatever! I'll be back tomorrow after I get my hair twisted." I told her as I got up to leave.

"Goodnight!" she sang easily before she shut the door behind me. I got back in my truck with a smile on my face. Everything I felt before I went to see my daughter was gone. That's why I called her my light. I walked into Jasmine apartment with enough light for both of us. Jasmine needed it too. It was like ever since Kevin died she carried a dark cloud around like a flag. I figure having Jasmya around would brighten her day the same way she has mine. Hopefully, I could make that happen soon. I thought before I showered and went into the room I made my own. After Kevin died, Jasmine had become uncomfortable with me sleeping in the bed with her. I didn't trip. I just bought a few things and made her mother's old room mine. After I got used to having my own space again, I was alright with the arrangement. She seemed to like it that way so I went with it. Only sometimes it bothered me to know she no longer needed my touch. I lay awake at night trying to figure out what happened. The only thing I could come up with is the fact I became a father. Before that happened, everything was good. I tried to make the best out of every event that happened after that. We went places and celebrated each others birthdays together. My obligation to the streets prevented me from being with her as much as I wanted to be, but I did the best I could to make her happy

Jasmine

I was alone. Even when there were people around me I still felt like I was all by myself. Nobody could understand what I felt. It was lonely and no matter how many times MyKing asked what was wrong, I couldn't tell him. Beyond the fact he wouldn't believe me, I didn't know how. I couldn't tell him how I felt without explaining why. I just wanted to forget it. I kept my mouth closed to avoid it slipping out. I felt lonely, but I didn't want anyone around me. I can't explain how that makes any sense, but I would rather be by myself. Not because I didn't need the attention I craved so much from MyKing. But because I felt disgusting. I felt unworthy of it. I felt like dog shit under the bottom of the nastiest pair of shoes to exist. No matter how many times I washed, I still felt nasty. Whenever I had to be around people I could sense they knew. Everybody could see me nude and I was ashamed. I hated my body and I hated being me. I felt like a prisoner trapped in a filthy shell. I was on display for the world to see. There were so many things going on around me my mind ran constantly. Even though I was nothing but a ball of rare emotions. I still felt numb. It had been nearly two months, but I was still emotionally exerted. I just didn't know how to be after everything that happened.

"Bae, damn you're killing me. It's cold as fuck in here." MyKing said as he pulled his hair back into a ponytail.

"Oh..I needed some air, I'd gotten nauseous. You can turn the air off since we're about to leave." I told him as I pulled my bag from the couch and headed out the door first. He locked the door behind him before walking towards me at the elevator and we exited the building together. It was getting warm outside and the sun shined despite the darkness I carried around. I jumped in the passenger seat of the truck and made myself comfortable. MyKing strapped his seatbelt and took into the street like today would be his best day. I took out my phone and played Tetris a while until he stopped at a red light abruptly. Now the sudden stop wasn't unusual considering the ticket lights notoriously known in Chicago. But the stop brought about a rush of nausea that sent everything I'd eaten for breakfast right back up to my mouth. I quickly pushed the door open and emptied my stomach right out onto the street.
"Damn! What the fuck Jas? You aight?" he asked with a disgusted look on his face. He rubbed my back and I pushed his hand away.
"Hands-on the wheel" I spat.
"But the car ain't even moving. What's wrong Jasmine? Talk to me. I closed the door and he pulled away from the light.

"Yeah...I just don't feel good. Had to have been something I ate." I told him as I swished water between my mouth and spit it out into a cup. I felt like shit. I was disgusted with myself, but his questioning gaze made me straighten up in my seat. He took his eyes off me and starred at the street in front of him. It was an awkward silence and I didn't plan to speak again.

"We don't have to do this today. We have another two weeks to get ready." He said.

"No, might as well get this over with," I told him seriously as he drove the rest of the way to the store. We arrived at the boutique I purchased my prom dress from. The alterations were done last month and now it was time for me to pick it up. The final fitting was supposed to be exciting and I'd imagined this moment since I was a kid. Prom is a big deal up north and even though I was raised in the boonies, I still looked forward to bringing the heat to the senior prom. I purchased a long gold and hot pink mermaid styled dress with a high split and the entire back out. The shimmering gold embellishments were simply gorgeous. I loved everything about the dress when I saw it and even though I wasn't feeling my best then it brightened my day. MyKing was over excited to see me wearing the dress and he sat on the other side of the door encouraging me to step out. Only I pulled the dress on and realized there was a problem with the way it fit. I walked out of the dressing room into the mirrored sitting area where MyKing sat. He smiled when he saw me.

"Dammmnnnn. That dress sexy as shit. You gone kill it, bae, you look good." He said easily. I smiled for two seconds before the seamstress came back to help me. The look on her face wiped the smile clean off mine.

"Oh honey...that fit is all wrong. When did we do your measurements? She asked as she frowned in confusion.

"Last month. Couldn't have been but three weeks ago, if that" I told her as she tugged on a part of the dress to see where she'd made the mistake.

"No, that's impossible. I must have written them wrong because I'm not convinced you've gained so much weight in just a few weeks...Can you even breathe?" she asked jokingly. I didn't laugh. She actually hurt my feelings and when she realized she tried to smooth it over.

"Oh honey, I'm joking. Is it your cycle that's causing the bloating in your midsection? I don't remember you having much of a tummy. Just a whole lot of behind back there." She chuckled to herself. I looked up into the mirror as she tugged on parts of the dress and wrote every so often. I stared at the beautiful gown in the mirror and at myself and a pain so deep ripped through my chest I thought I'd pass out. I stood there staring in the mirror silently as hot tears spilled down my face. My King's smile faded and he rose to approach me.

"Bae...what's wrong? Don't cry. She was just playing. She can fix it. Can't you fix it?" He asked her seriously.

"Of course, honey! I'm sorry. I didn't mean any harm, aww don't cry." She said sincerely as she placed her paper down to hug me. Only I didn't like to be touched and I pushed her away the moment she brought her body in for a hug.

"No, no thank you!" I told her sternly as I held my hands up in front of me to keep her away. My sudden hostility made her hesitant and she apologized again.

"I really am sorry. I didn't mean any harm. I can fix this in no time if you allow me." She said humbly.

"No! I'm not going to the prom. Forget it!" I cried as I stepped down from the mirror and made my way back into the dressing room. MyKing attempted to console me but I snatched away from him ashamed of my body. I knew exactly what they thought of me. How they all would look at me at the prom and I wasn't going. Fuck it! I quickly took off the dress and pulled my clothes back on. As soon as I was completely covered, I sat on the small bench in the dressing room and buried my face in my hands. I let out the tears that were clouding my chest and balled right then. I knew exactly what this was. After I cried a while MyKing came to knock on the door.

"Come on bae, I promise we can fix it. I thought you looked amazing in the dress just the way it is. I can't wait to be standing next to you in my Tux." He said. I could hear his smile through the door. I quickly wiped my face and pulled the door open to leave.

"No…I'm not going. You can still go though…" I told him as I stepped away from him as he stood there completely confused. I walked towards the door because the room was starting to close in on me. I just wanted to leave.

"I don't mind giving you a refund. I'm really sorry the dress didn't fit but if you change your mind I won't hesitate to make the corrections." She said genuinely.

"No, it's alright. Keep your money. The dress is beautiful. Just how I pictured it. Give it to someone who will wear it and appreciate it as much as I do." I said as I turned and walked right out of the boutique. I waited for MyKing to unlock the truck and got in as soon as he did. He jumped in and turned towards me.

"Jas… I will do whatever you need me to do to make you happy. I don't know what's wrong but you been tweaking lately. Tell me what you need." He said seriously.

"I just want to go home." I cried.

"Okay, I'm bout to take you home now." He said before he pulled off into the street. He didn't say another word and I could tell by the look on his face he was tired of me. I was tired of myself. I cried the whole way home. He pulled up to the front of our building and let me out.

"I gotta run, I'll be back later. Call me if you need me.

"Be safe," I mumbled before I shut the door and walked up the walkway counting every step I took towards the elevator. I end up having to walk up the pissy stairwell and I was winded and angry by the time I'd gotten to my floor. I opened my door and walked in sick with grief. I slid down the back of the door and pulled out my phone. I quickly dialed Bebe for help. Although we'd not known each other long, I realized she was the closest friend I had. Especially since Candice suddenly wanted to be friends with Val. It hurt to know our friendship was over because I wasn't going to be fake with her. Her man was an evil, nasty nigga that deserved death and I couldn't be the friend to lie to her and pretend she loss someone special. He was sinister and even though he hadn't popped up again, I know he's lingering around here. I could still feel him in every touch I feel. I am reminded of him with everything I do. I couldn't be the friend Candice needed but Val was a far cry from that too.

Hello….Helloooo! Jas!" Bebe sang aggressively.

"Bebe?" I asked confused.

"Ah yeah…you called me. Why you just holding the phone? Wassup?" she asked.

"Oh…I guess I forgot I was calling you. Where are you?" I asked.

"Out. What's wrong?" She asked knowingly.

"Can you please come over here? I..think somethings wrong." I told her.

"What? What is it?" She asked.

"Have you ever been pregnant before?" I asked her nervously.

"Yeah…What does that…Wait, I told you to go to the doctor. You promised you would. They have medicine that prevents pregnancy after rape. You said you went!" she said seriously.

"I tried…they were just asking too many questions and I got nervous and left. I didn't go back after that." I revealed.

"Damn, you think you're pregnant?" She asked seriously.

"I hope not." I sniffled.

"I'm on my way. "She said before she hung-up quickly. I got up to turn the air back on and wait for her arrival.

When she got to me she wore the look of anger. I knew it was at me but under the circumstances, I understood why.

"Here go take this test real quick." She said as she handed me the pink box out of her purse. I didn't object. Instead, I walked into the bathroom and read the directions on the box. After I urinated on the stick, I threw it back in the box. I didn't need a test to tell me something I already knew. I hadn't seen a period since right before Kevin raped me. I was sick and gaining weight faster than Flo joe. After two months, I couldn't ignore it anymore. I stepped out of the bathroom and handed her the box back. I got into my bed and cried. It didn't matter what I wanted or what I did. I was doomed anyway. Bebe reached into the box and pulled the test out to look at it.

"Damn...G, what are we going to do?" She asked. I shook my head and no words would come out. Just tears.

"You need to just tell your man. I don't see this getting better no matter what we come up with. Either choice is gone cost something. All imma say is I'm here for you." She said seriously.

"I want an abortion! There are no other options. I'd rather die than have a baby by him. Just help me get rid of it." I begged.

"Okay...I know just the place." she sighed.

CHAPTER TWENTY-THREE: TIMES PAIN

Jasmine

I waited until that following Monday to go see a doctor. When MyKing got up for school I was sick as a dog. I convinced him to go without me because I was ill. I watched him and Candice load into his truck and leave before I left right behind them to meet Bebe at the clinic. I rode the bus the whole way there expecting to have the parasite removed from me immediately. After a two hour wait, I was finally asked to follow a nurse to be checked. After running what I assumed to be standard test and a billion questions Bebe and I were sat in a small room to wait on the doctors. I was instructed to remove my clothing and put on this thin paper gown. The moment I had come out of my pants the cold air hit my ass and reminded me of how nasty I must look. I glanced at Bebe who didn't even blink. It was something in Bebe that had made her completely immune to feelings. That bitch never sweated. She was always hard. The situation was so scandalous we sat quietly in our own thoughts. I kept thinking I'd die before this was all over.

The doctor came in with a smile despite the displeasure I displayed on my face. She shook my hand happily and introduced herself to me and Bianca.

"I'm Dr. King. How can I help you today?" she asked. Her chocolate skin caked up with makeup and perspiration. She was extremely short, and her salt and pepper hair color convinced me she was older than she looked.

"I'm pregnant," I stated dreadfully, and I figured she'd catch my complete disgust and offer to help me end it right then.

"Yes...I did have the nurse run another test to be sure and you are definitely pregnant. I understand your last period was about two months ago, right?" She asked easily.

"Yes." I nodded.

"Okay, I would like to do a quick exam and we can go over options after I've figured out where we are. That alright?" she asked nicely.

"Sure," I responded as her nurse assisted her with giving me a full exam. Bebe sat quietly in the chair to my right as solid as they came. She pressed and examined my breast first which were tender and sensitive to touch. I winced as she came across my raw nipples. Her expression wasn't clear to me as she moved towards my abdomen.

She carefully pressed and rubbed my belly as if she was looking for something. It felt weird and the look on her face made me nervous.

"You sure it's only been two months since you've had a period?" she asked again as her nurse looked on knowingly.

"Positive. It's been two months." I stated plainly.

"Alright." She stopped suddenly and moved towards the edge of the table I was on top of. "Move your bottom all the way to the edge so I can take a look." She said easily. I did and even though I was uncomfortable I hoped this would be over soon. She spread something cold on her rubber gloves before I felt her fingers enter my vagina. It wasn't painful, but I kept my eyes closed to avoid having to make eye contact with Bebe. I knew better then to wait as long as I did to get checked out after what happened, but my fear is what kept me away. I was simply afraid.

"Okay, I would like to go ahead and do an ultrasound today. I am concerned about the size of your belly with you only being about eight weeks. You look to be much further along. Is it possible you remember when you think you conceived?" She asked. "Yes. It was two months ago. I hadn't had sex before or after." I stated aggravated that she kept asking me the same fucking question over and over.

"Okay, no problem. Let's go ahead and do the ultrasound then." She stated as she removed her soiled gloves and replaced them with new ones. I scooted up and laid flat on my back as she spread the cold jelly over my bloated belly.

"Okay, let's see what we can see." She encouraged herself. I didn't give a fuck what she saw. I knew this nasty muthafucka was coming out of me regardless. Just waiting on that part of the conversation. She placed this machine handle that reminded me of roll-on deodorant over my belly and rolled across the lubricant like it was fun. She used one hand to type and one to roll. The tapping she did on the keyboard calmed me. I started to count every time she hit the keys.

"Oh...I see." She smiled like she was amused.

"See what?" I asked seriously.

"You're having twins!" she smiled widely. I sat up off the table to look at the screen.

"Bullshit, I want these muthafuckas out of me right now!" I spat angrily. She had me fucked up if she thought I wanted twins. I didn't want one baby by that muthafucka, let alone two.

"Oh..well I'm sorry. I didn't realize you were considering termination...is that what you're saying?" she asked as if she herself was disappointed.

"Yes. I don't want them. Please take them out today. I'll pay you however much it cost. I need an abortion!" I cried.

"Well..If that's what you want, I can have one scheduled but we won't be able to do it today. There are a few preparations we must follow before that can take place.

"Fine. Let's start preparing today." I stated and meant it. I got home mad that I was still pregnant! I could not believe my luck. Fucking Twins! I yelled as I slammed shit around just for the hell of it.

"God, what did I do to deserve this shit! Why must you torture me?" I cried out in pure pain. By the time I'd finished my tantrum I was too exhausted to do anything else. I put on a big ass T-Shirt and jumped my fat ass back into the bed. I planned to sleep the rest on the day away.

I heard a noise in my room and popped up to find Candice standing there. Her presence only bothered me because I thought of Kevin.

"What are you doing here?" I asked seriously. We hadn't talked lately and it was suspicious that she randomly ended up in my bedroom.

"Oh..King asked me to prom and he needed me to stop by and pick up some cash." She stated easily.

"Okay...how are you?" I asked nervously.

"I'm doing better. What about you?" she asked almost instantly.

"Alive." I retorted before I eased back into a more comfortable position and closed my eyes. I didn't want to talk anymore.

"Well, Bye! She said before stepping out of my room. "Bitch" she added under her breath. I didn't react. Sometimes it doesn't even make sense to do so. I already knew we were no longer friends. I didn't even understand the friendship that had seemingly developed between her and MyKing but I was too fucked up at the moment to address it. Fuck her! I thought.

On the day of my scheduled appointment, I couldn't get in touch with Bebe at all. I was nervous as shit. I did the whole I'm sick trick with MyKing and waited until he left to make my way to the bus stop. I called her the whole ride to the hospital, but she never answered. I was already freaked out at the fact the procedure could not be done at the clinic I went to for it. I actually had to go to the hospital for an outpatient procedure. I was scared as shit. I walked in and filled out any additional paperwork I needed too and waited to be called. The whole process was really simple but my nerves were shot. I'd had to change my attitude completely by the time they let me back and asked me to undress. I convinced myself that the seeds inside of me were not a part of me. I cleared my conscious before I placed on the paper gown and rested on the cloth table in the room. All I could focus on was getting my body back. I wanted to rid my body of the constant annoyance of being pregnant. I was bloating and gaining weight quickly. My nipples were sore and raw and I had to pee more than I could stand. Not to mention the sickness associated with these demon seeds. I just wanted them out of me. I've never felt more peaceful than when they administered that drug and put me into the deepest sleep I'd ever been in.

I was back home, in my old estate, in my old bed and I could smell my mother cooking all the way from my room. I stretched, got up, and slid into my slippers before jogging down the stairs. Daddy was in his office with a newspaper in front of him.

"Hey, Daddy!" I spoke, and he looked up excitedly.

"Hey Princess!" he smiled as I kept moving towards the kitchen. Everything was right in place as I entered the kitchen and my mother in jewels and a full face of makeup was fixing breakfast.

"Hey Jazzy! I thought you were gone stay in the bed all morning! The boys are hungry momma!" I smiled but looked around to see who she was referring too.

"What boys?" I asked confused.

"You're babies." She said matter of factly.

"Babies! I don't have a baby!" I screeched.

"Nope..you have two!" She stated. When I looked into her eyes, the rest of the mansion faded away. She stood in front of me with missing teeth in a raggedy T-shirt and nasty jogging pants.

"Mommy!" I cried.

"You are the mother now. Best thing in the world, ain't it?" she asked before I jumped up out of my sleep. I tried to raise up off of the bed to see where I was, but it felt like I was being tied down. I had an Iv attached to me and for a split second, I couldn't remember what I was doing.

"Its alright, you're okay. Everything went smoothly. We gave you medication to numb your lower half. You shouldn't be feeling any discomfort." The nurse said.

"Oh..I'm not pregnant anymore?" I asked.

"No ma'am, we successfully removed them." She whispered. I laid back thankfully and rested there until I had to empty my bladder. The fact that I could feel my bladder shoulda been a clear indication the drugs had worn off. However, that didn't register until I sat up and the soreness in my midsection sent me straight back down. I moaned at the crampy feeling I had.

"You are going to be feeling a little discomfort as the medication wears off. We will send you home with a prescription and you can leave as soon as your ride gets here." She said easily. I attempted to move my legs off the bed and it was torture. I felt like I was on the worse day of my cycle and I could feel it everywhere.

"Slow down, Hun. You must move slowly. Let me help." She offered but her touching me caused me more discomfort. I hated to be touched.

"No! I can do it. I have to use the restroom" I stated pushing her hands away. I stepped off the side of the bed and nearly hit the floor. I grabbed on to the side of the bed and she grabbed me and helped me back unto the bed.

"Um huh.. are you going to continue to be hard headed or let me help you to the washroom?" She asked. I stared at her but didn't respond because I did need her help. She assisted me into the stall in the bathroom just right of the room I was in and helped me pull down the diaper draws someone had put on me. She backed out to allow me the privacy I needed. In the underwear I had on was the longest hospital pad I'd ever seen. I was disgusted at the sight of blood and the smell of antiseptic. I felt used and yucky and I emptied my bladder into a fit of tears. I just cried, and I wasn't even sure what I was crying for. It seemed something in my heart had awakened and for a split second, I regretted what I had just done. I had no desire to have Kevin's babies but the idea of ridding my own flesh made me sick. I didn't think my life would go back to normal if I would've kept them but, at this moment, I knew I'd never be the same. I had no intention on ever having an abortion again.

I sat in the waiting area of the hospital's main entrance to wait on my "ride". I called Bebe, but her phone was going straight to voicemail at that point. I didn't know who else to call besides MyKing and I wouldn't because I couldn't explain to him what I was doing. So, I sat there contemplating calling a taxi before I heard my name.

"Jasmine?" She asked happily as she carried the car seat like a pro.

"Hi," I stated plainly as I looked away to avoid eye contact.

"Oh, come on, don't be like that! What are you doing here?" she asked. I quickly looked towards her afraid of what she might assume.

"I've been sick as hell lately. I just got to the point I couldn't take it no more." I told her.

"Hmm yeah…I know that feeling? Are you waiting on MyKing to pick you up?" She asked.

"Umm yes, but he hadn't answered yet. I'm so tired I'm about to call a cab." I told her.

"Come on, you can ride with me. I'm on my way home. Jasmya just had a check-up." She said. I looked at her and then down at the car seat she'd placed in front of me and shook my head. All I could think about was what I'd just done.

"Fine," I said as I stood carefully and followed her out. When we had gotten to her car she unlocked it and placed the baby in the base of the seat.

"You still want to fight?" she asked as soon as she closed the door. I sighed miserably.

"Yeah, just not right now…" I told her.

"Okay, just checking." She chuckled before we both got into her car and she pulled off.

MyKing

Just when I thought things were getting better shit got worse. Tevin had gotten arrested for driving under the influence which quickly turned into murder when they retrieved the guns from Kevin's car. He was held without bond and I was mad as a muthafucka. Plus, being back in our territory meant I was losing money. Shit got bad real quick and I knew if I didn't come up with a plan I was gone be in some real trouble. I had stashed some cash and figured if everything went left I'd have enough to run it back. However, I wasn't a drug dealer. I only did the shit to back my brothers. One was dead, and one was going to prison. It didn't matter what I could've done for Tev at that point. That nigga was going down regardless. I ain't like it but I figured he was better off there than dead. I didn't know what the fuck I was gone do forreal. I was winging it like a muthafucka. My first thought was to quit. I was satisfied with the money I made and thankful I wasn't already fucked up. I had done enough to be in deep shit by now. I was just always as careful as I could be. And I had brothers protecting me from the bullshit. Now, I was alone with a gang of niggas trying to kill me because of what Tevin had done. Not only had he waged war in retaliation to Kevin's death but we moved right into these niggas territory like some fucking dummies. No amount of money was worth what the shit had caused. It wasn't no telling what else that nigga had done in P-town before getting arrested. I knew the first thing that needed to be done had to start in P-town. Against my better judgment, I went to the trap. I had left something there that I needed. In my mind, I was going to walk away and operate as we did before upping our load. I didn't like the idea of trying to roll alone but I figured I could control my fate a little better if I took shit back home. P-Town wasn't my shit and I should've spoken up when that idea was brought to the table. I wanted the money, but Kevin might still be alive had I just said no. I knew better than that. "In any war, somebody has to die," I thought as I crept into P-town like a thief in the night. I got an eerie feeling in my gut the moment I got on the block and I had been through too much shit lately to ignore my gut. I passed up the trap and drove thru the alley. I thought no one would see me if I went through the back door. I planned to collect my shit and take my ass home. I pulled my truck into the backyard lawn and stepped through the high grass and broken concrete. The sun hadn't shined in a long time but it wasn't dark out yet. I touched the butt of my pistol to calm my racing heart. I didn't even know what had me so anxious. I ran up the stairs and opened the back door to the trap. It was musty as fuck inside and I quickly ran through to retrieve what I'd come for and vacated for good. I never intended to be there again. I stepped off the back porch and got to the last step before I realized that musty smell had followed me out. It was rank like spoiled meat and I was sniffing around to see where it was coming from. I was finna say fuck it until I peeped somebody propped up on the side of the house. That was my cue to vacate and I quickly stepped towards my truck. I tucked my shit in the glove box and walked around to my side. I jumped in and pulled out the yard, but I couldn't pull off. The nerves in my stomach would never let me sleep. "Fuck!" I said as I exhaled loudly and stepped back out the truck. I walked back over towards that stank smell and right up to the slump on the side of the trap. I covered my nose when the smell had gotten unbearable. I frowned at the thought of being so high a person could shit on themselves. The figure before me was ripe. The clothing hung off the gaunt, ashy, body like they were wet. I couldn't tell if it was a male or female initially because the hair was matted and nasty on top of a nodded head. The body slumped awkwardly in an odd position.

"Aye!" I attempted to break their nod while keeping my mouth closed to keep the funk away from my personal space. They ain't move so I had to step closer and I nudged em with my boot. The body slumped over and fell heavily against the concrete.

"Oh, shi…" I started before tears welled up in my eyes. I stepped closer and squatted before the body that had stiffened in the position it had been locked in against the wall. She had to have been dead for days to smell as bad as she did. I touched her leathery neck to make sure before I dropped the tears that were coming regardless. She was so frail I barely recognized her. I closed my eyes in despair because I couldn't save her.

"Damn Jen..." I said as I quickly wiped my face with an open hand. I stood up sure she'd come here for me and I pulled out my phone to dial the police.

"911, what's your emergency." A lady answered abruptly.

"It's a dead body on the side of a white house on 68th and stone," I said before I hung up and threw up in the grass the moment the thought processed in my head. I got back in my truck. I hated to leave her like I did but I had no choice. I wasn't about to stay and wait for the police to come and catch me with no problem. I had to vacate and dreaded having to go home and tell Jas her mother was never coming back. I could only recall my last words to her being not to come back until she got her shit together. I felt guilty as a muthafucka. I was sick.

Jasmine

I was tired but feeling better than I had been for a while. It had been almost two weeks since I had the abortion and my feelings were getting back to me. I cleaned up the house and even decided I'd cook. MyKing was out as he always was but I was preparing to have dinner done when he got home. We hadn't been spending as much time together lately and it was my fault. I felt flawed after Kevin raped me and I have been trying to mask that ever since. The pregnancy only pushed me further away but somehow, I figured by getting rid of the babies I had gotten a second chance. I was planning to allow him to sleep in my bed tonight. He came in loudly. He almost stomped his way through the apartment. When I looked into his face I knew he found out about what I'd done. I figured Mia had told him about the ride she gave me.

He walked up on me close and my breathing started to fluctuate.

"MyKing...What's wrong?' I asked nervously.

"Sit down Jasmine. Let's talk." He said as he shook his head back and forth. He grabbed my hand caringly and pulled me toward the couch. He sat down and pulled me onto his lap. I looked at him with tears gathering in my eyes. He knew! He pulled me closer to him and wiped his face. His eyes watered, and I couldn't take the pressure anymore.

"Bae...your mother is gone. I'm sorry. I tried to help her, but I couldn't. She died." He said as he held me tighter.

"No...no she...what happened? She was supposed to get better... No..I moaned as the tears fell from my face. I buried my face in his chest and sobbed. He held on to me and let me cry and I cried myself to sleep wrapped into his arms.

When MyKing took me to claim the body she looked horrible. She died of a drug overdose but her whole body told a story. From her broken off mangy looking afro to the needle tracks that ran from her neck to the crust that accompanied her feet. I looked over my mother's decomposing body and felt numb. She had died like a stray dog in the street. The woman who had taught me to love myself lay cold and ugly before me. My heart broke to admit their Jane Doe was indeed my mother. However, after they released her, MyKing handled everything else like the guy I fell in love with. He paid to have her buried classily and we had a private burial. It seemed he held me the entire time and I needed it. I was hurt but I needed him again. He was there in a way I hadn't felt since the beginning. I realized the love I had gained for him was real. He was the love of my life. He made the pain bearable.

CHAPTER TWENTY-FOUR: A NIGHT TO REMEMBER

Candice

I was happy when King asked me to prom. I didn't understand his explanation as to why he wasn't taking his bitch, but I was happy about it. I even enjoyed the look on Val's face when I revealed I was going with him. That bitch was jealous. I laughed to myself as I eagerly pulled on my sequin rose gold and nude gown. It had a sexily stitched pattern that ran straight up the front of the dress. The split was high enough to see my rose garter belt and the straps that held my dress together shined like fine jewelry. I was so happy I didn't know what to do. My mother and family all helped dress me while laughing and joking like ole times. It seemed lots of people came out to support the prom sendoff King gave my momma the money to set up. She ordered fried lemon pepper wings and fries and decorated our apartment with balloons and banners. Frankie Beverly and Maze played in the background as Tasha added the final touches onto my made-up face. The dress I chose was perfect and matched King's nude tux to the T. He came into the apartment joyfully as I admired his freshly twisted hair and expensive jewelry. From the shirt he wore under his suit to the socks that sat in a pair of nude Versace Loafers, he matched me head to toe. He smiled the moment he saw me and wrapped his arms around me without hesitation. He didn't give it a thought as his baby mother and Jasmine both stood behind him.

"Dang Candice, you know you look good!" He exclaimed. He handed me the rose and gold wrist corsage proudly and even help me put it on.

"You too!" I said as I adjusted his bow tie. I side eyed Jasmine who didn't mumble a word. She looked pitiful. I looked at her almost feeling bad for what I had planned for her. But the fact that she lost her mother couldn't curve the hate I had for her. I wanted the bitch to suffer and I would see to it that she understood what it felt like to lose her man. I didn't give a shit that she was pregnant.

"Come on let's take some pics!" he said excitedly as he pulled me to him to pose. The cameraman snapped what felt like a thousand shots of us and our family. Even his mother seemed happy to be invited. Right before it was time for us to go he left my side to retrieve his daughter who he held as the cameraman snapped away. He gave her back to her mother and turned towards the couch where his sulking bitch had retreated miserably.

"Come here Bae!" he called, and she pouted his way.

"Come on and take some pics with me." He smiled at her and she perked up at his undivided attention. I couldn't stand her ass, but she was still pretty in her Victoria secret's Pink jumpsuit. She smiled as he held her around her waist. I hated the love he had for her bitch ass.

"You know I love you right?" he asked completely comfortable with everybody hearing him. I could've gagged, and this wench had the audacity to get teary eyed.

"I love you too" she sniffled as he pulled her face towards him to kiss. The moment they did my insides started to boil and I huffed loudly and pulled him towards the door. I realized then Jasmine was getting exactly what I dreamed of with Kevin. King was taking care of her and he'd probably love her more if he knew she was pregnant with his baby. They'd be happy, and I couldn't stand the thought. As much as I cared for King I just could not let him be happy with Jasmine. I knew I had to find a way to fuck their relationship up. I had to.

"We gotta go, King!" I insisted as he chuckled and bid her farewell. He promised he'd be back later, and I had every intention to make sure he broke that promise. The custom painted creme Camaro with peanut butter leather seats surprised me as it sat running and waiting on us to get in.

"Aww, I love it!" I screeched, and he smiled and helped me into the car. After he got me in, he happily jumped into the roofless car instead of opening the door. I laughed as I rode shotgun. My mother and family had come down to wave and the sendoff went well despite Jasmine's presence. We laughed and talked the whole way to the downtown hotel that hosted our high school prom. I was happy. We got to the prom and made one helluva entrance. He literally treated me like Cinderella the whole night and I was grateful. I didn't even think he had it in him. But he turned out to be a completely different nigga than I remembered him. When Kevin was killed he stepped up and had my back. He always tried to cheer me up that way. During our last dance he pulled me close and danced like the night would last forever.

"You really looked beautiful tonight, G.," he said easily.

"You ain't look bad yourself, Prom King." I smile as I glanced at the ridiculous crown that adorned his head. This nigga was a real piece of work. But you couldn't help but love him and I did. Now more than he knew. When it was time to go home he guided me back to our beautifully rimmed carriage and drove into Downtown Chicago like he owned it. I didn't even care that he drove opposite our home. I just road completely satisfied with the day. When he pulled unto the navy pier dock, he parked and helped me out. I followed with no question. He held my hand as we boarded a small boat. The sailor smiled pleasantly as he pulled out onto the open water. I was nervous as a muthafucka. I had never been on a boat and the thought of drowning quickly invaded my head.

"Aye, I know you ain't scared G." he laughed as I tucked myself in a seat as far away from the side as possible.

"Come on, I'm trying to make this special for you. This is some shit Kevin woulda did. Come on." He said with an open hand as he led me to the open edge where the hum of the engine sung, and the view of the Chicago skyline was clearer than it had ever been to me. Here I was floating in Lake Michigan staring at the lights of downtown Chicago.

"Damn its pretty out here," I said as my eyes welled up with tears.

"Word." He said as he pulled me close to him.

"I miss him so much," I admitted.

"Shit me too. In many ways. I'd gladly trade places with him if I could." He said. I believed him and could sense his sincerity.

"Thank you for your support King. Tonight, was a night I'll never forget." I told him as he wiped a tear away.

"Don't mention it. He said as he ordered me a glass of sparkling cider from the waiter that happily handed it to me. I drank it and we talked like best friends. At the moment, I forgot about Jasmine and he hadn't mentioned her the whole night. By the time we got back to the Camaro, I was floating. We road back to the Ps as Jagged edge's promise played amongst us. We arrived home and it was well after midnight. I was sure everyone was asleep. We got on the elevator and I wasn't ready to go home.

"I don't wanna go home yet. You sleepy?" I asked innocently. He looked at me but couldn't fix his mouth to say he was.

"Nah, you can come upstairs." He said easily. The elevator stopped on his floor and he let me out first and I strutted right past Jasmine's apartment and walked next door.

"Where you going? You know I don't be there no more. My mama ain't even there most nights because she be at her nigga house.

"Okay...I don't wanna wake your bitch. I ain't planning to go to sleep no time soon." I smirked.

"Man, you and Jas need to squash that shit." He chuckled shaking his head, but he pulled out the apartment key and opened it anyway. I thought it was obvious what I had planned to do in the apartment. As soon as we walked into his old room, I was all over him. When I kissed his lips, it caught him off guard. He fell back onto the bed and I fell right on to of him. He pushed me back gently, but confusion was all over his face.

"Aye, what the fuck you on, G?" he asked seriously.

"What?" I asked.

"What you on? You drunk cause I coulda swore I told that bitch to give you cider." He said in disbelief.

"No... I'm not drunk...I'm horny!" I smiled nervously. He exhaled loudly and stood to his feet moving away from me.

"Candice, you know it ain't like that with us. You tweaking... This what you came in here to do?" he asked seriously. His tone showed how displeased he was, and it angered me.

"King, are you forreal? I thought...you'd want me as much as I want you." I retorted.

"What? I only took you to prom because my brother couldn't, Jasmine wasn't up to it, and I thought I was being a good dude by stepping in. I ain't never been on that with you shorty. How you think that?" he asked. I was devastated. I could not believe the biggest man hoe of my time was rejecting me. I was so mad I couldn't just walk away.

"You bogus as hell Candice, my bro loved you and you in here tryna fuck me. That's some disloyal hoe shit. Thought you were better than that. Plus, my girl next door. You think imma lose her by fucking you? You tweaking shorty." He said angrily.

"Oh, so that's how you feel. Now I'm a hoe?" I asked pissed off.

"Candice just gone home and go to sleep. I had fun. I won't say shit to Jasmine about this misunderstanding." he said easily.

"I don't give a fuck what you tell that bitch. I'll stomp that baby right out her pregnant ass! She already knows what these hands do!" I spat angrily.

"Baby? Bitch get the fuck out! You don't even know what you talking about." He said cluelessly. I laughed.

"Ha! She ain't tell you about the baby huh?" I laughed. I had peeped the pregnancy test in the trash can I knocked over the day I went to pick up money for prom from King. I figured I'd ruined her chance to tell him about their baby and piss the both of them off. It would have to do since I couldn't break them up like I planned. Realization crossed his face and real anger followed. Before I could even think about my next move King had wrapped both his hands around my neck and squeezed.

"Bitch!" he hissed between clenched teeth. I stumbled back towards the wall as he choked me out angrily. His face contorted seriously, and he didn't even attempt to loosen his grip. When it registered that he was trying to kill me, I started scratching at his arms and hands.

"I...Ca..ntt...Bre..Ki.." I sputtered. He knew and had picked me completely off the floor by my neck. I start to feel faint and at my last attempt to break his trance I started banging my feet against the wall hoping someone heard and came and got the crazy nigga up off me. I ain't understand his sudden hostility. It was a simple argument that should not have resulted in an attempted murder. All I did was tell him he's expecting another baby. I was about to die for that?" I thought as I nearly slipped into unconsciousness.

"Bae, what the fuck are you doing?" Jasmine burst into the room. He let go the moment he heard her voice and tears fell from my eyes as I pulled in as much air as I could. I coughed as my body adjusted. I couldn't move immediately but the moment I could I stood on to my feet and hauled ass out of that apartment.

Jasmine

I watched MyKing off to prom with Candice and I was sad. I hadn't wanted to go to prom but seeing the big grand gesture he granted her made me envious. I was selfish not to go with him and I knew if I showed my disdain I'd ruin this experience for him. I sucked it up because I knew he didn't deserve that. He was a good guy and he always made sure I was good. My 17th birthday had been a big event and since the moment I let him in he had been the perfect guy. When he held me down after the death of my mother I knew I had been handling him all wrong. I was convinced we'd marry after college and figured he would grant me a bigger wedding than the senior prom. I loved him and I enjoyed seeing him happy. When he left, I walked back into the building with Mya following.

"So, are we gone box or what?" she asked with a smirk.

"Bitch ain't nobody trying to fight you." I chuckled as she came up to my apartment with the baby in tow. I held the baby close to me on my chest. I loved the smell of her hair and her soft light skin. She was beautiful, and I knew what I loved the most about her is the fact she was his. I couldn't wait to have his children one day. I thought, as the twins I aborted quickly crossed my mind. Guilt rose in my gut as Mya took the baby because she got ready to leave. So, I was left alone in my own thoughts. I sat in the house thinking about my future with MyKing until I got sleepy. However, I couldn't fall asleep. Thoughts of my mother invaded my mind and I started to cry. MyKing held me every night so I was used to having someone here and tonight I felt so empty without him. I cried until I fell asleep. I was awakened by someone arguing but I didn't move initially because I figured it was MyKing's mother and her boyfriend. I reached out for him to go over and see what was up, but he wasn't lying next to me. I sat up and groggily got out of the bed to go to the other room where he slept alone sometimes but he wasn't their either. The closer I got to the door the louder the noise and I finally heard it cease but it was shortly followed by a loud banging against the wall.

"What the fuck?" I asked myself as I slipped on my house shoes and made my way next door. I reached for the knob and let myself in going towards the knocking. A few seconds after I walked in I realized that MyKing might've been in here fucking Candice but quickly erased that thought. I opened the door in confusion as MyKing held Candice against the wall by her neck. He was mad as fuck by his demeanor and I knew I had to help her.

"Bae, what the fuck are you doing?" I asked confused. I stepped closer to him and he dropped her. He turned towards me and the look on his face took my breath away. He stared at me evilly and I stood in shock.

"MyKing...Baby...what's wrong?" I asked as he stepped towards me. Candice jumped up on her feet and ran out and I stood there trying to understand why he was so upset.

"You cheated on me," he stated through clenched teeth. His eyes watered angrily.

"Wait...what?" I asked confused. I had never cheated on him nor have I ever thought about being with someone else.

"BITCH! YOU FUCKING CHEATED ON ME!" He said agitated with the fact I didn't know what he was talking about.

"What! No...MyKing I would nev..." I started before he cut me off?

"HOW THE FUCK YOU GET PREGNANT THEN?" He asked angrily like he was about to hit me. At the mention of my pregnancy, my eyes watered. I never intended for him to find out but now that he had I figured I'd fess up, but nothing would come out when I tried to speak. He looked on knowingly.

"What's wrong Jasmine? Cat got your tongue HOE? Who the fuck did you cheat on me with because I ain't touched you? Who does that baby belong to?" he asked loudly. He had become belligerent and disrespectful. I reacted with tears. I was shaking trying to figure out how to tell him.

"Can't even tell me huh? Well since you don't know who, can you at least tell me why? After everything I did for you, tell me why you did this shit to me?" he asked as he pushed me towards the wall he had just had Candice up against. I shook my head no because he had to have known I'd never hurt him.

"MyKing...it was Kevin. He..." He cut me off again.

"BITCH! YOU BETTER NOT FIX YOUR NASTY ASS MOUTH TO BLAME MY BROTHER!" he yelled in my face and he snatched the pillow away from the bed and in one swift move stuck the cold gun in my face. I trembled under the metal as tears wet my whole face.

"Go head Hoe! Say my brother name again. Spit it out so I can blow your fucking head off!" he gritted coldly. I didn't attempt to say shit else out of pure fear. He wouldn't believe me if I told the truth and I was convinced he'd really kill me. I held up my hands to his chest to calm him.

"MyKing..." I cried.

"What? What bitch? Don't fucking touch me! " he said as he muffed me with the pistol. I just knew he'd make a mistake and the loaded gun would go off in my face. I sobbed miserably knowing I couldn't do anything to fix this.

"Fuck!" he gritted. "You and your bastard ass child can get the fuck out of my life. If I ever see your black dog ass again I promise I am going to kill you. Now get the fuck out you nasty slut bitch!" he hissed as he grabbed me by my neck and pushed me hard towards the door. Once I caught my balance I couldn't help but turn back to him.

"MyKing!" I cried. He swelled up as tears filled his eyes. He cocked the gun and pointed it at me.

"Get the fuck out Jasmine!" he spat. I dropped my head and held my hands up in defeat as I rushed out of the apartment. I ran next door and quickly threw on some pants, grabbed my bag, and left like I was told. I was too afraid to stay after what had happened. I rushed out of the building completely defeated. I had nothing and no one and the man I thought I'd spend the rest of my life with had turned on me. He wouldn't even allow me to tell him the truth. This had turned out to be the worst night of my life. I got onto the bus and watched as the Slater Mills housing Project disappeared from my view. I didn't even realize then it was the last time I'd see it.

MyKing

I angrily threw shit around as I released the pure pain I held back. I was devastated at the thought of Jasmine betraying me like she had. I changed for her. I did everything to prove what I felt for her and she took my heart and crushed it like t wasn't shit. Then she had the audacity to accuse the death of my brother as her motive to cheat! I could not bring myself to picture her and Kevin fucking around behind my back. He wouldn't have done that shit to me. I was mad as fuck! I sat in that room for a long time until I calmed down enough to go to sleep. I knew I had to get myself together. Shit was happening in my life and I couldn't let my feelings get in the way of that. I had a new baby and I had just put all my money into my next shipment. Every penny I saved went towards making sure I had what I needed to take care of my business. I ain't have time to be dealing with Jasmine and her bullshit. But when I woke up the next morning, she was the only thing on my mind. I had calmed down and thought about what had happened. Last nights events replayed over and over in my head and even though I wanted to hurt her, I couldn't. I got up to go to her next door. I needed to know the truth. But she was nowhere in sight. She had left, and I was mad all over again. I figured she went to be with the nigga who got her pregnant and vowed to cause some real damage if I got my hands on her again. My hate for Jasmine developed then and I needed it. What I had to face next was not for a soft loving ass nigga. That cheating bitch bore a beast. I can honestly say that night was when I remembered who the fuck I was. I'd never again forget. My name is MyKing, but everybody calls me King. And Imma run all of Chicago!

The End!

BONUS CHAPTER: PROLOGUE TO QUEEN

Jasmine

I got off the bus on 79th with less than fifty dollars in my pocket. I thought to take money from MyKing's stash but thought better of it. I was shaking. My thoughts were clouded from all tonight's unfortunate events. Survival was my only option and I was right back where I started. Only this time, I ain't have my mother, so I had to do what I had to do. I didn't know where to look exactly and I felt foolish for even trying, but Bebe was my only option. I had nobody else to help me. And I needed help. I was afraid that if I attempted to go to my family before it's time, they would turn me away.

It's evident MyKing doesn't want anything to do with me now... He didn't even allow me to explain myself. I wiped a lone tear away from my face before I walked up to a big brown skin woman with the shortest skirt on I'd ever seen. I knew the fact her whole ass was hanging out the bottom of it meant she was probably someone who could help me.

"Hey sweetheart, you see something you like?" She asked seductively after she realized she had my attention. I would've gagged had I not needed her to give me information.

"Um, hi...I'm actually looking for my friend, Bebe. She usually hangs around here. Do you know where she might be?" I asked sweetly.

"Oh yeah, she went for a ride. It won't take her long. Just wait right here, she'll be back in a minute." She said nonchalantly. I thanked her and stepped all the way back off the street. I leaned up against the side of the building so none of these fools would think I was out here tryna sell my ass. I mean mugged any guy that even looked at me. The big lady was picked up by some man in a blue pick-up truck. I stood alone until Bebe hopped out of a black SUV. She smiled as soon as she saw me standing there.

"Wassup bitch? I missed you!" She smiled as she walked up and pulled me into a hug. It was always something about Bebe that made me comfortable. Like we were family. Nobody but my own parents had truly made me feel like family. Before she let me go, I broke down in tears.

"G, what's wrong with you? What happened?" She asked concerned.

"It's a long ass story and at this point, I need some place to stay. Just until I turn eighteen. I can go back home when I turn eighteen. Can you please help me?" I cried.

"Bitch...you know I stay with Cash. I know you ain't tryna go there. I'm down to help you the best way I can though." She said seriously.

"You think I could just ask him to let me stay for a while. I'm already seventeen. I won't be there that long." I cried desperately.

She shook her head no before speaking. "Cash is a pimp, Jasmine. Ain't no way he gone give you shit without selling or taking your pussy. You want to do that?" She asked with her eyebrows raised in surprise.

"No, but it doesn't sound like I have a choice...this is my only option. You are my only option." I said seriously.

"Damn, what the fuck happened?" She asked as she led me down the street.

"He thought I cheated on him because he found out I was pregnant. Candice and Val set me up. He put a gun in my face and kicked me out of the apartment. He wouldn't even let me explain what really happened." I told her miserably.

"I'm sorry, I thought if you told him he'd understand. You should've said something from the beginning because just letting him find out on his own made him come up with his own conclusion. The same way you did when you found out he was having a baby with that light skin bitch. Ain't no telling what those snake ass hoes put in his ear about you. I just can't believe he put his shit in your face though." She said shaking her head.

"He did. I was so scared I couldn't even breathe. I don't know why he would even think I'd cheat on him. I love him. I would never cheat on him." I cried.

"Damn, I hate that for you girl. I know how much he means to you. After all the shit he put you through, it's crazy he wouldn't even hear you out. That's some bullshit." She said bitterly.

"I don't have anyone else," I said slowly as I allowed the tears to fall. I felt empty inside and all I could do was cry about it. Bebe stopped suddenly and turned to me.

"You got me... I don't have a whole lot of money and I ain't got half of what you did when you stayed with him but I'm your friend. After everything you did for me, you deserve my loyalty. I owe you a whole lot and I'm always gone have your back the same way you had mine when I needed you. It's really hard to find good hearted people and you have one. I will give you anything I have if it'll help you." She told me sincerely. I smiled as my broken heart fluttered a bit.

"Thank you...I just need you to get me in the house." I said seriously. She dropped her head before exhaling loudly.

"Jasmine, you are so much better than this...I got two hundred dollars stashed at the house for a day when I don't feel like being out here all night. But you need to take that money and go home. I know your people will let you come back. Your mama ain't even alive to be an issue. Just go home." She begged.

"I can't...I chose where I wanted to be, and I think if I go back now it will be a mistake. They nearly threw us out of town. I can't go back with nothing." I exclaimed.

"Jasmine..." She started.

"Bebe, take me to the house. I just need to talk to the man." I cut her off.

"Jasmine, I know you don't want this. I'm trying to protect you because once you start tricking it's going to make the situation worse. Just go home." She said as tears built up in her eyes.

"I have no home now...take me to Cash," I said shortly as I wiped the tears away from my own face.

"Okay." She said as she dropped her head and walked me up the block.

We walked down two blocks to 82nd street. The apartment building, we stopped in front of was a red bricked three story. Nothing at all about it looked like a whore house. But I was still nervous as hell. I walked up the walkway towards the front door.

"Bitch! What the fuck are you doing? You tryna get me killed? Don't go up the stairs. This way!" She whispered aggressively. Her eyes bucked wide opened as she led me towards the side walkway. And down a short slab of concrete steps to a thick steel door. She went through her little purse and got her key. She unlocked the door and we walked into a short hall with mirrored walls. She closed the door behind me and walked me into another door. It led into a kitchen with no appliances. It was merely just a room with a kitchen sink in it. I followed her through that kitchen and down another hall. She made a right into a room and closed the door behind her. She turned on the light and sat on the bed I presumed to be hers. I quickly glanced around the room that was tidy and neat. It looked perfectly normal and was comfortable if you look past the old furniture and a hole that had been knocked into the wall. All it needed was a fresh paint job and a furniture readjustment. I hadn't got permission to stay yet but I knew this was going to work out for me. I took a seat on the bed next to her. My feet were tired, and I hadn't sat down since I left my apartment.

"So...what's next? When do I talk to Cash? Is he home?" I asked.

"He rarely leaves the house... Everything he does is calculated. He is the type of man that thinks before he speaks. Before he even questions you, he will have already determined the answer. You'll be crucified before you can even explain your innocence. He's a dangerous man. You have to understand this isn't going to go the way you plan." She said as she looked at me more worried than I'd ever seen her.

"What are you so afraid of? He's a man. The worst thing he can say is no and I will leave." I assured her.

"No, the worst thing he can say is yes. He won't say no. You don't seem to understand what you are about to walk into. This man is as close to Satan as a person can get to alive. When he pulls you into his world it will change you and..."

"Bianca!" I cut her off as I glared at her. "Just take me to him," I told her seriously. She shook her head before she got up off of the bed.

"Just wait here. I'll bring him to you." She said before she left out of her room. I exhaled the air I'd been holding since I walked in this house. I was nervous as shit. Still shaken up from being dumped and having a loaded gun stuck in my face. Now I'm sitting in a whore house about to consent to sell my ass. The tears started to build again before I heard footsteps. I quickly wiped the water away as I stood to greet the infamous Cash.

Bebe opened the door with worry all over her face. I could feel her heart pounding in her chest from across the room. Behind her stood a tall dark man that looked directly at me the moment he entered. He had a face of stone and no expression at all. His skin was dark but only a shade lighter than mine. His eyes were the sweetest color of hazel I'd ever seen but his gaze only reminded me of a snake. Before he was close enough to harm me, I was terrified. He looked me up and down and the closer he got to me the further away I wanted him. I took a step back each time he came closer until he backed me into the wall. That seemed to entice him and when I couldn't go any further he pressed his body right up against mine. He looked right into my eyes as if he was trying his damnest to hypnotize me. He scared me so bad I knew he could feel my body shaking beneath him.

He breathed deep and his warm breath grazed my nose. But he wouldn't speak.

"Cash this is my friend.." Bebe started before he turned away from me so quickly, I felt a breeze. He snapped his head towards her and she shut up right then. He looked at her for a while before slowly turning back to me.

"What's your name?" He asked suddenly. His voice deep and smooth.

"Ja...Jasmine." I said slowly. I hadn't stuttered but I was shaking so hard it came out as if I had.

"Hmmm". He stared. I was his target and he didn't even attempt to look away. He barely blinked. I was so uncomfortable I wanted to run but had nowhere to go. I shut my eyes tight to avoid his creepy gaze.

"I have come here because I have nowhere else to go. Both of my parents are dead, and I have no home. I have nobody but Bebe. I need for you to let me stay here...I won't stay longer than my 18th birthday. I won't be any trouble and I will do whatever I have to for you to let me stay. I can get a job and pay you if you allow me to get myself together first. I will stay out of your way, sir." I said as I opened my teary eyes when I felt him back up off me. He looked at me seriously and after a few moments passed he straightened up his posture and knocked imaginary lent from his shirt.

"Okay. B, show her around." He simply said as he did the cleanest about face in front of me and slid towards the door. The look of relief washed over my face as soon as his back was turned. However, Bebe looked to him for mercy. She was still afraid, and I didn't understand why. He had gotten all the way to the door before he stopped suddenly in his tracks.

"You sleep up top." He said easily as he walked out and shut the door behind him. I exhaled in relief before Bebe broke into full tears.

"What? What the fuck just happened? What did he say? I was confused at her reaction. In my head, I was thinking maybe there were bunk beds somewhere and I had to sleep on the top bunk. I had no idea why she was crying. She shook her head before sitting on her bed again.

"The top is upstairs." She said dreadfully.

"Okay...What's the problem?" I asked her stepping closer to her.

"Hoes don't sleep upstairs where Cash sleeps...." She said slowly.

"Okay, Bebe so tell me what that means because you are scaring the shit out of me. What does that mean?" I asked her again.

"You are going to be a slave." She said as more tears fell from her face.

"A slave?...Like a maid or something?" I asked.

"Bitch a fucking slave! You are about to work, cook, clean, and fuck like a bitch from the 1800s." She exclaimed.

"Okay..well that doesn't sound so bad. I think I can do that." I said easily.

"Jasmine black people ain't like slavery two hundred years ago, what makes you think it's gone be enjoyable today? Slaves ain't free! He gone lock your ass up the moment you cross that threshold. I won't ever see you. I won't be able to protect you and you will have no way out. You are property now. The chances of you ever leaving this house are none. Whatever he wants to do to or with you is not even a choice that you have. You will never leave this house again, Jasmine. At least not alive." She cried. I pulled her into my arms into a hug. I honestly thought she was being dramatic. I couldn't even picture what modern day slavery would be like let alone being held captive.

"It's alright Bebe, I'll find a way out when it's time," I assured her.

"I hope you do." She smiled as if she knew it would never happen. But she got up and wiped her face and led me out her bedroom door anyway to show me the rest of the house.

Acknowledgement

First, I'd like to acknowledge God. Without him, I would not have been able to do anything. I am unworthy of all he has done for me but so grateful he has.

I want to thank my **Family and Friends** for supporting me. I love you all!

Additionally, I want to pay homage to the city of **Chicago**. I have a great appreciation for the lessons the city taught me. Regardless of where I go, it will always be home.

I must acknowledge my personal go team for believing in me and encouraging me whenever I needed them. I could not have done it without you guys. I love you all!

Antrae' Roshanique Kirkland, Cheretta "Cookie" Perry, Onisha McCarty, Chris "Sister" Hinson, Angelica Norman, and Latonya "1st Lady" Jones

Also, Thank you to the **MyKing Review Board** for my initial review. You guys are MVPs. Thanks for being on my team!

Jacquelynn Pettigrew, Kristin L Taylor, Nicole Madison, and Courtney Jones

Additionally, I would like to acknowledge **Kanika "K.K" Harris** for her talent and ability of creating quality covers. Thank you Chick!

Lastly, I would like to shout out all of my **Wattpad followers and readers** for your continued support.

ABOUT THE AUTHOR

Kane

 Shekinah Denham-Taylor, also known as Kane is an African American author and entrepreneur. She was born July 30th, 1992 and raised on the Southside of Chicago, IL. There, in a local library, she discovered her love for urban literature and writing. She grew up reading and writing for fun and excelled in her English and reading academics. After being awarded the Edgar Allen Poe award in highschool, she was inspired to take her love for literature further. She majored in English and minored and Speech and Theatre. She earned her bachelor's degree in arts from Jackson State University and decided to pursue her dream of being a writer. She is dedicated to publishing creative literature worthy of royalty. She is excited to provide a world of literature in the future.

Facebook & Twitter:Kanetheauthor
Instagram:The_Legendary_Kane
Website:www.Kanespublishingcompany.com